It's not over... until it's over.

SWIFT

Kindred Book Four

SCARLETT FINN

www.scarlettfinn.com

Also by Scarlett Finn

NOTHING TO...
NOTHING TO HIDE
NOTHING TO LOSE
NOTHING IN BETWEEN: ONE
NOTHING TO DECLARE
NOTHING TO US
NOTHING IN BETWEEN: TWO
NOTHING TO SAY
NOTHING TO GAIN
NOTHING IN BETWEEN: THREE
NOTHING TO YOU
NOTHING TO THIS PREQUEL: ONE WILD NIGHT
NOTHING TO THIS
NOTHING IN BETWEEN: FOUR
NOTHING TO DO
NOTHING TO FEAR
NOTHING IN BETWEEN: FIVE
NOTHING TO DENY

GO NOVELS
GO WITH IT
GO IT ALONE
GO ALL OUT
GO ALL IN
GO FULL CIRCLE

KINDRED SERIES
RAVEN
SWALLOW
CUCKOO
SWIFT
FALCON
FINCH

EXILE
HIDE & SEEK
KISS CHASE

THE EXPLICIT SERIES
EXPLICIT INSTRUCTION
EXPLICIT DETAIL
EXPLICIT MEMORY

THE FORBIDDEN NOVELS
FORBIDDEN DESIRE
FORBIDDEN WANT
FORBIDDEN WISH
FORBIDDEN NEED
FORBIDDEN BOND

WRECK & RUIN
RUIN ME
RUIN HIM

MISTAKE DUET
MISTAKE ME NOT
SLEIGHT MISTAKE

THE BRANDED SERIES
BRANDED
SCARRED
MARKED

TO DIE FOR...
TO DIE FOR TRUTH
TO DIE FOR HONOR
TO DIE FOR VIRTUE
TO DIE FOR DUTY
TO DIE FOR LOVE

RISQUÉ & HARROW INTERTWINED
TAKE A RISK
FIGHTING FATE
RISK IT ALL
FIGHTING BACK
GAME OF RISK

FORBIDDEN PREQUEL DUET
ALL. ONLY.
ONLY YOURS

LOVE AGAINST THE ODDS STANDALONE COLLECTION
SWEET SEAS
HEIR'S AFFAIR
RESCUED
MAESTRO'S MUSE
GETTING TRICKY
THIRTEEN
REMEMBER WHEN...
RELUCTANT SUSPICION
XY FACTOR

LOST & FOUND
LOST
FOUND

ONE

KADIE HARRIS COULD feel him watching.

It didn't matter that she couldn't see him, she could feel him lurking. The prickle on the back of her neck wasn't unpleasant anxiety, it was agitated anticipation building to fever pitch. Somehow, somewhere, he was here.

Walking through the deserted park on her way back to work, she took one measured step after another, listening to the tattoo of her high-heels and speculating about when he might choose to show himself.

Being without him tortured her every day they were apart. Their agonizing periods of separation were interrupted by sudden concentrations of intensity that were often cut short. Passion and love exploded when they came together to make up for every second he'd spent away from her side and it defined their pained farewells.

Their apartment was nearby. She considered whether or not she should go home just to try to draw him out. But she'd learned long ago to trust him. He knew how to play her, how to torment her, how to be patient in the face of her zeal. Only in his own good time would he appear to her, and he'd make sure it was worth the wait.

Experience taught her that he always made their reunion memorable, but that didn't assuage her eagerness. Kadie had never been particularly good at holding her horses. "Come on, Hotshot. Where are you?" she muttered to herself.

It had been too long, and she needed him. She didn't want to wait anymore. Weeks had passed since she had last heard from him. Worrying was ridiculous because the man she loved was capable of defending himself. Yet somehow that never quite alleviated the concern that plagued her every day she didn't receive word.

In the five years they'd been together, he'd spent weeks, sometimes months, away from their life, but he always came back to her and she had to make herself believe that he always would.

After another half dozen steps, Kadie stopped. A spike of adrenaline told her he was close, closer than he'd been all day. She'd learned not to ignore her instincts. Sure enough, when she spun around, there stood her love, right on her heels.

"This is your version of a hello?" Kadie asked, trying not to show any joy. "Some people would call it stalking." Usually when they came back together after a period apart, there was elation in his affect. Today, there was nothing but blank intensity, and that wiped the grin from her face. "What? What is it?"

One of his arms came around her waist, and without further ceremony, she was tugged to his body. Tucker Holt's mouth took her words and sanity. She should have known better than to try to think or reason when Tuck had made up his mind.

There she was in his arms, pressed against the broad, solid chest that had served as her pillow on so many nights. This was what she'd been waiting for and she was going to enjoy it.

All too soon his mouth left hers. Drifting on the memory of their previous goodbye, which had lasted her all these weeks, she had to convince herself that this was real and not another of her lucid dreams. Sometimes when she woke in a sweat, coiled in their sheets, she would reach for him because the sensations in her dreams had been so real that she'd be almost convinced they'd just made love. But he had never been there, he so rarely was.

Releasing her tension, she slid a hand from his shoulder to his bicep and let her fingers slip under the fabric of his tee shirt sleeve to pinch his flesh with her long nails.

"All real, Toots."

His heated words rested on her lips. Try as he might to convince her everything was rosy, she could tell that he was carrying a burden heavier than any she'd seen on his shoulders before. Her head was still swimming. His presence made her heady, making it difficult to think and questioning him even harder.

Just having him with her, safe, alive, holding her, gave her an endorphin boost. He had come back to her just as she'd known he would. The only thing that would keep him from her side was death. He joked with her about having a return to sender tattooed on his ass in case of the worst. While he found the idea funny, she did not.

If he wasn't going to be forthcoming about what was on his mind, she was going to have to be creative about getting her answers. "Two weeks," she said, punching his shoulder with the hand that had just caressed and pinched. "I haven't heard a peep from you in two weeks!"

He didn't decrease the stranglehold of his embrace. "I told you I'd hit a delay."

If she cut him any slack, he wouldn't recognize her. "And you were nowhere near a server of any kind? Somehow I doubt that."

Shoving out of his clinch, she sprang back when his arms flexed then locked. Tuck would let go of her when he was ready and not a single heartbeat before, "Are you sulking?"

Unwilling to relent just yet, she considered his question because her answer would depend on his reply to her next query. "How long are you home for?"

Crouching lower, he smelled her hair. Burying his face in her locks, he moved it side to side reveling in the texture. Tuck could be affectionate. He'd learned how to trust her enough to act on his emotional impulses in the same way he would to physical threats: on instinct. Their usual greetings were teasing and flirtatious, and sex was high on the agenda. This man, squeezing her, seeking comfort, was troubled.

Reducing her rankle, she wanted to be what he needed, but he so rarely let her in. "Anyone would think that you missed me," she murmured, stroking the back of his head.

"You have no idea."

When he kissed her again, he cradled the back of her skull and dipped her until her balance was entirely at his mercy. They'd kissed a million times over the last five years, but the chemical reaction that their bodies created when combined hadn't become any less combustible.

As he eased his lips away, he didn't put her back onto her feet. Kadie didn't care about her physical balance, she'd forgotten where she was, who was here, and her very reason for being. In his presence, Kadie's world shrank, just as his did. Together, their universe reduced itself to two occupants and that was all they needed. With each other, anything could be achieved. He made her feel that she could take on the world. Not that she would ever need to because he would do it for her, every time.

Forcing herself to open her eyes, she absorbed his features. Every minute together was so precious that she felt the need to cling onto every nuance. "You are something to look at, Tucker Holt," she whispered.

Lean and always ready for action, Kadie knew just how ripped every inch of her man's body was. Not that the light-brown hair, presently a little on the long side, with its sparkling natural blonde highlights and his penetrating blue eyes were anything to shrug at.

Pulling her upright again, he held her close and squeezed her so tight that there was no denying something was plaguing him. The stubble on his chin dragged and snagged on her hair, but she enjoyed the familiarity of the friction.

"Let's go home," he said and began to pull her toward the path that would take them to their apartment.

Ah, this was more like just-come-back Tuck, single-minded and overbearing, edgy until he released himself into her. Kadie laughed. "I have to go back to work. I have a meeting and—"

"Dempsey can handle it," he said and when he took her hand and tugged her along, she followed.

While scurrying along behind him, she tried to make him see sense and remind him of their responsibilities, even though she wanted to go home as much as he did. Except making his life hard was what kept things interesting between them. Ubiquitous banter was synonymous with foreplay. "Dempsey and I have a meeting this afternoon, with a company we've been courting for a while."

Dempsey, her cousin, had been the one to introduce her to Tuck. Since then, she and her cousin had run Tuck's firm while he gallivanted off to take care of less reputable practitioners. Truth was, she didn't know what he did when he wasn't with her and she didn't like to ask. Maintaining their often separate lives never made her doubt their relationship, having him sometimes was better than having him never.

"The meeting has been canceled," Tuck called over his shoulder, still dragging her along. "They've hit a digital snag."

Her brows rose. Tuck was a planner. Always had been. He hadn't met a hiccup he couldn't thwart with his superior tech skills. "A digital snag?" she asked. "What is that code for? What did you do?"

"They might have a little virus problem."

The amused pride in his voice didn't surprise her. "A virus," she said and stopped, pulling her arm up and down to shake it out of his hold. "Tuck!"

The company's duty was to find weaknesses in corporate security. Tuck was the brains behind the operation, she and Dempsey ran the company for him and were the public face of it. None of their clients knew who Tuck was because he did his hacking from external locations. He was the faceless wizard behind the curtain. Once he'd poked holes in their client's electronic security, he gave reports to Dempsey, who then worked with the client to toughen up their barriers.

That was what Tuck's legitimate company did. The work that took him away for such long periods of time wasn't exactly on the books… or the up and up from what she gathered.

Tuck wasn't dissuaded. "The system will reset in twelve hours. By the time they're enjoying their morning coffee, everything will be back as it should be," he said and came back to put an arm around her waist to get her moving again.

She kept on going until they were out of the park and down the block on their way to the apartment she shared with him when he was around. Having an apartment that bordered the park was her dream and Tuck delivered. Everything he did seemed effortless; nothing was too much for her. She could ask for the moon and he'd find a way to give it to her.

"Only you could come up with that solution," she said as they ran up the external stairs to their place. "I tell you that I have an appointment with a client—our client—and what do you tell me? That you've already infected their company with a computer virus, ensuring that my appointment has been canceled because the whole place is in disarray."

Her key slid into the lock and his hands landed on her shoulders from behind when she turned it and pushed through the glass paneled wooden door that opened into their dining kitchen.

"It was only a little virus," he said.

"A little virus," she said, going inside and dumping her purse on the table. These teasing exchanges were missed when he wasn't around, not that this was the time to tell him that. No, this was the time to read him the riot act. Ruffling her feathers got him going and she'd learned the carnal value of ruffling his. "Dempsey has been working to improve their security. They're our client, now we look like idiots."

She spun around to glare but received no apology. "I did it for a good cause," he said.

The predatory tone in his voice matched the look in his eye. She hadn't even taken her jacket off and he was onto the seduction.

Resisting with disapproval was her role. "To free up my afternoon so you can get laid is not a good cause. Do we have to talk about your boundary issues again?"

He snapped the lock on the door, shirked his jacket, and began to stalk her. "Depends on your perspective. I say it's a good cause," he said. "And you're going to get laid too."

He knew her too well. Boy, had she missed him. Edging back as he advanced, she could never escape him when he was this hungry. "You expect me to give it up when you haven't answered my question?" Her spine hit the wall beside the fridge just next to the corridor that led to the bathroom… and their bedroom.

"What question?"

The most important question, the one she always asked: how long did she have with him before he deserted her again? Now, he was upon her, gathering her into his arms, forcing her weight to her tiptoes. He knew what she wanted to know and that saying goodbye was always a raw sorrow, so she could forgive him for not wanting to address the issue, especially if it would have an answer that might upset her.

Shallow breaths and a pliant soul signaled her surrender, she was his, in every sense. "Tuck," she murmured, pressing her hands to his chest, reminding herself again and again that this was real. She couldn't wake from this dream and be disappointed again. Speckled shivers darted through her skull as her body grew heavier, he didn't hesitate.

"Shh," he reassured, covering her hands with his and then bringing them to his mouth. "You've got me, baby, I'm home."

"For real?" she asked, daring herself to believe he meant it. In time he would go, he always did, it was the nature of his occupation. It could be days, weeks, sometimes months, but eventually he would leave and they would do this all over again.

"For real."

Bending his knees to line up their mouths, Tuck let his eyes linger on hers for half a beat before he leaned in and pressed his mouth to hers. Alone at last, in the home they shared, Kadie could forgive him for threatening the contract with the client. She'd forgive him anything as he collected her into his embrace and began to maneuver her backwards toward their bedroom. Joining, connecting, savoring their time together, he was her only priority.

Their relationship was what kept her going. Despite the distance, she was never lonely because he would always be there for her. If she demanded that he drop everything and come home to her then he would. Kadie had never done it, recalled him on a whim, but she had full faith that he wouldn't hesitate if she did.

"I've got a lot saved up for you, Toots. You ready for a ride?"

They entered the bedroom and he gave the door a shove to close it. After scooping her legs from under her, it took him two strides to reach the bedside where he tossed her down to the mattress.

"You're stalling, Hotshot," she said, pouncing to her knees and whipping her top off over her head. "Get your dick over here now, and I'll take exactly what I need."

Tuck stripped down at the same time she did, racing her to naked. "You're not going to outlast me, Toots."

"We'll see about that," she said, leaping up off the bed and into his arms.

They lived their lives in a power struggle with each other. It was yet to be determined which of them was actually the dominant one. Maybe that was because the truth didn't really matter as long as they were together.

The way he kissed her told her so much about his mood. When they came together after spells apart, their unions were frantic, and this time was no different. Laying her on the bed, Tuck suspended his weight above her, except she didn't want that, she wanted to feel the full length of his ravenous body stimulating every part of hers.

Biting his lip to get his attention, she smiled at the glare he returned. "You're holding back," she teased. "Get with it."

"Oh, I'm with it," he said, seizing her waist and rolling their bodies over to put her in the dominant position.

"You could work a little harder."

If he was trying to rile her, she'd take it. After half a decade together, she had nothing to prove to him between the sheets and there were few surprises. But she had what she wanted, control over the body that starred in her fantasies.

Working her hips until his dick was nestled deep between her folds, she pinched and rubbed her nipples, stopping when she wanted to slide her hands over his ripped torso. There might be no surprises, but that didn't mean there was no effect. He'd been working hard on his body since they saw each other last, leaving her curious about where he worked out and if he did it alone.

With her nails, she stimulated his nipples, then let them glide down to circle his belly button, before taking them lower. But when she tried to slide her hips away, he caught them and raised her up, and the head of his erection followed. She'd tested his patience long enough, just as she knew she would. Kadie had pleasured herself in front of him before, and he loved nothing more than watching her hands go from her tits to his torso.

This time, he pulled her down onto him and there was no more teasing, he was all the way inside and after a satisfied exhale, she laughed. "Doesn't it feel good to be home, Hotshot?" she asked, rocking her hips, relishing his intimate occupation, and reminding him of the warm constriction she provided.

"It sure does, Toots," he said, flipping them over in a slick maneuver that allowed him to begin pumping into her before she was even flat on her back.

Sex with Tuck was different every time and exactly the same as well. Their connection, the security, it heightened every luxurious stroke of his powerful shaft that demanded satisfaction through to his soul.

Kadie wanted to be fucked by him, wanted his body to take advantage of everything hers could offer. But the speed of their union slowed and when she released her lip from her teeth and opened her eyes, she saw him staring down into her, still moving, but preoccupied by something that wasn't the pleasure of sex.

"Tuck?" she asked, touching his face.

Taking her wrist, he moved her palm to his lips and kissed it in a long tender moment that re-inspired the concern she'd sidelined earlier. When he released her, a new determination took over his expression and his actions. He was thrusting harder than before, faster. So fast that it only took a minute more for them both to come together, panting and shouting for each other in ecstasy.

He was here, he was home, and when he took her into his arms and kissed her again, Kadie didn't want to think about anything negative. Being his girl had its disadvantages, but they were all erased in moments of post-coital bliss like this one.

Whatever was bothering him, whatever was different, they'd deal with it, she'd always be here for him and he kept coming back, proving that he knew he could rely on her. Even when they fought and teased, it was submerged in love, they had real, unshakable security, maybe all he needed was a reminder that no matter how much she riled him, she loved him even more.

TWO

THE KINDRED TOOK up most of Tuck's life. Kadie had given up asking him about what he did when they weren't together. For the first time, he wished he could tell her everything. Just a couple of days ago, he had watched Art die in the Atlas warehouse. Brodie's pain might be subdued now, but the loss was going to change everything.

Tuck had to leave the manor, Zara could probably have used his support with Brodie, but he had done his duty and needed to get out of there for his own sanity. He'd helped her to secure the device and given her a quick rundown of the manor systems, then he'd split. Driving without aim, he planned to head for a dive bar and a cheap motel, except he'd come back here on autopilot. To Kadie.

Hacking her calendar didn't take him long and when he saw the meeting she had scheduled, he'd dumped the virus into the client's system to make sure that appointment wouldn't be going ahead. Watching her wasn't enough, which was odd. Playing with her, stalking her from afar, had been a hobby he'd always enjoyed. Tempting himself with the sight of her, while resisting making direct contact, he placed bets with himself each time on how long he'd be able to keep his hands off her, it was a game. But it was one he hadn't enjoyed playing the previous day. As soon as he saw her, he needed to be in her arms, which meant he had no patience to let her go to business appointments.

Seeing Art die had changed something in his bones and a desire for comfort had overwhelmed him. Kadie was the only person who'd ever had a grounding effect on him when his world went off-kilter, which was probably why his aimless journey had steered him to her.

Going back to work after spending the night with Kadie was bittersweet. Tuck liked to see that the place was doing well, liked to see how Kadie kept the place fresh and made adjustments to the décor. Every time he came back here something was different. His woman wasn't so great at keeping still, she was a bee, always buzzing around, getting things done, keeping busy. For so long he'd been encouraged by her optimism and enjoyed picking out details simply because he knew it would give her a thrill that he noticed them.

This time was different. Coming back, he'd wanted home comforts and familiarity with the belief that they could make him forget the tragedy in his other life. Being intimate with the woman he loved gave him an anchor and erased the images of his latest Kindred mission. Kadie had always made him feel like he was a good guy worthy of her love and that he was capable of giving her what she deserved.

But he didn't feel like that anymore. Not after what had happened to Art. Losing his mentor and witnessing the implosion of his closest ally brought the consequences of Tuck's risks into harsh focus. He couldn't shake the feeling that this life he had with Kadie was on borrowed time.

The brownstone he'd bought years ago as a base for his company, housed vital equipment and contained more electronics than any passer-by would assume, which was exactly the point. Dempsey and Kadie didn't see clients here, they went to their consumers premises. Keeping their base low-key didn't draw attention to their operation and the art of deception was something he'd gotten good at in his time with the Kindred. Occasionally, those lessons transferred to his life with Kadie, though he tried to limit their impact.

Kadie had left him in their apartment this morning to come into work. He'd been not too far behind her and had spent most of his morning in the brownstone basement. That space was his private lair, the one place in the world he could call himself king. Filled with his machines, the dark cavern was out-of-bounds for anyone except him and Kadie.

Dempsey had been coming in the front entrance just as Tuck was walking upstairs. Greeting his old friend was a strange kind of normalcy and they'd gone out to the coffee cart to catch up. Coming back inside, they ascended toward the first floor where their main offices were. "I don't give a shit," Tuck said.

"I do," Dempsey said. "You can't miss my sister's birthday party."

"Why not?" Tuck asked, taking the steps two at a time at Dempsey's six. His colleague stopped on the stairs with his hands stretched to each banister and glared over his shoulder. "I'm more interested in figuring out what's up with your cousin."

"Your re-entry is always bumpy. Kadie's just thinking about when you'll waltz off again… Which is all the more reason you should come to my sister's birthday party. Gwen always has great parties and you can make some memories with Kade."

"Gwen hates me," Tuck said.

Dempsey smiled. "Most everyone who knows you hates you. It's what comes from being an enigma. If you won't let people in, they won't trust you." Dempsey let this hang in the air and finished mounting the stairs. "Give me a minute."

The wooden stairway hadn't changed, although if he didn't know better, he would say the walls up here had been re-plastered. Being paid to be observant meant he was positive he was right. Given the number of zeros on his bank balance, he'd guess he was good at details. Dempsey had disappeared into their breakroom. Tuck didn't wait.

Heading forward, he opened the double doors to enter their outer office. From here, the other four doors led to their offices and the file room. Inspecting the frame, and moldings, he ran his hand up the seam of the hinge and peered up at the ceiling. If something was different, Kadie needed him to notice.

Lifting his head as he moved into the office, he noticed there was a male on the chrome-footed leather couch under the window, probably in his early twenties. He could be younger than that, he looked it, especially in his current pose. Sunk into the three-seater, his feet and knees were tight together, and he clasped a leather binder on his lap with two white-knuckled hands.

The stranger stared right back, but there wasn't any attempt to intimidate in his returning stare. This dude was firmly on the receiving end, fear was all he portrayed. The boy blinked, shifted, blinked again, and swallowed once, twice. He was nervous, in fact he was sweating. Tuck grew more curious.

"Can I help you?" Tuck asked, giving the door a shove, and sending it clattering into its frame.

Tuck didn't flinch at the noise, he just kept staring. If there was one thing the Kindred were good at, it was getting to the bottom of mysteries.

The stranger blinked again, twice, then again, then there was another swallow. "I—"he croaked, coughed and cleared his throat. "I…"

"You what?" Tuck asked, widening his stance and folding his arms. "No one gets in here without a reason or a security clearance. Explain yourself."

"I—"

The file room door opened behind him. Though the boy shifted again, Tuck kept his scowl steady. The boy tried to push up from the couch but slid only an inch to the edge. The seat was too soft and too low for a reason. It was meant to keep people uncomfortable, it looked like luxury, but its purpose was intimidation.

Tuck didn't need to turn around to know who had opened the file room door. The shoe heels clacking on the oak floor told him who it was. A moment after a door closed, the unmistakable scent of her perfume dosed him. Fighting the urge to close his eyes and let the scent drug his senses, Tuck gritted his teeth against the knowledge that even just the smell of her made his jeans shift.

She didn't say a word, although her heels continued to click on the floor. From the direction of the occasional movement, he imagined she was at one of the two filing cabinets between the doors on the far wall, opposite the couch that the boy sat on. Tuck didn't miss how the youngster tried to peek around him to the woman Tuck couldn't see.

He was subtle, or at least trying to be. He didn't lean too far, but the slight movement of his eyes, and the constant shifting on the couch, told Tuck exactly what their guest was trying to do. The stranger wanted to see Kadie, he wanted to watch her while her back was to them. Under other circumstances, Tuck may not blame the boy because he understood the effect she could have on a male. But he didn't like strangers, he liked them even less within their sanctuary, and he liked them less than that when they took an interest in Kadie—understandable or not.

"You got a problem?" Tuck asked.

Still, the boy said nothing, though he had returned to swallowing and blinking. The kid squeezed his cracked lips together, nervous didn't begin to explain this guy's state. The nature of what he did with the Kindred meant being suspicious was a necessity. Tuck had been told he was a formidable guy, but this reaction was extreme, which made him wonder if this boy had something to hide.

"I need you," Kadie's voice carried to them. Relaxing his rigid form, he was ready to accommodate his woman. But when she walked past him and he moved to follow, she spoke again. "Not you, Hotshot," she said over her shoulder without making eye contact, then nodded to the boy on the couch.

The boy scrambled to his feet, dropping the binder, then tripped over himself to pick it up. Tuck watched him run to Kadie who stood at his office door holding it open, she bestowed the youngster with her most accommodating smile. With a shrug of her shoulders, she laughed, and shook her head.

"Take your time. I'm not going anywhere," she soothed.

The boy nodded and darted past her into the office. Kadie followed him in and closed the door. She didn't look at him, not once. And she closed the door! That was his fucking office! Tuck took a minute to replay events.

Every time he left her, he counted the seconds until he was home again. Dempsey was right that his re-entry was always bumpy, but Kadie was his smoothest transition. It might take time for him to get back up to speed and into a routine, but this, strangers in his office, wasn't something he wanted to get on board with.

Deciding that it was time he took charge of what was his, the steel returned to his spine. He marched to his office and opened the door without hesitation. A laugh died on Kadie's lips. The boy was in his chair behind his desk. Kadie had one hand on the desk, and the other on the back of his chair. The youngster was doing everything he could to keep his tongue in his mouth, and his eyes off of her cleavage, which was on display a couple of inches from the thick rimmed glasses that had appeared on his face from somewhere.

The boy's mouth dropped open when he registered Tuck's presence, his Adams-apple bounced again. The boy's obvious initial reaction was to flee, but Kadie's position trapped him in. A laptop was open in front them, both had to have been working on something because they were both positioned to see the screen, and the youngster's hands still rested on the keyboard.

Bad enough that the boy was at his desk, drooling over his woman, but Tuck sucked in an audible breath when he recognized that the laptop was also one of his. Jesus! Give the boy the keys to his apartment, turn down the sheets, and give him Tuck's credit card for the rubbers, why not? What was wrong with everyone?

"Can we help you?" Kadie asked, not moving an inch. The boy's impulse was to look at her, so he found himself once again lost in her cleavage.

Guys had to drool over her all the time and he wasn't usually here to see or police that interest. Watching this performance made him consider installing cameras just like the ones at the McCormack Manor. "This here is my office, Toots," Tuck said.

"We can move," she said, pushing away from the desk to stand up. "You won't mind if we go down to the lab if you're in here, will you?" He and Kadie were the only two with security access to his basement lab. To his knowledge no one had been in there except them, the key being: to his knowledge.

Was she playing or was something eating her snatch? "Hey now, Kade—"

The sly slink of her smile grabbed him by the balls, she was playing, and if she wanted satisfaction, he'd deliver. "It's that or I take him home with me."

Sauntering a few steps inside, he hooked his thumbs into his jeans. "Neither of us are home enough to take care of a pet, Toots. We've had this discussion."

"I—"The boy tried to rise, but Kadie moved behind the chair and pushed him back down into it.

"Don't let him bully you, I told you he would try to intimidate you," she said, massaging the boy's shoulders, this time treating Tuck to the vision of her cleavage. Much as he wanted to enjoy it, the knowledge that the boy had been spoiled by the same view made him grind his teeth.

This kid was in the middle of their foreplay, but Tuck didn't give a shit about his feelings. "You have to show them who's boss on day one," Tuck said.

An almost smile quirked to Kadie's lips. "He knows who rules the roost. He's my new intern and it's about time you two met. Tuck this is Howie. Howie meet Tucker."

"It's an honor, I—"

Again, Kadie pushed Howie back down when he tried to stand. "You're not supposed to name them," Tuck said, not diverting his attention from her. "It's how you get attached."

"Someone woke up on the wrong side of bed this morning," she said. "Or was it the draft that bothered you?"

So that was her game, she was playing tit-for-tat, usually it was her waking up alone in their cold bed after he'd abandoned her to go back to the Kindred. This was payback for all of those times, giving him a taste of his own medicine.

Tuck took one step toward the desk, Howie tensed,

and Kadie released the youngster to round the desk and match Tuck, step for step, until they were toe to toe. "Are you playing with me, Toots?"

"Moi?" she asked, her manicured nails grazed her breast, as she gaped in mock indignation. "We're only trying to get some work done."

"Work on what exactly?"

"Now, Tucker," she said, touching his sternum with those same fingernails. "I taught you how to ask nicely, do I have to explain it to you again?"

Seizing her upper arms, he stole her breath from her lungs causing it to flood his chest as he yanked her against him. Panic made the kid move fast. Howie bounced up from the chair, causing it to ricochet off the wall under the window behind him.

"Oh!" Howie exclaimed, going no further, proving he had no idea what action he was supposed to take to save his mentor. "I—should I—"

"Scram, kid," Tuck growled, glaring down at the woman in his clutches. She didn't need saving from anything except his devotion to her, and Howie wouldn't be able to combat that with any success.

"I—But I—"

"Howie," Kadie breathed, matching the ferocity of his stare. "Lesson over."

The words barely had time to leave her lips before Tuck snatched her up on the ends of her toes and forced his mouth down on hers. The grasping, desperate tangle of her tongue on his raised their heart rates until their hearts seemed to be trying to switch bodies. He didn't know if the boy had left but when he pulled his mouth from hers, she sucked in a sob on her breath.

Leaving her to sleep alone in their bed was as tough for him as it was for her, and he couldn't let her forget that. "Damn you, Kadie Harris," he huffed and kissed her again. "You're my fucking world, my—"

"Oh, shut up, Tuck." Grabbing his shirt in her fists, she pulled him to the desk and shoved everything out of the way to perch up on it.

The boy had gone, and he'd taken the laptop with him. Tuck would get to the bottom of that, and get his property back, but not before he reclaimed the most important thing in his world. Kadie shoved up his tee shirt. Gathering it in her fists, she reached to try to remove it. Helping her out, he whipped it off and groaned when her hungry, eager lips began to taste the width of him.

"Kadie," he said, driving his hands into her hair, but she ducked lower, kissing down to his diaphragm before he got hold of her again and thrust her away.

She fumbled with the buttons on his jeans. Too quickly, she freed his solid want and her fingers curled around him. Panting out his name, she dipped her head, but he couldn't let her taste him or he'd be done before they got started. Capturing her wrists, he pinned her down on the desk and flattened himself against her. "I missed you, Toots. You've got no idea what you do to me, what the thought of you gets me through."

"Tuck," she said, wriggling her hands out of his grip. "Shut up and fuck me."

She unhooked her belt and tossed it over his shoulder, then got to work on her shirt buttons. He knew his woman and the mischief she could get up to. After five years of dedicating himself to her, he knew exactly what she liked. Taking hold of her lapels, he ripped the shirt open and unclipped the front clasp of her bra. Stooping to suckle one nipple, he massaged her breasts closer to his mouth, deeper, until she squirmed beneath him and whimpered out his name, then it was time to switch sides.

"Tucker," she sighed, pushing her hips up, seeking out the bulge she'd had her greedy hands on moments before. But he wasn't about to let her take control. Backing off enough to flip her over, he gripped her thighs and dragged her closer, forcing his erection against her ass. He knew how she loved to feel the effect she had on him, and sure enough, she moaned and tried to push up. Tuck held her down and forced up her skirt. Tugging her underwear down her thighs, he probed his fingers between her folds, and let himself bounce against her as he stroked himself in time with the rhythm of his caress of her slick sex.

"You always did get off on screwing the boss," he said. The sound that came from her was a cross between a laugh and a whine.

"So far the boss hasn't screwed anything today," she said, elevating her rump.

Tuck clamped her in his grip, taking hold of her hips, so he could lift her for ease of access. "Consider this your bonus." Just like that, he slammed into her center and she cried out.

A scream that loud would vibrate the foundations of this structure. Everyone else on the premises knew exactly what they were up to, but that suited him, interruptions were the last thing he wanted when he was this deep inside the woman he loved.

***

RESTING HER FOREHEAD on the solid desk beneath her, Kadie let her eyes close, and tried to quiet her panting breaths. His hand slid from her waist to between her shoulder blades and he circled the clasp of her necklace with his thumb.

"I knew you were trouble the first second I laid eyes on you," she whispered. Proximity made her lips sample the texture of the wood. "Do you remember the night we met?"

Still stroking her upper back, his voice stayed low. "Have you ever known me to forget anything important to us?"

"I couldn't breathe when you looked at me. You ate every inch of me with that lethal gaze. You hadn't said a word, we weren't even in the same group, but I knew my life would never be the same."

"I haven't disappointed you, have I?"

His hand slid down her spine, and covered half of her behind, giving her a squeeze before he let his member slide from her body. She stayed put, bent over the desk, her hands tangled in her shirt somewhere at her hips. He moved across the room, those heavy boots of his clumping on the floor, he hadn't taken off his jeans, and she imagined that his tee shirt had to be in a twisted mess somewhere on the floor.

The bathroom door opened, and she listened to the water run before rolling onto her back. Sitting up, she shrugged her shirt back to her shoulders and fastened her bra. Her torn underwear lay on his tee shirt, which was clear on the other side of the room. In no hurry to button her shirt, or retrieve her lost underwear, she sat in the middle of the desk, and tried to think about how to explain herself. As much as she'd avoided him, and the discussion, thus far, she knew that she couldn't avoid it forever.

Tuck returned to the room with his jeans buttoned again. Rubbing his face dry with the towel, he hooked it around his neck when he was done and leaned against the doorframe. The damp locks of his hair on the periphery of his face stuck to his temples.

"What are you trying to say to me, Toots?"

What a picture he made. His perfect form was draped with such confidence, it was hard to tell if the wall held him up, or if it was the other way around. Over the years, she had lost count of the number of times she'd seen him naked, yet as she examined the ridges and grooves of his abdomen, and the trail of hair that disappeared down into the band of his underwear peeking over his jeans, she wondered if she would ever tire of it. Somehow, he was never something she had taken for granted. Seemingly, he didn't feel the same.

"I don't know if I can do this anymore," she said, and saw the muscles in his stomach bunch in time with a hissing intake of breath.

"Do what, Toots?"

"This," she said. "What we do—you gone half the year, me wondering where you are, what's going on, if you're safe, who you're with—"

"Hey now," he said, shoving away from the doorjamb. "Don't get crazy. There's no one else, there couldn't be—"

"This isn't about that," she said, shaking her head.

"But you don't trust me?"

Peering, she tried to see his mind. "Do you think this is about sex, Tuck? Do you think that's what I'm worried about? I don't even think you'd be able to perform with another woman. You're the most honorable man I know. You always come home to me, always. And you always will."

"So what's the problem?" he asked, maintaining his position on the defensive.

"Do you know what it's like never knowing? Sitting home alone, and—"

"Dempsey looks out for you."

"Is that the same?" she asked. "If it is then explain it to me, because I don't get it."

He went quiet, and still, so very still she couldn't see, or hear him breathe. Despite their long-term relationship this stoic side of him still made her shiver. It was like a visual off switch. One minute he was there, animated, in the moment, and the next he went on pause. He crashed, that's how she put it. Like a computer that freezes as it tries to sort through the multiple processes it's been overloaded with, he didn't move, react, or respond until order had been formed, only then did normal service resume.

Sometimes he stood like this for half a second, but she'd seen him like this for as many as five minutes at a time. Knowing better than to try and get anything out of him at this time, she pushed her weight to her hands and swung herself off the desk. Wriggling her skirt back down over her thighs, she buttoned her shirt and retrieved her useless underwear along with his tee shirt.

"Is this about the marriage thing?" he asked.

Taking a deep breath, she took her belt from the hat stand it had hooked itself onto. "That's what you came up with?" she asked, pulling the stretchy cinch belt around her waist, and breathing in as she hooked the ends together.

"If it's the baby thing, that's easily fixed—"

Pinning him with her own icy stare, she shut him up. "Do you think that I would have a child in this relationship? I know how painful it is to watch you go. To wait, and wonder if you'll come back, when you'll come back, what state you'll be in when you get here."

"Are you saying you don't want to have children?" he asked.

"I'm saying I wouldn't put a child through that torment."

"So you're saying you don't want a kid with me, is that it?"

This was going to descend into an argument, and not the fun kind. She'd have to be careful not to trigger his anger or she'd never finish saying what she had to say. "Do you think I would carry another man's child?" she asked. "Do you think that's what I want?"

"Right now, Toots, I have no idea."

"Clearly," she said, tossing his tee shirt at him as she strode past and went into the bathroom. Leaving the door open as she washed up, she gave him another chance to regroup.

"Do you want me to give it up?" he asked from a place closer to the door than he had been. If she had to guess she would say he was leaning against the wall just outside, but he didn't invade her privacy. That was a joke, there had been no privacy between them from day one of their relationship.

Opening the drawer next to the sink, she retrieved fresh underwear and pulled them on. This wasn't the first time that her underwear had been a casualty of their prolonged time apart. Straightening her clothes, she opened another of the long narrow drawers he had built into the vanity just for her. With a swipe of mascara, and some lip gloss, she was back to normal—almost.

"You can't give it up, Tuck," she called to her own reflection in the mirror. "You would never be able to give it up. You told me that in the beginning."

"You've been patient," he murmured. "We never talked about marriage and kids."

"I knew that those were things you never wanted." Tuck had never been typical, or had it in his life. Staying at home, stuck in one place, trapped, that would be the quickest way for them to lose their spark. "What did you think the first time you saw me?" she asked.

"I've told you that before."

Yes, he had, but the sound of his voice soothed her. Hearing that she'd had an impact on the man she coveted never got old. "Tell me again," she said, keeping her tone neutral.

"I found my reason," he said.

The mumble in his voice wasn't embarrassment, anything but. Tuck wasn't one to get embarrassed, ever. The concept was foreign to him. She could picture him exactly, arms folded over his chest, shoulders hunched back against the wall, his feet far from the baseboard, one ankle crossed over the other.

From the tone of his voice, she knew everything about him—his position, his mood, even his thoughts. They had nothing left to learn, they knew everything there was to know about each other's personalities and demeanors. It hadn't always been easy, but patience and trust paid dividends time and again.

"You were the first thing I saw when I walked in. You were it. My reason for being. Everything I had been for my entire life had been for you. It was the most illogical moment of my life. Since then, every moment with you has been a tie."

It didn't matter how many times she heard it. He always said it with such conviction it was like he dared her, or anyone, to challenge him. Still basking in his words, she was knocked off kilter by his next declaration. "I won't leave you again. You're right. It has been unfair. I'll give up the job."

"That's not what you want," she said, still speaking to herself in the mirror, his disembodied voice could have been in her head. Knowing him as she did, she could have played this argument out in her mind, playing his part as accurately as her own. What she wanted was for him to be honest about whatever had happened in his life before he came back to her.

Until now, she'd always believed he kept his dealings secret to protect her. Now she could see in him that something was wrong and yet, he wouldn't share his pain with her. Gaining that knowledge allowed her to admit that their relationship wasn't as real or as whole as either of them wanted it to be, because there was a huge part of their lives that they didn't share.

The Tuck she knew was always certain. Except since he'd come back this time, he hadn't been as assured. Kadie wanted to know what was weighing on him, wanted to be the one he leaned on in his time of need. Whatever he'd endured, he was carrying that burden alone and that made her feel like a failure.

Keeping his unknown grief a secret was a symptom of what she wanted to remedy between them. Tuck had been the only man in her life for five years, he shouldn't be a mystery to her, not like this, not at the detriment of his own emotional well-being.

"I want you," he said. "I would do anything you asked me to. If that's what will make you happy…"

Again, her eyes closed. He might as well have pierced her heart with a blade. In that moment, his words hurt as much as a physical injury would. "I want you to be happy," she said.

"My happiness shouldn't come at the expense of yours."

"Nor mine yours," she said. "I want you to keep doing what you do with the same conviction you've always brought to the job."

"So that's it. We're over?" he said. "You expect me to turn around and walk away from you, the only thing I've ever known to make sense?"

Everything in his world made sense, she knew that. He worked with logic and reason on a daily basis. His bread and butter were the classifiable, predictable lines of nonsense to the rest of the population.

"No," she said, nipping her lower lip between her teeth. "I don't expect you to do anything. You're not the one who has to change." She had to change. She had to stop being the girl in port he visited when it suited him. Kadie wanted to be his whole life, not just a small part of it.

"Are you guys in here?"

They hadn't locked the office door, being that they were rarely discreet, the others knew to listen at the door before walking in. Although the excitement buzzing in Dempsey's tone made her wonder if he'd even paused.

"We're in the middle of something," Tuck answered.

"Doesn't look like it to me," Dempsey said. "Looks

to me that you're in here all on your lonesome. You need privacy for that, you take extra time in your morning shower." Her lips quirked up, and she heard Tuck's exhaled laugh. "I have something to show you."

"Show me later, this is important."

Leaving her reflection, she pushed the door out of the way, and found she had been right, Tuck was against the wall next to the door. "So is this," she said.

The conversation between them continued in their eyes for a few seconds. Time wasn't on their side right now, but they would get there. Linking her fingers between his, she leaned up and touched her mouth to his.

"We're not finished here," he said.

"We have to work," she said nuzzling against his neck, tipping her lips toward his ear. "We'll talk after the party tonight."

"I'm not going to the party," he said.

Stepping away she smiled and started to pull him toward the other two men loitering inside the door. "Of course you are. Gwen will expect you."

"Gwen hates me," he said.

"I need a date," she said. "If you can't make it, I'll have to ask Howie."

Much as it aggravated him, her smile stretched further when he huffed. "Fine, but we're getting an early night."

"I'd expect nothing less," she said. Spinning, she pulled his hand to the small of her back and leaned her shoulders on his chest, as though he was her own personal leaning post. "Now, what's all the excitement about?"

Maybe there were still things to say, and maybe things were about to get tough. But she wouldn't let anyone into their relationship. They had clear boundaries between them and their colleagues, their friends. No one messed with their relationship, and everything that happened between them in their alone time was private—everything.

THREE

THEIR CONVERSATION HAD been interrupted, and she'd been desperate to finish it ever since. Something about the way Tuck hadn't stopped frowning made her edgy. Whatever was on his mind was reaching critical mass and yet, he still wasn't sharing it. The point she'd been trying to make had been lost and he'd withdrawn when he thought she wanted to finish their relationship. Now Kadie panicked that she'd planted a seed in his mind that was blooming into an idea she didn't want him to embrace.

Gwen's birthday party was next on their to-do list, and she almost wished that they hadn't committed to going. After leaving the office, they'd grabbed some food and got ready. Now they were in the car, driving to Gwen's nightclub party. Tuck hadn't said much, so she figured it would fall to her to make conversation.

Except, before she could, something buzzed and his frown got deeper. Rooting in his pocket, he pulled out a small black earpiece, which he hooked onto his ear in rapid time.

"Swift," he answered.

Why he would use that greeting, she didn't know. Usually he held his conversations in secret, the ones that weren't related to his life with her at any rate. Trying her best to stay still and quiet, Kadie hoped he'd forget she was here and might say more that could reveal some of his other life to her.

"Is it in the kitchen?" he asked.

Kitchen? His other life came with a kitchen. She would give anything to hear the other side of the conversation right now, especially when he smiled. "You want to get us both into trouble, Swallow. I can patch you into the chief's room, but you know Rave will go crazy if he catches you in there."

Swallow. Another name? Another bird? The chief had a room of his own and no one else had access to it. No one except Tuck. Kadie didn't know anything about his other life, but she'd long ago concluded that his skills stretched far beyond beefing up boring corporate security.

"You'll have to give me a couple of hours, I'm not at my terminal." He smiled again, and a curl of jealousy heated Kadie's belly, could it be another woman on the other end of that line? "I'm not at any terminal… No, I'm not sick or doing anything stupid, Zara, don't panic." So it was another woman. Kadie's fists tightened. Whoever she was, she worried about him. "I'm going to a party… Yes, I do go to parties." His smile faded and a grim glare took its place. "You know I'll come back for that. But you're trying to do too much too fast, you can't fix this. You have to know that, right?" His attention left the road for a minute, and she got the sense he was warring with himself again. "I don't want you to even think about Saint. We'll deal with him when we have to. Together. You're not alone, Zar. I'm still with you. You can call me any time. What's priority one?"

Kadie wanted to know what priority one was, but he'd never tell her. "I'll call you tonight when it's done, okay?" he asked down the line. "He always pulls through. This is just gonna take time."

There was no further farewell, he took the piece from his ear and tucked it back into his pocket. They drove another block. "She's my best friend's girl," Tuck said. "Before you start cooking up shit in your head."

That was supposed to make her feel better about his

fidelity. But she hadn't worried about where he put his dick when they weren't together, she knew it belonged to her. His explanation didn't make her feel better. It reminded her of how little she knew about what he did in his life beyond her. How could she be in love with him and in a relationship with him for five years and not know his best friend?

Little reminders like this cropped up all the time and she accepted them. Until she wanted to support him and he shut her out.

"You care about her?" Kadie asked.

He stopped at a light. "I don't know her that well yet. They haven't been together long."

Twisting to face him, she ventured a question. "What's he like?"

Reluctance made him tense, she could see it straight away, how his body got rigid and his expression blanked. "I can't talk about him, Toots."

Using her pet name after denying her his trust seemed ridiculous. When she switched focus back to the windshield, he tried to take her hand, but she pulled it away. "He's more important to you than I am?"

He scowled. "Don't do that, don't make it sound like that. He's not more important. He's dangerous and if I revealed his secrets to you—"

"He'd hurt me?" she asked because unless that was the case, she couldn't understand his hesitation.

"No," he snapped, glaring in offense. "He'd kill to protect you. He'd give up his life for yours."

Whatever they did, it was serious. She'd tried to convince herself that he didn't do anything life-threatening, but it was a lie and a part of her always knew that.

"How do you know that? He's never even met me. Why would he put himself in harm's way for me?"

"Because it's what I'd do for Swallow." Tuck would die for the woman he'd just been talking to on the phone. She felt sick. "It's what we do, Kade."

"Die for strangers?"

"Protect our own. Swallow would die for you too. She'd die for me."

Tuck had always asserted that he kept her separate to protect her and she bought that. Learning that there were other women on the team changed Kadie's perspective. She could give her life for him and for his colleagues, maybe, if she knew what they were all about and was given the chance to learn and prove herself.

"What's priority one?" He tensed even further and pulled into the club parking lot. They got a space and he turned off the engine, but before he could get out and avoid her question, she lunged over and grabbed his arm. "What's priority one?"

Unable to avoid it, he made eye contact and his gaze softened a fraction. Maybe it was pity that made him feel sorry for her, or he was pained at the position she'd put him in. "I can't, Toots. I have to be careful. You have to be careful. If you said those words to the wrong person—"

"What about Swift, Swallow, the chief, or Rave—" He grabbed her shoulder.

"Don't ever even hint at those names around anyone." Letting her go, he banged his hands on the steering wheel. "This is fucked up. I shouldn't have come back. It was too soon."

Evidence that she was right. Something was wrong. Taking off her seatbelt, she stroked her hand across his knotted shoulders. "Why weren't you ready? What happened that—"

Snatching her wrist, he hauled her off him. "Don't you dare fucking manipulate me, Kade. I won't betray my kin."

"But you'll betray me?"

"I love you."

Until now, those words had always been enough. When she believed it was work that took him away and nothing else, she could cope. But she could see it was more than that, there were people he cared about, people she'd never met. People he kept her from. She couldn't exist in a bubble like a fantasy woman he could return to whenever he needed a break from his reality.

"We better go inside," she said, and their hands slid

away from each other's bodies.

"Yeah," he mumbled. "I guess we better."

All they could do was show up and smile for the others. Kadie had grown up with Dempsey and Gwen, her own mother had abandoned her as a baby and she'd never known her father. This was as close to family as she got. Tuck didn't usually complain about socializing with them when he had to. The party was just going to give both of them more time to stew, but Kadie was determined to get to the bottom of his mood.

***

THEY'D BEEN AT the party for an hour and she'd barely seen Tuck. He'd done his duty and got her drinks, but he'd found a spot in the corner of the room and had avoided talking to anyone. Kadie watched him sulk but deflected questions from Gwen and her friends about his mood. Most of them didn't know how close she and Tuck were and tonight she was fine with that.

The next time she glanced up, Tuck was wearing the earpiece again, and his lips were moving. The group of people she stood with were chatting and laughing, but she was trying to read his lips, even though the low lighting and flashing lights made that next to impossible.

"What's eating him?" Dempsey asked at her shoulder. Her cousin hadn't missed their separation, despite his presence.

If only she knew the answer. "It's complicated."

Tuck began to move, he left his corner position and headed for the exit. He disappeared into the throngs of people. Those who didn't know him read danger, and wanted a piece of it, she hadn't been much different at the start. But Tuck ignored anyone who looked his way.

Dempsey was still in her ear. "Are you guys fighting?"

"Maybe," she said, still looking at the mass of people who had closed in on Tuck's wake.

"Something is going on," Dempsey said. "If it's going to affect business—"

"That's not why you want to know," she snapped, and turned to glare at her cousin.

None of this was his fault. She couldn't place blame on anyone. Tuck did a good job of withholding the truth, she didn't know why his mood was so erratic, and that was why she was testy. She couldn't identify the cause of his brooding, and he didn't trust her enough to offer an explanation. Anger was easier to grasp than heartache, and targeting her cousin was safer than confronting her love.

Dempsey wasn't offended by her outburst; his look became pitying. "Kade—"

"Sorry," she said, swigging from her bottle then handing it to her cousin. Despite the looks she got from the others they were with, she retrieved her purse from the bar, threw the strap over her shoulder, and began to follow Tuck's route out.

When she found him, he was around the back of the building, pacing a narrow strip of grass in front of the chain-link fence at the boundary.

"You quit smoking when you were eighteen," she said, leaning against the concrete roughcast surface of the nightclub building.

Tuck stopped pacing and saw her. Not that he hadn't known she was there, he knew. But those eyes of his saw her now. Black as night beneath the hard set of his jaw, she read his struggle. The torment riled him, making him feel out of control, which he didn't like. So this was what she got. Hard lines, and the immovable man, not the man who held her, and whispered words of devotion after making soft, slow love with her.

Her statement went unacknowledged. "Just in case you forgot," she said.

"It's time to go."

The party was never going to get any better and that wasn't a reflection of the company or the club, Kadie just wasn't in the mood to feign smiles. "If that's what you want," she said, pushing away from the corner. "I can go and tell everyone we're going home, and—"

Remaining cold, he didn't move. "Not you. Just me."

In one chilling reflex, her throat parched and her shoulders pulled her back straight. The idea that he was leaving again so soon, and without resolving any of their issues, scared her. "No," she breathed and took one long step toward him. Even when he was being a prick, she still wanted him around. "You just got here."

"Can't be helped, Toots."

"When did this happen?" she asked.

"Inside," he said, in that damn blank tone of his. He hadn't budged an inch, hadn't flinched, how could he say this as though he were dishing out directions to a passer-by?

"You've never…" she said, taking a less steady step toward him. "It's never been this quick before. You usually have at least a week…" her words drifted off because there was no point, the decision was made.

Forcing Tuck to stay here while he was in this dark place would be detrimental to them. All she could do was let him go and hope he'd work through his issues before he came back to her again. Answers were never forthcoming when she tried to coerce them.

Sometimes he stayed with her for months, sometimes it was a few days. Just as he could be away for a weekend, or a season. Once in a while, he came to her in the night, made love to her, and then slipped out, like an apparition. But if he hung around long enough to come into the office with her, he would usually be around for a while.

Arguing with him wouldn't help the friction that had built between them. So she steeled herself to accept the inevitable. "When are you coming back?" she asked.

Her lips didn't taste the words. All she was aware of was the ball of bile threatening her throat. Shifting her feet, she watched her sandals be enveloped by the damp grass. Ice ran through her in place of blood, and she wished for some sign that this was as difficult for him.

"I'm not."

Her grasp of the English language faltered. The phrase, "hear it but don't believe it," seemed to be applicable, but she had never experienced it, not like this. "What?" she sobbed on a laugh because she couldn't figure him out.

Making herself look up, she wanted to lash out when she saw that he was blank, vacant. He'd switched off, completely detached himself. That ability was what made him good in his line of work—he'd never done it with her. "I don't understand—"

"Dem is right," he said, his tone ratcheted into aggressive. "Hell, Toots, you got it on the money."

Though her jaw moved, she couldn't say a word. The thud of her heart in her stomach chilled every drop of blood it fought to keep pumping. Her head swirled knowing that this wasn't real, it couldn't be real.

"Take care of yourself," he said and marched forward.

He was going to pass her; he was going to walk away. Once he disappeared around the nightclub, he would be gone, and this time he wouldn't be coming back. "Wait," she said, grabbing his arm with both hands to halt him beside her.

She sucked her bottom lip, and salved it up and down with her tongue, buying herself some time to try to think of something to say. As soon as she released her lip, it dried in the bitter night air again. The moon was bright tonight, shining a glorious white, spotlighting this moment for the stars to observe her torment like onlookers of a tragedy on the stage.

"You always come back to me," she said, forcing herself to look at him, even though she knew her eyes reflected that moonlight in her glacé desperation.

Though he held himself rigid his hand came up, then hesitated. He never hesitated in anything. Never in his life, never in all the time she had known him. Snatching his hesitant hand with both of hers, she pushed it to her cheek and rubbed it back and forth, reminding him of who she was, of their connection, of his right to touch her in any way he pleased.

Keeping him with her for as long as possible might be the key to breaking through this shell crackling around him. "You don't have to go now," she said, pressing her lips to his palm. "We have our routine before you leave me. And we were going to get an early night, remember?"

"Toots," he said, and his eyes softened as he took his hand from her face. He tried to step away, but she grabbed the sides of his leather jacket and pulled him against her.

Feeling him pull away was worse than seeing it. Holding on to him was the only way she could keep her heart beating. "I don't understand what—"

"This was never meant to be forever," he said over her, probably because he knew if she started to beg, he might relent. Manipulating him into staying with her might not be best emotionally, but it was better than giving up without a fight. Tuck was better at holding his ground than she wanted him to be. "I told you that. You remember the night of your birthday?"

"Yes," she whispered. "The night we met."

"You remember what I said to you?"

For the first time, she didn't feel safe at this proximity. "You told me to be sure," she said, staring into his chest. "You told me you were going to hurt me one day."

"And, here it is," he said. "To the people I roll with, 'one day' means death. It means the end, and that's what this is."

But she wasn't ready to lose him. "No," she said, shaking her head, and finding his eyes. "No, I don't believe it. You're not that person. You're not the monster you make out to be."

Shadows crept over his face. "You have no idea what I do when I leave here," he said. "No idea what I'm doing. Where I am or what's going on. You don't know if I'm safe… or who I'm with…"

Immediately she started to object, then she realized, he was right. All this time she'd believed that they were exclusive, there was no evidence to suggest he screwed around, but she didn't question him about his fidelity either, meaning he could get up to whatever he liked.

"What does that mean?" she asked, dropping his jacket from her grip.

The glimmer of his sinister smile decreased her confidence. "Do you think I waltz away from here, and go without for months? Toots, you're good but—"

No, her man wasn't cruel and he wasn't a liar either. He had no reason to string her along with promises of exclusivity if he wasn't in love with her. She couldn't believe that their whole relationship had been a lie. "Why are you doing this?" she murmured, figuring that the only reason he was resorting to cruelty was in an attempt to wedge them apart.

"Time to walk away," he said on a shrug. "You know I don't like complications."

Six months was a complication, that would be the time a woman might start to get too clingy for a player's interest. Having been with this man for half a decade, she knew how to see through his indifference. "I'm not a complication," she said. "You love me. You've loved me since the first time—"

"Toots, let's call a spade a spade," he said, dropping some of the act with withering patience. "You're not happy, I'm not happy. Let's make everybody happy and walk away with dignity."

Now she could get angry because without the bullshit, she had to wonder if cutting her loose had been on his agenda for a while. "Are you implying I'm making a fool of myself?"

"I'm saying we're done, and I don't want a long, drawn-out scene. We're good, you're a good girl, smart and sassy, we've had a good ride."

She deserved more than a clichéd goodbye. "And, now it's over," she said, stepping away. "Just like that."

"I'm not going to marry you, Toots," he said, stepping into her, so she stepped away again. "I don't want kids, or a house, or a broad who wants to "talk" whenever I get a few days of shore leave, you hear what I'm saying?"

Her back hit the wall, and she realized he had walked her onto the gravel surrounding the nightclub. The eaves of this lean-to rear section hung only a foot above his head. "You're scared," she said on a wavering breath. "I think you're a coward."

The corner of his mouth tipped up. "If that helps you sleep, Toots, hold on to that thought. You think of me any time you need help to get through the nights."

His eyes dragged down and up her body, lingering both times on her cleavage, usually the heat in his gaze made her shiver and wet all at the same time. Now, she just felt violated.

Poking holes in his story, she challenged him. "If you were so sure you didn't want me, why didn't you tell me any of this when you got here?"

"Like I said," he leered and leaned in until his lips touched the top of her ear. "You're good."

She knew him well enough to know that his harsh words weren't real, at least not real enough to detract from what they'd shared together. Pressing her hands against his chest, she closed her eyes and took a long inhale of his scent. Something had been up his ass since he got back, maybe a job went south or he was frustrated at not making progress with a task.

Either way, if lashing out at her was going to make his life easier, she'd take it. Making a point not to be a complication in his life had always been her default. Even when times were desperate, she fell back on the confidence she had in their love.

"If you have to go then go," she mumbled, touching her lips to his neck. The unexpected move startled him and he leaned away from her. "You know I love you, Tuck. If you want to walk away, I'm not going to stop you. I've never stopped you."

"This is exactly what you wanted," he said. "You're free to do what you want, with who you want."

So that was what he'd taken from what she said in the office about not doing this anymore. His head was up his ass and once he got over his sulk, he'd realize that. Way back at the start of their relationship, before it really was a relationship, he'd tried to tell her that he wasn't a good bet as a boyfriend. After she accepted that, he got belligerent and told her he wasn't going to leave her on the open market. She expected this experience to play out the same.

"Thank you," she said, flattening her hands against the wall at the small of her back. "I suppose that means you are too."

"Right then," he said, taking a reverse step.

"I'll be seeing you, Tucker."

What could have been pity in his eyes morphed into melancholy then in a flash it was gone, leaving his stare blank, black, vacant. He didn't say another word, just looked for a second, turned, and left.

Taking a long, loud breath, she closed her eyes and told herself it would be okay. He might have accepted a job, but he'd never accepted one then vanished in the same hour. There were things of his at the apartment that he would need, and in the basement of the office too. This was a man she knew better than she knew herself and he'd have preparations to make before disappearing from her life, which gave her the chance to make him see sense before he was gone.

***

EXPLAINING TO DEMPSEY that they were leaving only took a few seconds, her cousin assumed that Tuck was outside, so he accepted that she was safe. Except Tuck wasn't outside and the car they'd arrived in was gone. Kadie couldn't ask for Dempsey's or he would know that Tuck wasn't giving her a ride.

Getting herself to a main road took longer than she thought, but eventually she got there and found a cab. The driver took the long way around for a shortcut, but she didn't mind as it gave her a chance to think about what she was going to say.

Of course she wouldn't tell Tuck that she had followed him. Instead, she decided to go with the work angle. Saying she was ill would make him baby her, so he wouldn't talk to her, which was what she needed. There were files at home that needed her attention and Tuck wouldn't know that they weren't urgent.

When they finally got to her apartment, she trawled the cars, but his wasn't there. Asking the cab driver to wait, she ran up the stairs just to double check. Nothing was out of place, not until she went into the bedroom. Some of his clothes were gone, but that didn't alarm her. What alarmed her was the electronics, or rather the lack of them. He'd taken all of his toys, all the computers and gadgets that were usually locked in the bottom drawer of his long secure cabinet under the bed.

The solid metal case was pulled out, unlocked, and emptied, there was nothing left. Her knees gave way and she sank to the bed. Had she just made a mistake? She let him go without a fight because she thought there would be time for the fight here, in their home. After all the arguments were done, they would be in a private place to have wild, make up sex… Except, he wasn't here.

The blare of a car horn woke her from her daze, and she bounced to her feet. If he wasn't here then he would be at the office, there was nowhere else he would go. That Tuck was working fast to clear out gave her the fire under her ass that she needed. Running for the door, she didn't even lock it, she just hoped that the latch caught when she slammed it. Getting to the office before Tuck could leave was urgent, nothing else came first.

Slamming the car door, she gave abrupt instructions to the cab driver, then promised him an extra twenty if he stepped on it. Sinking back into the seat, she closed her eyes and tried to calm herself, Tuck couldn't have more than a forty-minute lead on her. Of course, he was in his own vehicle, and could drive as fast as he liked, and on whatever route he liked. But this was crazy thinking, she couldn't let herself believe that he was trying to get away from her in such a hurry. There was no reason to think that he wouldn't be in the office basement.

Sure enough, when she got there his vehicle was outside and relief relaxed her muscles. She paid the cab driver and got out. Straightening her clothes, she reminded herself of why she was here, work, nothing else, if he happened to be here, so what. At least, that was what she wanted Tuck to think.

Ignoring the niggling worry that she didn't see any lights on, even in the narrow basement windows that showed on one side of the building. She convinced herself that he didn't need to have lights on and the glare from the computer screens wouldn't show because of the angle. Also, he'd tinted the window slats to conceal what was inside, so there would be no light.

Unlocking the door, she frowned at the flashing alarm panel. While punching in the code, she forgot all about a cover story, and ran down the stairs. Only she and Tuck had ever been in here, the whole building was his but this section was only for them. It was filled with flashing lights and gizmos he wouldn't trust anyone else to see.

Only one corner contained anything approaching comfort. It had a large top-of-the-line sofa bed, and a huge-screen TV that he had brought in for them to watch movies while he was working with one of his systems that she didn't understand. Sometimes he could be down here for days, but when that happened, she just moved in with him and they simply stayed here, together. There was a small bathroom that was nothing more than functional, and a few kitchen necessities, but this was his lair. There for them to enjoy each other while he worked, nothing more.

Typing in the code, and giving her fingerprint, she waited for the door to open. It beeped and whooshed open, and she didn't hesitate. The moment she stepped into the dim haze, her heart froze. The usual beeps and flashing lights on the panels and screens around the room were silent and dark.

He'd shut everything down. He never did that. Never once, in all the time she had known him, had he turned anything in this room off. These machines were his babies and always doing a dozen things each and every second. He used the servers he nurtured in here to piggyback many of the things he did when he was working here or away.

With another step inside, she saw a large brown envelope on the nearest facing desk, "Toots" was scrawled in his script, and then she knew. He was gone.

FOUR

Eight months later

WHEN YOUR MAN leaves you alone in a nightclub parking lot after telling you he's never going to see you again, it stings. Kadie decided, not too long after her heart broke, that she wasn't going to take his declaration lying down.

For too long she'd accepted his excuses and sat at home waiting for him. Bringing up their situation in the office was supposed to be a move toward changing it, to integrating her deeper into his life. It wasn't supposed to finish their relationship.

After wallowing in self-pity for a few days in the basement, where she locked herself up alone, she'd given herself a mental shake. If she wanted to talk to Tucker Holt then there was no goddamn reason that she shouldn't be able to, she deserved at least a conversation with him.

Tracking him down wouldn't be easy, she'd been under no illusions about that. One reprieve was that the business was never going to excel in the same way now that the real brains had abandoned it. Dempsey was good with computers, he had qualifications and knew procedures, whereas Tuck had an instinct that put him at one with the machine. Without her job to worry about, she had plenty of time to find her ex.

Tuck was careful about not leaving things lying around, which was how she was so sure that he wanted to divide her from his other life, but she'd known that there had to be something that would point her in the right direction. He might not be expecting her to stroll up and present herself in front of his colleagues, but he had no right to dump her ass and take off without any follow-up discussion, not after five years together.

Determination was inspiring on a mission. Kadie had learned that making a plan and focusing on how to implement it was more productive than lying around whimpering about how her life had gone wrong.

The apartment was a dead end. She'd stood in the middle of his basement lab, surrounded by the silent machines, and known her journey to find Tucker would start right there.

Wishing that she'd paid more attention when Tuck was doing his hacking, she made little progress with the computers. Frustrated, she wouldn't let herself be beaten and decided to take advantage of her intern. Without telling Howie who the computer belonged to, she told him they had a digital forensics job and asked him to pull up any names or addresses that might lead to contacts of the computer's owner.

Staying out of Dempsey's way was easy, he had enough business to keep him occupied. Almost immediately, she could tell that Howie was suspicious. Given the level of security on Tuck's machine, and probably the kind of encryption too, it had to be obvious that the computer belonged to a person who knew what they were doing and one who didn't want to be snooped on.

Still, it took the kid just a couple of hours to pull up one file. It was a document containing spotty background information and incomplete observations that she guessed came from surveillance. It gave her one name: Nykiel Sikorski.

On gaining that information, she was confident it wouldn't take her long to find the man who would be her first link. Turned out she was wrong, for months she'd chased down leads and just when she was about to give up, someone found her. Howie.

The kid had been tailing her, which was sort of embarrassing because he was such an awkward geek, in no way a pro. She'd like to think that she would have noticed him schlepping along behind her. In her defense, she'd been distracted by the various bars and clubs that she had to frequent to try to find Nykiel Sikorski.

He wasn't an easy man to track down, and when she did, she was struck by such elation that she might as well have found Tuck himself.

"He's here?" she asked, and the barman she'd been talking to nodded to the corner.

On a raised section in the corner of this pounding nightclub was a booth filled with people. Bulky men stood around it in poses suggesting they were security agents. There at the head of the booth was her man: Sikorski.

Not wanting to get too close, she ordered a drink and began to edge in the direction of the booth. Striding up there would be impossible with all of the security men standing around, and she didn't want to ask Sikorski about Tuck until she was sure they were friends.

This was the first concrete link she had found. The first connection to her man in months. So many times, she'd been ready to give up and grieve for the relationship, but without him, she had no purpose. Getting up in the morning depended on her belief that she would see him again, that she would find him and prove to him that she couldn't be cast aside.

What he had done wasn't fair, and someone had to tell him that. It had occurred to her that he may have moved on with his life. He may have a new girlfriend or be screwing around with a posse of females. There was also a chance that he had no interest in rekindling their relationship either. With what she'd been through over the last seven and a half months, she wasn't sure that she wanted him back anyway.

Love still warmed her, but she ignored it because she couldn't trust him, not after what she'd been through. Anger was easier to find and at first, she'd believed it was unsated passion, a pent up, rageful lust aimed at the man who she resented for still having control over her. Even now, after months apart, he dictated her life and it was like he couldn't care at all.

Since she'd packed a bag and snuck away, she'd made only a brief call to her cousin, Dempsey, to tell him that she was getting out of town for a while. Confused as he was, she could tell from his questions that he believed she was with Tuck, and she didn't correct that assumption. Dempsey would never have let her come on this kind of a mission alone.

Edging down the bar until she got to the end closest to the booth, she noticed Sikorski looking in her direction a few times. She smiled, blinked her eyes away, and looked back, playing the furtive but interested onlooker. Straight away, his lips began to curl, not in attraction as such, but in satisfaction that he'd been spotted.

Okay, so he had an ego, she could use that to her advantage. Flirting it up, she kept the little eye dance going and hid her mouth in her drink letting him think that she was loose, maybe a bit tipsy. All she had to do was get close, if she could talk to him then she could figure out what kind of a person he was and why Tuck might want to associate with him.

The idea that Tuck might appear just because she did also crossed her mind. If what she'd seen on the computer were surveillance records then it was possible that Tuck was tailing this guy. That being the case, Tuck could see her here and intercept her before she spoke to Sikorski. So far, that hadn't happened.

Sikorski got the attention of one of the security men and spoke to him while keeping his focus on her. She had him. Trying to remain clueless, she didn't look straight at the security guy as he came over to her.

"The boss wants you to join him for a drink," the oaf said when he leaned in to grumble in her ear.

He didn't wait for an answer, just grabbed her upper arm and began to pull her along beside him. So much for civility. Kadie maintained her smile, as if she was perfectly fine with this idiot manhandling her. Tuck sure could pick his friends. It stood to reason that he kept her away from this aspect of his life when it was so dangerous. Though she hadn't faced it while they were together, the only reason to maintain a barrier between her and the truth of what he did was because it might hurt one of them if he didn't.

Adapting to the caliber of people her ex worked with hadn't taken her long, she'd grown up in poverty, surrounded by crime, and bounced around several foster homes before her aunt, Dempsey's mother, took her in. The duration between past and present shrank to nothing when she started questioning people on how she might find the man in the booth she was being dragged toward now.

Tuck had given her a good life, set her up with responsibility, and made her feel important. Now she speculated that it had all been a trap, a gilded cage, meant to seduce her away from making her own decisions, keeping her right where he wanted her. Manipulation came in many forms, Tuck had never been violent, always let her have freedom, but the chain on her ankle had been loose enough for her to miss its presence for half a decade.

Her anger came back. Locating Tuck was supposed to give her closure. Initially, it had been meant to win him back. Now, all she wanted to do was smack him in the face. She felt used, abandoned, and didn't like being vulnerable because a man walked away from her. But he had been her whole life and she'd lost sight of her own dreams because she'd been too busy deferring to his while being the dutiful housewife, sitting at home, waiting patiently for her man to return and indulge her with his presence. She wasn't sure who she angrier with, Tuck or herself.

"Good evening," Sikorski said, half-standing to take her hand so he could pull her around the booth and seat her beside him. "Your eyes are mesmerizing."

The thick accent wasn't attractive, not that she expected to feel any sort of sexual pull toward this man. Instead of being exotic or commanding, it just came off as cold, just like the eyes he was trailing over her body.

Touching her collarbone, she slid her hand up into her hair. "Thank you," she said. "I feel very privileged to be here." Ego, she'd noticed he had one, now it was time to appeal to it.

"You are," he declared, proud of his superior position in the room, and the respect of those around him. Those who were at his table said little and what they did say was in low whispers. Either these people worked below him or were terrified of him, maybe both were true. "Sapphire."

"Excuse me?" she asked, not understanding where the word had come from.

"It's what I'll call you."

Like she was a pet. Her eyes were a striking blue, very brilliant, and she'd been told that before, so the name didn't surprise her. It also served her interest that he played this game because it meant she didn't have to reveal herself to him. Being a passing fancy was fine and she could play a role for one night until she found out what she needed to know.

Widening her smile, she nodded, trying to seem pleased that she'd been named by him, rather than insulted. Whatever game he wanted to play, she'd play it, as long as he kept his hands to himself. Maybe after another drink or two, she'd ask him about what he did and who he worked with. A drink or two for him that was, not for her. Kadie had never been much of a drinker and with so many variables floating around, she wasn't going to take the risk of putting herself in too vulnerable a position.

Right now, they were in a bustling nightclub. At any time, she could excuse herself to the ladies' room and depart if she felt unsafe. Protecting herself came before obtaining any information Sikorski might have, and if she didn't get what she wanted from him then she'd find another avenue to get it.

If this man, who could be dangerous, knew who she was, he might link her to Tuck. More likely, he'd link her to Dempsey, who was sitting at home unaware of where she was or what she was doing.

Although she didn't plan to upset the man sitting beside her now, rubbing her thigh, she also didn't know enough about him to trust him. Dempsey wasn't expecting an Eastern European criminal to come busting in to kick his ass, so she wouldn't give Sikorski any ammunition to want to hurt her.

As back-up, she'd make sure he never knew her real name, and she'd left all her IDs at home meaning no one would be able to trace her family. As long as everyone she cared about was safe, and she was the only one taking risks, she'd push forward and take the precautions she needed to ensure her own survival.

Though her desire to track Tuck down was waning, she could only go so far before she had to admit to herself that Tuck didn't want to be found. A few months of looking for a man she'd loved for five years was acceptable, much longer and her desire for closure would come across as obsession, and she didn't want any man to sneer at her with ridicule.

While formulating a plan for how to extract the information she needed without giving too much away, Kadie almost didn't see who was approaching with a second security guard. When Sikorski moved his attention from her to them, she was horrified to see the youngster next to the goon.

"Who is this?" Sikorski asked, impatient about the interruption.

"He says he's with the girl, that he looks out for her."

Kadie had told Howie to go home. Coming to her rescue was probably his idea of heroism, but she didn't need to be saved and now she had someone to worry about other than herself. Howie was awkward, not at all social, and his charisma ranked alongside that of an amoeba. Kadie found his gawkiness endearing and he was so eager to please her that she made concessions for him too often. Her kindness was coming back to bite them both.

Sikorski looked at her and then at Howie before he gestured for Howie to sit down. Howie did as Sikorski requested and she scrunched her nose. This wasn't going to finish as clean as she wanted it to. Howie wasn't a bodyguard; he didn't have bulk. Sikorski would view him as suspicious, either he was a kid in love with a woman out of his league, or a boy with an agenda who wanted an in.

Whatever Sikorski thought, Kadie sighed. She couldn't leave this table, or Sikorski, until she could take

Howie with her. Given his lack of perception, she would struggle to hint at him to take a course of action. Complications. Tuck hated them and now she understood why.

***

"WHAT ARE YOU doing here?"

Howie had made the mistake of telling Sikorski about his talent. He might not be in the big-boy leagues, but Sikorski seemed intrigued by the idea of a computer whizz at his table. They talked so much that she was largely ignored. Sikorski didn't drink much because he was too engrossed in the conversation with Howie, and she had no opportunity to flirt information out of the Russian.

Toward the end of the night, Sikorski got up and declared that they were going back to his mansion. Kadie had no choice but to accept because Howie was already being escorted out.

"I thought this was what you wanted, to be here," Howie said, coming over to sit beside her.

They'd been left in this large room with a bunch of other people who were all chatting and admiring the décor in this space designed for entertaining. Couches were scattered around with tables full of drinks everywhere. For an impromptu gathering, it was remarkably well organized. An open fire on the far away wall blazed up an immense chimney breast that was decorated with tiny glass tiles.

The room was gorgeous and the atmosphere was warm, but already she wanted to leave. "You can't tell him who you are or who I am. As far as he's concerned, I'm a dumb ho attracted to power."

Something about the offended confusion he exuded made her want to shake him and hug him all at once. He had no idea what he'd just walked into. The people around them gave them cover to talk without being listened to and she needed to seize this chance while she had it.

"Tell him we met in a bar somewhere, that we were friends, that you liked me," she said, taking his hand and pressing it onto her knee. "If you tell him the truth, or ask about Tuck… just trust me, Howie, please."

Sikorski came in and began to greet everyone. Because every other soul in the room got up to gravitate toward the leader, she took Howie's hand to force them to do the same. Walking into Sikorski's private home was not part of the plan. During the ride over, she'd noted how secluded the building was and the grounds were vast enough that sneaking out would be tough, especially with the number of guards she'd seen.

As long as Howie was here, she was here, and maybe he was right. If he was inside, he could find a way to hack Sikorski's system and collate what Sikorski knew about Tuck, in the same way Howie had done for her with Tuck's machine when they ended up with the Sikorski information.

"We have to stick together," she said, pulling him close. "Whatever happens, Howie, we can't be separated because if we are, we're never getting out of here again."

FIVE

One month later.
Present day.

IT WAS DARK, and dirty, and loud. Just like every other time he'd pushed through the scarred wooden door, the smell that assaulted him was of alcohol, urine with a hint of blood, and a dollop of body odor. Hell's Waiting Room, even the devil himself couldn't come up with better. The scum of the world, the has-beens, and the never-weres mingled in the sound of heavy rock, punctuated with the clatter of pool balls ricocheting, and every curse word known to man.

The game never changed, the music stayed the same, the faces hid different souls, but they all meant the same thing. If you were here, you didn't belong anywhere. Whether this had been your haunt for a week, or a decade, you still didn't belong. Not here, not anywhere.

Anything went in a place like this, rules didn't exist, the patched up furniture and gouged floor testified to that. The sound of flesh on flesh was as likely to be carnal as it was to be angry. Never a night went by that there wasn't a brawl of some sorts. The sound of a woman's feigned pants, accompanied by the groans of a john from the corner with the busted lightbulb, told him that tonight was business as usual. Not that Tuck had come to expect anything less.

When Tuck slapped a hand on the bar, the long-haired, leather-clad barman, who was chewing on a toothpick, glanced up. "You seen my friend?" Tuck asked.

The barman, who he knew as Linc, spat out the cocktail stick, without thought for where it would land, and reached beneath the bar for a stained glass. "Not tonight, man," Linc said. "But it's early."

"You expect him?" Tuck asked, watching Linc pour out a stingy measure of sour mash.

"In this place," Linc said, shoving the glass over the bar.

"Has a habit of confounding expectations," Tuck said, propping himself on a stool and casting an eye around the establishment, using the reflection in the broken bar mirror behind Linc.

"You never told me what you wanted with him," Linc said, fishing another stick from his pocket.

Tuck wasn't going to answer that question, just as he hadn't answered it the other three times Linc had asked. "What's going on there?" he asked, sipping the liquor and nodding toward the reflection of a huddled group in a faraway corner.

Linc glanced over his shoulder at the reflection then looked past Tuck to the actual group. "Fresh meat," he answered. "A stray, don't think she knew what she was walking into."

Tuck had distracted Linc long enough. Another patron stumbled to the bar looking for service. Linc plucked the stick from his mouth and wandered toward the customer, calm as you like, despite the newcomer's obvious impatience.

Women weren't common in here and those who did show up knew what to expect. Most of them came looking for trouble or payment. This was a place where men could lose big. Drugs were sold like candy and everyone had a price.

Linc's description of her as a stray meant she was unlikely to be a working girl, but if the crowd of men around were anything to go by, she was holding her own, at least so far. There was zero chance that those men would let the woman walk away without giving up what they wanted from her—virtue included.

For now, they were entertained, but eventually they would get bored of her and take what they wanted. In another life, he might be concerned by that, he might have even tried to help her out, but his days of playing martyr were long gone.

Twisting the base of his glass back and forth between his thumb and forefinger, he looked down into the molten liquid displaced by the rhythmic motion. He couldn't rescue a woman he didn't know from a fate she might end up enjoying.

Funny thing about the women that came in here looking for trouble, they didn't have to look hard and more often than not it changed their lives, one way or another. This place was far enough away from anywhere decent that Tuck didn't have to worry about the woman being an innocent. If she had been underage, Linc would have thrown her out to save her from the clutches of the evil they all knew loomed here.

Linc was almost as broad as he was tall. This place was his and he knew exactly what went on here. That didn't mean he saw any of it, especially if someone came looking to ask questions. Tuck had been frequenting this place and had learned that as tough as Linc looked, he still had some morals, though he'd probably lost count of how many times they'd been compromised. Linc didn't care about much, but what he did care about he was vehement about, and no one wanted an enemy like Linc.

Still, this wasn't a place that had local law enforcement on speed-dial. In fact, Linc paid a lookout who loitered in the parking area, looking out for any trouble-vanquishing force. Being part of the Kindred meant there were circumstances in which he could've been accused of playing vigilante, exactly the kind of guy they didn't want around here. But this mission was too important not to take the risk of being discovered by these crooks.

He'd been reminded of what it felt like to have nothing to lose and it freed him up to take all kinds of risks without blinking for thought. Being an island might make him untouchable, but it did funny things to his conscience. He'd lived like this before; his life had been nothing but this until…

Glancing up from his drink, he found his own reflection, and tried to imagine her smile, or what it had been like to smile at her. With nothing to lose, there was nothing to smile about, so his facial muscles had forgotten how. The scowl served him well, it told people to back-off, to mind their own business, and to leave him alone. He was alone and now he always would be.

Pity stung his throat, so to disguise it, he flung the measure of liquor back in one gulp, then slammed the glass onto the bar. He'd had it. He allowed himself to think of her once a day, no more than that, otherwise she'd consume him. Not that he was under the illusion he'd ever left her command. His fingers twitched and he balled them into fists against his palms. He'd thought of her smile, he couldn't think about her body, about her skin under his touch, how she'd writhed and responded to him, how her eyes closed and her lips parted when he laid her in their cool sheets—no, once a day, now he had to stop.

Lifting the glass to give it a shake, he indicated he needed a refill. Linc came over and filled it from the label-less bottle he was holding. Tuck threw back the measure and gestured for a third.

"Got a problem?" Linc asked, pouring out the measure.

Tuck usually nursed his drink because he liked to be in full control. But he always tipped big so that Linc wouldn't fling him out when he needed to be here. This was the waiting part of the game. That was fine, he would wait. The Kindred's bidding was his sole purpose now.

Where this part had always frustrated him in the past, he'd known it was because he wanted to get back to his girl and waiting to pounce delayed that. Now, this part nearly killed him because he wasn't going anywhere, and certainly not anywhere near her. Even in his internal monologue he wouldn't acknowledge her name. If he said it, or thought it, he would have to acknowledge it was real, that he'd left her.

Shaking his head, he took a sip, and dropped back

into the stool he hadn't realized he'd left. Normally, she was never far from his thoughts, but tonight was a plague. The last couple of days had been harder than usual, though he had no idea why. Maybe because it was only days from being nine full months since he'd seen her. Was she still living in the same place? Had she moved on? Who took her to bed now?

The sound of splintering glass assaulted his ears, no one else flinched, which was evidence of the regularity of such a noise and how feeble this one had been. Linc tossed a ragged towel at him, and Tuck realized the shattered glass was in his hand, he'd crushed it in his fist. He was bleeding, not badly, but he hadn't noticed the strength of his grip, not while the thought of another enjoying her body played in his mind.

Linc swiped the broken glass from the bar, and Tuck pulled a piece from his skin dropping it in the trash can Linc held up. Tuck wiped the blood from his palm and pushed the towel against the wound to stem the bleeding.

Tonight wasn't his night, and no amount of hanging around was going to be fruitful, he could tell. Apart from the gnawing in his gut, he'd heard rumors of a deal going down, but they hadn't confirmed the location or exact meet time. This was a shot in the dark. He and the other Kindred members were all in separate locations trying to find their mark. If he went back to their base, he could find out if the others had had any luck.

A chill crossed his shoulders, and he sat up, examining the mirror again trying to see who had entered, but no one had, the door was closed. What had he missed? What was he missing? That awareness, the biting knowledge somewhere at the edge of his superior brain told him to look, told him something more was here than he was seeing.

But the place looked the same. The faces were familiar, the decor hadn't changed. It was subtle, something subtle...

A flash of memory took him back to her twenty-fourth birthday party, that first night he'd clapped eyes on her. His heart had stopped dead in his chest. She hadn't said a word, she didn't have to, and for some reason, neither did he.

Squeezing his eyes shut, he had to physically make

himself erase the sound of her laugh, and the image of how her smile lit up the room. Her laughter bewitched him, reached into the depths of his being to parts of him he hadn't known existed, and in one instant he'd been hooked. Like a junkie in need of a fix, his hands were shaking now, and the crush of cramp conquered his gut. Willing himself not to double over, he shoved the drink and the towel away, while his stool fell to the floor behind him.

Fumbling for his wallet when Linc came back to him, Tuck managed to sink a couple of twenties onto the bar. Linc didn't hesitate to take the cash, but a curious concern swept his expression. "You don't look so good," Linc said.

Tuck shoved the wallet into his back pocket. "I'm good."

"If you're gonna have a heart attack, can you wait 'til you're off my property?"

Although he knew Linc was joking—maybe—Tuck could barely nod in acknowledgement, because again the cackling assault filled his ears. He shook his head, as though trying to free his ears of water, but it wouldn't shift. He'd been told this would happen, by doctors who had poked, prodded, and probed his mind since before he could walk.

Madness. Madness was inevitable they'd said. He'd taken it with a pinch of salt at the time, knowing that madness would be hopeless, heavenly oblivion. For as long as he could remember, he hadn't wanted the gift of logical, intelligent thought, then she'd made it okay. Suddenly, there had been something to stay sane for.

Except he hadn't expected this. If madness meant the torturous reminder of his solitude, he didn't want it. He couldn't think of her every minute of every day. When he did let his mind fixate on her, he became homicidal… or suicidal. Never in his life had he been afraid of anything, not until he had her to lose.

Now, he didn't have her to lose, but the only torture he wouldn't be able to withstand would be reliving every second of every day they spent together. He'd never again see her smile, hear her laugh, touch her… why couldn't he get her out of his head tonight? Why couldn't he finish this job? He'd finish it, then surrender to the glory of madness if he had to. But he couldn't let his kin down now. He hadn't expected the descent into insanity to be so sudden, so complete, this was like someone flicking a switch.

"I think he's actually gone and done it," Linc mumbled.

Tuck saw that the bartender was no longer looking at him, he was looking past him again to the group that had been huddled in the corner. With a shout, and a hurrah, Tuck narrowed his eyes at the celebration, what were they all so happy about?

"Think I'll be closing up early," Linc said. "Get yourself out of here before I have to throw this mob out."

Linc didn't mind the drugs or the gambling. He didn't even mind women trading under his rafters. Illegal or not, if it was consensual by all parties, Linc didn't care. The only thing that Tuck had heard from whispers of tale-telling that Linc wouldn't tolerate was rape of any flavor.

Knowing Linc could handle himself, Tuck bent and picked up his stool to right it again with intentions of taking the bartender's advice. In his periphery, he noticed the group separate. A few members disbanded, and Tuck stood up to see three guys who all looked rather pleased with themselves. The center member had his arm around a woman's waist. After hooking her dead arm around his neck, the lowlife held on to her hand, keeping her body on his.

Her head lolled forward; she didn't have all her faculties. The men laughed as they stumbled forward with the obviously unconscious woman. But that wasn't what made him pause. As horrific as the scene was, and knowing what that laughter meant to the miscreants, any reasonable human being would be disgusted.

But, no, that wasn't what made him sick and furious. Drunk, drugged, violated, tormented… no woman deserved those things, but complacency taught him a lesson in that second. Those who suffered, that were victimized and brutalized, those people mattered to someone. They were someone's daughter, sister… cousin, friend, lover. The victims weren't faceless, someone loved them. The mental slap, the ice-water of reality made him recoil. The lesson couldn't have been taught in a harsher way, because this one, this unconscious victim only minutes away from being violated, this was the one he loved.

"Put her down," Tuck said. He'd crossed the room to get between the door and the lowlifes who appeared just as shocked by his interference as the rest of the bar patrons did. Tuck didn't have time to be stunned, his wits had seen him through with narrower odds. Except that wasn't on top of three shots, which was certainly enough to warm his blood.

"Hey, it's Mr. Moody," the guy closest to him said.

The second was still holding her, and the third backed off. While it appeared that the third might be having second thoughts, Tuck wasn't going to take it for granted. He'd be ready to take three of them if he had to. He doubted anyone else around cared enough to get involved on either side of this fight. All the same, he kept his eye on the bar mirror in case anyone chose to come at him from behind. If he'd been alone, he wouldn't have cared about being cold-cocked, because there would be nothing to lose. Except right now he had something to lose, someone to lose, and she was relying on him.

"You want a piece of the action?" guy number two said lifting his shoulders, and in the process shaking the lifeless form at his side.

Just as Tuck began to worry that they might have given her too much of whatever they dosed her with, her head rolled to the side, and she muttered something inaudible. So at least he had confirmation that she was still alive, for now.

The guys intent on violating her, weren't so concerned with her wellbeing. "We've got to get going. This one's going to be a fighter, I can tell," he said, drooling in delirium.

Inhaling sharply through his nose, Tuck tried to be calm, tried to remind himself that calmer heads prevailed, that he could reason, use his intelligence— "Screw it," he said, throwing a perfect knockout punch on the closest guy, knowing he wasn't ready for it.

The second guy swore and dropped his prey. Leaping

over her, Tuck pushed his opponent off target, and spun on the spot to put himself in front of her motionless body sprawled on the floor.

"Who the fuck are you?" the guy who had dropped her demanded.

The third had disappeared, at least for now. When the speaker came at him, all Tuck had to do was move aside and given the guy's inertia, he bowled himself face first into the solid wooden column by the doorway. He hit the deck as his friend groaned beside him, apparently regaining consciousness. Tuck didn't hesitate, he bent and picked her up in one motion, throwing her over his shoulder.

"Sorry about the mess," he said to Linc, who was still behind the bar, as bemused by the sequence as everyone else.

Tuck carried her out, grateful for her safety, and thankful that he'd been there to ensure it. But those weren't the strongest of his emotions. Anger pounded in his head, he wanted to spit and scream, what the hell was she doing there? How the hell had she got herself into that position? When had she become so stupid?

But, God, he had to question if he was any better than that pond-scum who had drugged her. While he marched down that dark road, she mumbled again, and his head slanted toward her body of its own accord. Pressing his cheek to her thigh, he groaned to himself. Even fizzing with anger that was aimed at her static form, he wanted her.

There was no way on earth he could ever let her know the strength of that desire. He couldn't have her, which only made his want intensify. The forbidden fruit was all the more tempting because it was just that… forbidden.

SIX

WITH WHAT FELT like cotton wool in her mouth and her ears, Kadie tried to pry open her scratchy eyes, only to snap them shut at the instant stab of pressure and pain between them. She didn't know where she was. She didn't know how she got here. She couldn't even remember where she'd been. The blankets around her were stiff. The pillow was so flat that the stuffing had long been worn out, and the place smelled fusty, like old fetid mold meets sweat, and sex, and… something. A long distant memory maybe, a vague recollection of a scent, something precious, safe… loved.

"Tuck," she whispered through dried lips.

Another dream, it had to be, she couldn't take much more of it. This wasn't the first time she'd woken up with him in her senses, with the dream of his hands on her skin on the cusp of her memory. Waking up with the imprint still in her consciousness, it was so vivid that she could feel his fingerprints still all over her. Frequently, she heard his voice in her memory, felt his breath on her neck. Remembered the sweet, tender view of him, of his eyes on her, devoted. The taste of his tongue still tantalized her, warm, slick, enticing, promising her the whole world without uttering a single word.

This wasn't one of those mornings that she could

surrender to the memory, turn herself over to her mind, and her practiced fingers. This place wasn't safe, or at least she couldn't establish whether it was or not until she could recall how she got here. She couldn't. She remembered being in the car, driving, and the bar, he was supposed to be there. Except she didn't remember the details of the bar, had she gone in? Had she been in an accident? No, this wasn't a hospital, it smelled too dirty for that, but where was this? Turning onto her back, she took one deep breath and made herself open her eyes, one increment at a time.

To one side there was light, to the other there was dark, and her eyes struggled to adjust to the disparate illumination. Her head hurt, her eyes watered, and her ears were ringing now. Her tongue darted out to moisten her lips but her mouth was parched, and it did little good. Taking stock, she noted that her elbow hurt, and her hip too. Certainly, none of the injuries seemed pressing, and although her head hurt, she wasn't lightheaded, so she couldn't have lost blood, at least not too much of it.

Now if she could just figure out—

"Drink something."

Her desperate breath blocked her throat. Lifting her head, she couldn't see him at first, he wasn't in the light. He was in the darkest corner in a tub chair, his elbows on the arms, his fingers linked under his chin, with one ankle propped on the opposite knee.

"You've been out for fourteen hours," he said in a flat, emotionless tone.

"Tucker," she wheezed. She couldn't pick out his features, but she didn't need to, that voice was like velvet on her skin and she'd recognize it in a heartbeat anywhere.

"There's water beside you," he said.

He could be right, but she didn't take her eyes away from him. This could be another dream and she didn't want to lose sight of the image of him, not when it felt so real. "What are you doing here?"

"Babysitting," he said. Leaving the chair, he picked up a small duffel bag that must have been on the floor at the end of the bed. "Drink the water, drink lots of it, slowly. Sleep it off. The room's paid for the next two nights, but if you can get out of here sooner, do it."

He slung the bag over his shoulder and headed toward the door, which was next to a curtained window that was doing a poor job of keeping the daylight out. Shoving onto her elbows, she managed to sit up. "Wait," she called, and he halted a few feet from the door, but he didn't turn around. "You can't just walk out on me."

Excruciatingly slowly, he looked back over his shoulder. "Watch me," he growled. "And this time don't come looking for me."

The truth of her actions and motivations was too much to cover in the next few seconds and if he was heading out, that was all the time they had. "I wasn't looking for you last night," she said. Ignoring the pain in her eyes, she pushed herself back to lean on the headboard that was nailed to the wall. That wasn't a lie, she hadn't been looking for Tuck last night. Her mission to seek him out was a distant memory. In her predicament, she tried to think of Tuck as little as possible. "Dempsey didn't send you?"

She'd guessed it was only a matter of time before her cousin figured out she and Tuck weren't together. Given how hard she'd tried to find Tuck for so many months, it seemed unlikely that a coincidence had brought them together. Her ex hadn't sought her out, so someone must have prompted this connection.

The question brought his confusion into line with hers. "Dempsey?" he said, turning his body toward her. "I left you with Dempsey, why would he…"

Establishing whether or not he'd been home would give her an idea of what he knew about what she'd been up to. Knowing how this man worked was her greatest advantage, she wouldn't give him the chance to block her out. Kadie was trying to get herself and her friend out of a dangerous position, Tuck's involvement would endanger them all further and the situation was volatile enough. She had to get him out of here, get him away from her, it was the only way she could continue working toward freeing Howie.

If Tuck knew where she had been and who she'd

been with, he'd demand that she never go back. Kadie had made Howie a promise, the kid was infuriating in his naivety sometimes, but he'd been there for her, had risked his safety for her, she wouldn't abandon him.

"You're right," she said, watching the cogs turn behind his blank gaze that signaled his mental crash, a state that accompanied him putting puzzle pieces together. "You should get going. Thanks for… whatever, and I'll figure it out myself. It was good to see you."

Taking the plastic tumbler from the bedside, she drank all of the liquid in it in one go without realizing how thirsty she'd been. When dizziness grasped for her, she pushed it away, and turned her legs out of the bed. Wriggling to the edge, her feet found the floor. Now she had her back to him, but he hadn't moved, hadn't made a sound.

Swallowing her apprehension, she closed her eyes, and prayed her legs would hold her when she stood up. Propelling upward, her hand jumped out in front of her, and she planted it on the wall to steady herself. The other joined it, and she took a deep breath, willing herself to maintain consciousness while darkness clawed at her.

"Lie down," he demanded from his side of the room. His words echoed in her skull like he was screaming them in her ear.

"No," she whispered.

"Do you want to pass out again?" he barked.

Her head swam and her eyes wouldn't open yet. There was something pleasant about the disorientation. The haze softened the harsh edges of her gray life. With the dizziness came nausea, and she shuffled a step to the side, then another. She swayed on her feet; her hands hadn't left the wall because she needed something to hold her up.

"Get into bed!" he said, in much closer proximity this time.

"No," she said again, unable to muster anything over a murmur. "You were leaving… You should… leave. Yeah, Hotshot just… you go, just go."

His first contact was to sweep her hair from in front of her shoulder to behind it. Still, she was unable to open her

eyes despite his presence looming at her side, hard, stable…
terrifying. "Please get into bed," he said.

If he was willing to soften, then she had to be too. "I
need to pee," she answered.

"Okay," he said. "Let me help you."

Yeah, because that wouldn't be mortifying. "You
were going, you—"

He didn't heed her protests. "I'm going to unzip your
skirt. It's too tight to lift. I'm not getting ideas. This isn't going
anywhere."

That, she didn't need to be reminded of. "You've
undressed me more times than I can count," she said, pressing
her forehead into the wall between her hands. Putting up a
fight with him wouldn't occur to her when she was fully with
it. Half out of it as she was now, he could do whatever he
wanted to and she wouldn't hinder him.

He didn't reply. The sound of her zipper was stark in
the silently fizzing room. Every atom of air crackled,
scorching the depth between them. His actions and proximity
boosted her flagging consciousness.

"Where is the bathroom?" she asked when he pushed
the skirt away from her hips.

She couldn't see properly, her ears rang, and her head
pounded in a solitary, long-forgotten lake of fog. Her body
wasn't in control of itself, yet she was aware of him. Every
fiber of her being knew him, knew this, remembered. Where
he was, his expression, his mood. She knew, and she'd barely
looked at him.

Her question went unanswered. In a swooping move,
he had her feet out from under her, and she curled into him,
resting her head on his shoulder. Yes, this was the man she
knew. Her mind, her body, her soul, he was everything to her.
And for the first time in months, she got to relax.

"I'm going to sit you down," he said. "You've got the
sink to hold onto on one side, and the bathtub on the other.
Will you be okay?"

She nodded and he bent to sit her down. Clutching at
the sink, she had to let him go, and a part of her screamed so
loud even the silence was erased. Opening her eyes gradually,

she saw the door close and wished she'd managed to look a second sooner. This would be his last memory of her, taking her for a pee because she was too out of it to do it herself.

As humiliating as the moment was, she was more unsettled because she didn't know how she'd gotten into this state, what had happened last night, and how she would protect herself from it happening again. Glancing at her watch, she saw it was just after three, that gave her time to get it together, she had to get it together.

Managing to wriggle out of her underwear, she answered the call of nature, and took off her top and bra before leaving the toilet. Now naked, she shoved the shower curtain to the side while she held onto the sink with the other hand. Stretching herself to the limit, she reached the shower and turned it on.

While she gave it time to heat, she closed her eyes and tried to steady her breathing. As the room fogged, her mind spun again. She'd hoped the sweltering steam would soothe her, but it was the cold she needed to enliven her. Reaching through the water she switched it to cold. Without giving herself time to adjust, she clambered over the edge of the bath into the shower. Remaining on her knees initially, her hands sought the solid base of the tub. The water was hammering her spine, soaking her hair, and her body shuddered in the cold.

Pain and shock awakened her. "This is helping," she said aloud, but didn't know if she was right.

There was no time to be sick. Giving in to weakness like this was ridiculous. All she had to do was stand up. Pushing up on her hands, she managed to get her weight onto her soles. Crouching under the thunderous jets, she closed her eyes again and counted to three out loud, then forced her legs to straighten.

She wobbled and clutched for anything within reach that could steady her. Her stomach revolted and after a few dry heaves, she planted her hands on the wall and opened her eyes. She could do this, get washed, then she could lie down again, just for a little while, before she had to think about the next round.

***

THE WHOLE PROCESS took quadruple the time it normally would. But eventually, she turned off the water. Very slowly and carefully, she climbed out of the tub. The only towel in the room was too small to be a bath towel. With the cold freezing her skin, she rubbed off the residual water she could reach and towel dried her hair. Except the rapid movement of that made her dizzy again, so she settled for wrapping her hair in the towel. It would do until she got back to the bed and could sit down.

A yawn made her cover her mouth, and she tried to calculate if she would have time for a nap. If she had her phone… where was her phone?

Her phone would be in her purse, she thought to herself upon leaving the damp bathroom. The air in the bedroom was warmer, which was an odd juxtaposition, opposite to the norm. But where was her purse? She stopped when she came around the corner to the bed because there he was, under the window this time.

His presence was unexpected, she was sure he'd have bailed by now. If the last time he'd left her was any indication, Tuck was desperate to be away from her. "You're still here," she said.

"You're naked," he said.

Because he was in front of the window, the light behind him concealed his features, so she could only see his silhouette. Not that she needed to see his features, his tone said it all.

Her body had been his to play with for so long that she couldn't bring herself to be modest about it. "Only had a hand towel," she said, pointing to her head. "I never realized how much energy it takes to have a shower."

"I'm surprised you didn't collapse and knock yourself out."

Maybe his conscience hadn't given up on her after all. "Is that why you waited?" she asked, flopping onto the bed on her back, she closed her eyes in the joyful embrace of its cradle.

"I was waiting for the crash."

"No crash," she said. "I took my time. I'm a clever girl, not as clever as…" Tuck was street smart and a brainbox to boot. She opened her eyes and rolled her head to look at him, he was out of the chair, standing next to the bed, looking down at her. "Well, you know, I'm not as smart as you… Believe it or not, it's not my goal to injure myself."

"What is your goal?" he asked.

"Uh-oh," she said, closing her eyes again. "Please don't tell me I've piqued the famous Tucker Holt curiosity."

But how could he not be curious. She was curious about why he was here with her and what his intentions were. "What were you doing in that bar last night?"

His questioning might give her the chance to piece together the fuzzy parts of her night. Getting rid of him hadn't been as simple as she thought, so she considered taking advantage of his memory. "So I did get that far," she muttered to herself and stretched her hands over her head to the headboard. "Did we leave together…? We didn't have sex, did we?"

"What do you remember?" he asked.

It would be a cruel irony having dreamed of his body so often in the time they'd been apart, that she would blackout during her chance to experience him again. "I asked you first," she said.

"We didn't have sex," he said. "Why would Dempsey send someone after you?"

Answering his questions would increase the chances that he'd bail on her and she had wanted him to leave. The shower had helped to clear her mind and she had to put together last night's timeline because if anyone had seen her and Tuck together, the damage may already have been done. Since he was still here anyway, she pushed for an explanation.

"We left the bar together," she said. "But we didn't have sex… I find that hard to believe." After being separated, sex was inevitable between them, at least, it had been while they were together. Flirting, or God forbid, making out, wouldn't have gone over well with her new employer. Any witnesses to that would have passed on the gossip to him by now, she just hoped Howie wasn't paying the price for her inability to control herself—drugs or not.

"Do you feel like we had sex?" he asked.

Opening her eyes, her hand moved to the neat line of hair above her center, and she considered his question. "No… but that was fourteen hours ago, fifteen now probably."

"You were unconscious," he said on a sigh. "Do I get off on that?"

"A lot can change in almost a year, Tuck," she said, rolling toward him onto her front. The man seated with her now used to belong to her. They hadn't been intimate in months and she was lying naked on a bed. Curiosity, and maybe her own ego, wanted to know if he was as indifferent to her as he was portraying. Her Tuck wasn't as cold as this man scowling at her now, not in her memory. "Are you horny?"

"What are you playing at?" he asked.

She peeked up at him. "I'm not playing at anything."

Enticing him to test his resolve, she wanted to know if he craved her like he used to and knew that softening him with their teasing was the best way to get him to tell her what she needed to know.

"You have no idea what happened last night," he said. "You're in a strange room, with a man you haven't seen for nearly a year. You're blatantly flaunting yourself, but you have no memory of anything. What would've happened if I wasn't there last night?"

"I can't remember anything, so I can't tell you what actually happened, let alone what *might* have happened. And as it turned out, you were there," she said. "And I'm not flaunting anything. I didn't think you would still be here after I got out of the shower. You told me you were going. I didn't come out naked to wave myself in front of you, there was no towel in there. You've seen me naked a zillion times, I don't get what your problem is."

He didn't hear her. "Why is Dempsey looking for you?"

"He's not," Kadie said. "As far as I know anyway."

"When was the last time you saw him? Why was that the first place your mind went?"

Filling him in on how she'd spent the last few months would lead to an explosive conversation that she wasn't ready for or interested in having. Tuck kept his secrets and she was learning the value of keeping her own. "As delightful as twenty questions is to play," she said. "I want to get some sleep. I have to work tonight, and—"

"Where are you working?" he asked.

His expectant attitude and abrupt manner were starting to piss her off. "You haven't answered any of my questions," she said. "And you expect me to answer yours. It doesn't work like that. If this is your room, and you want me to leave then say so. I'll repay you for—"

"I don't want your fucking money," he said, anger beating through his voice. "I want an explanation."

He wasn't the only one. Now he knew what it was like to be her throughout their entire relationship. "I don't have one," she said. "Not one I'm willing to give you."

"What is wrong with you?" he asked. "Are you in trouble?"

That almost made her laugh because it was the biggest understatement she'd heard in a long while. "Oh, all sorts," she said, managing a smile. "But it's nothing I can't handle."

"I'm not going to leave you here," he said. "If you need help—"

So sure of himself and his place in her life, it was almost insulting that he thought he could just take over and that she'd sit back and let him. As nice as it would be to have some support in the mess she'd gotten herself into, she wasn't willing to admit her mistakes to have him chastise and pity her.

Kadie had always been tougher than Tuck gave her credit for. So yeah, she was in deeper than she'd meant to get, but she'd survived on her own before he came along and gave her a job and a company to run. If they weren't together, it wasn't her responsibility to keep house anymore and she didn't have to follow his rules or compromise herself for him.

"I'm not your responsibility anymore," she said. "You dumped me, remember?"

"Fine," he said. "I get that you're upset with me, maybe your cousin can talk some sense into you."

When she saw that he was reaching for his phone in his jacket pocket, she leaped to her knees to grab for him before it was fully out. "No!" she shouted, wrenching his hand away from the device. "Don't phone Dempsey. Don't… you can't tell him about this, anything about this… Have you spoken to him?"

"Not since I left."

Her ex-boyfriend had no right to dictate to her, but her cousin still had all of his rights. God bless Dempsey for always looking after her, but if he found out where she was and came rushing in to save her, he'd get himself hurt or worse, and she couldn't live with that on her conscience.

"Oh thank God," she breathed. "You can't tell him you saw me. Please. You can't talk to him about me at all."

"Tell me what happened," he said.

"I can't."

"You can," he said. "You can trust me."

Shaking her head, she cursed the building heat of moisture behind her sinuses. "I can't trust you. I can't trust anyone."

One harsh lesson she'd relearned since they broke up was that looking out for number one was the only chance someone had to stay safe. "If Dempsey doesn't know where you are—"

"No one knows where I am… Not where I really am."

The confusion and concern bleeding from his expression was comforting, it proved that somewhere—even if it was deep down inside—he did still care about her. "What does that mean? Dempsey let you go? Are you telling me that your overprotective cousin isn't worried about you? About trouble you might get into, about your safety?"

She shook her head. "He thinks I'm safe."

"You're not safe," he said. "Why would he let you walk away from the company?"

It was true that if Dempsey had all the facts, he'd have been decisive in preventing her from walking away from her life. Keeping him in the dark saved her from having to explain why she'd run away.

Building a wall allowed her to walk into dangerous situations without addressing the emotions that could paralyze her at exactly the wrong minute. Facing his concern forced her to experience everything she'd kept locked behind that wall. "I don't need his permission to live my life. I don't need yours either."

"I created that company to give you a safe place to be," he said. "So that you didn't have to be out fending for yourself."

Such a lovely thought that her boyfriend coddled her and built a glass house around her just to protect her from herself. Before their relationship, Tuck did what he did and worked with Dempsey, but there was no official structure. Kadie had built the reputation of their company and kept it running as a legitimate enterprise.

At the time, she'd suspected it was a distraction for her. Something to keep her busy while Tuck did his real work. Now the concept was insulting. She didn't want to be kept separate from the evil he vanquished, she'd wanted to be a part of the solution.

Terrifying as it sometimes was, she was doing that herself now and it felt so much better to be taking an active role in doing the right thing, rather than living her life assuming that someone would take care of the world's problems for her.

Kadie didn't grace his statement with an answer, so Tuck spoke again, "When I think about what happened last night I want to murder someone and I still might. I've told you about that kind of trouble," he said, closing his hands around her face to let his thumbs wipe the tears that dripped from her eyes. "Men are a danger to you, Toots, all men."

Not all men. "You're not," she answered. "You don't want me anymore."

The corner of his mouth curled. "What gave you that crazy idea?" he said, tipping her head farther back, he lowered his mouth onto hers.

SEVEN

WHEN YOU'RE KISSED by the man that's kissed you more than any other, your body responds like it would to that first taste of chocolate after a diet. It's water in a drought, nourishment to the famished. That first taste is like sliding into your sexiest dress. The world ceases to exist and it's better than every dream you've ever had, because it's real. This was real. Her tears didn't stop, but her heart awakened from the slumber it had been seized by to begin pumping harder than it ever had before. This man had been hers, completely hers, and when he was, her life had been his. They'd been one. Complete. Perfection.

Grabbing for his jacket, she yanked him forward. Although he fell, he caught himself over her, pressing her deep into the firm mattress. Her nakedness was protected by his clothed form. The sensations were arousing. The zipper of his jacket rasped her nipple. Its leather stuck to her skin and she pulled him closer.

One of his legs found its way between hers, and she pushed down on the denim offering, enjoying the rough material over his muscled thigh against her moistening core. She wouldn't say no, she never had, and never would.

Releasing his jacket, she drove her fingers into his

hair, slanting his head to force his mouth deeper against hers. Tongues devoured, teeth collided, and breathing increased. Arching her body toward his, she found her sanctuary behind his fly. Long, thick, solid, and completely for her in this moment.

Wriggling her pelvis up closer to his member until her clit angled against the seam of his jeans, she recognized her own mew of pleasure. This was what her wettest, raunchiest dreams were made of.

"No," he mumbled, but didn't let his lips leave hers.

Shoving against her, he clamped her down on the mattress. Every inch of her body was covered by him. His hot tongue swept hers, wet and desperate. Tuck had always been amorous, but this… this was a desolate man. Could it be that he'd missed her?

His agony couldn't match hers, nothing would, or ever could. This was a stolen moment in time, a last connection between once upon a time lovers. She was here, she was naked, of course he would take what she offered, what man wouldn't? This union would mean more to her, it always meant more to her. But she'd take it.

Unwilling to dwell on her grief, she took this lifeline, this last chance, and she would ride it as long as he let her, because he would leave her again. He would walk away, just as he had all those months ago, and she'd mourn alone all over again. Maybe it wasn't smart to revisit this, ultimately she would get hurt. Yet even a single snatched second of his passion dominating her again would be worth taking the risk of emotional upset. He was worth it, he always had been.

Managing to wriggle her fingers between them, she unbuckled his belt. He pushed down again, trapping her hands against the bulge behind his buttons.

She didn't know why he was hampering her, but she wished he wouldn't. Her impatience was growing. "Let me," she said, but didn't finish her sentence before he kissed her again.

"No," he said, wrenching his lips away and dropping his forehead against hers.

Alone in this private space there was no reason for

them not to be intimate, and she could use the oblivion right about now. "There are condoms in my bag," she said. Considering neither of them knew where each other had been in the last few months, protection made sense. "Where is my bag?"

His eyes opened in a glower. "Why the fuck are you carrying rubbers around?"

Well, that was a ridiculous question. "They're a fashion accessory," she said. "Why do you think?"

"What do you need them for?"

So he was sticking with anger. He'd had her. She'd been his. Faithful for every second that they were in a relationship. To be affronted that she may have shared herself with another man after he broke her heart was more than a little unreasonable.

"Earrings," she said. "What do you think they're for?"

"Who's fucking you?" he snarled.

Given their current position, she'd have thought that question answered itself. "You," she said. "If you let me get my bag."

"What happened to your pills?"

So that was why he was annoyed, he wanted to take her bareback. Before, she wouldn't have blinked at that, now she couldn't trust the skanks he might have been with. "It's hard to get your prescription filled on the run," she said, preferring rubbers in her current situation. "Your aversion to children is greater than your aversion to latex, Tuck. I do remember that."

"I have no problem with condoms," he said. "I have a problem with you carrying them."

Was he voicing a double standard and expecting her to accept it? "Why?" she asked. "You always told me to protect myself as much as I could."

"I was talking about pepper spray and panic buttons," he said, his scowl was so deep it had to be giving him a headache. "Who are you fucking?"

The accusations weren't arousing. Their arguments that led to sex before were much more tantalizing. "I remember you being better at the dirty talk," she said, squirming under him. "Can we move things up a level?"

If he was focused on the sex, he should stop quizzing her. "What do you—"

"Touch me," she said, arching her chest up to draw his eyes down to her breasts. As she wanted him to, he studied her, examined every pore with those ravenous eyes, except he didn't touch her. "Tuck."

When she sighed, his eyes leaped to hers, then as quick as she'd ever seen him move, he was on his feet, with his back to her.

"Put your clothes on," he said.

Confused and unsated, new questions presented themselves. "You won't have sex with me because I carry condoms?"

"No," he said. "I won't have sex with you, full stop."

"Oh," she said, casting her eye over her body, speculating about what might have put him off.

Throughout their relationship he'd never been able to resist her, even when she was fully clothed. His appetite had been insatiable, and exclusively for her, at least that's what she believed. Her body hadn't changed that much since they'd broken up. If anything, she was in better shape than she had been last year, now she worked harder at it, she had to.

So either her body didn't do it for him anymore, or… comprehension struck. "Who is she?" she asked, without thinking the words.

"She who?" he asked, still standing with his back to her.

The question had burst out, but as she considered what she might find out, she closed the query up again. "I don't want to know," she said, clambering off the bed.

Wobbling on her feet, she'd forgotten about the aftereffects, whether her haze was caused by last night, or what had happened with Tuck on the bed, she couldn't be sure. Stars flickered in front of her, and she dropped to her haunches. Using the bed to stabilize herself, Kadie got to her hands and knees and started for the bathroom.

"What's the matter with you?"

He had to have turned, but she couldn't see him given her direction. "My clothes are in the bathroom."

"Jeez," he said.

Mid-crawl, she was ripped from her knees and tossed down onto the bed, as though she was nothing more than the lifeless pillow she'd awoken on. With a glare, he marched into the bathroom and returned moments later with her discarded clothes. Taking a seat beside her, he began to uncoil her underwear as she put on her bra.

"There is no she," he said, shoving her feet into the underwear and forcing it up her legs. He might not be the most graceful man in the world, but he could be gentle... except now wasn't one of those times.

Apparently, he hadn't gleaned that she didn't want to know about his present love life. "Of course there is," she said, popping her head into her top. If they were going to talk about it, she was going to be honest. "You always have a 'she' to go home to."

He stopped to look at her after feeding her feet into her skirt. "That she was you," he said. "The only *she* I ever went home to was you."

Kadie wasn't going to make this any more difficult by starting another fight. "Okay," she said, lying back to lift her hips so she could pull up her thong and her skirt. "You don't want to tell me, that's fine. I figure you wouldn't tell anyone you met on the job about me. It's a protection thing, I remem—"

"Stop it," he snapped.

"Stop what?" she asked, zipping her skirt on a deep breath then pulling the towel from her hair.

"You think because I won't have sex with you it's because I'm being faithful to someone else. Could it possibly have anything to do with the fact that you're still under the influence of a date-rape drug?"

Her fingers stopped in her tangled hair. "You think that you'd be raping me?" she asked, having never heard anything so ludicrous. "I undid your belt, buddy. I knew exactly what I—"

"You don't," he said. "You can't walk, how—"

"Date-rape," she said when his words caught up with her thought process. Drugs explained her blackout and how she'd ended up here feeling as groggy as she did. This new piece of information lessened the importance of their non-starter carnal interlude. "Who drugged me?"

"Losers at the bar," he said.

The bar, yes, she had been there. Memories came back as blurry pictures. She'd been talking to a group of men. They'd been flirty, she couldn't remember their faces or what they'd spoken about. One thing she knew for sure was that she had no interest in being intimate with any of them.

That they'd come so close to taking advantage of her made her feel sick. "Why did you tell me that?" she asked, staring at her own knees as she tried to control the churn of bile in her stomach.

"You need to learn to be more careful," he said.

She did want to know what had happened, what might have happened, but she couldn't claim that the knowledge changed anything. "Careful," she whispered. "Why?"

"Why what?"

Her eyes met his and she searched for an answer. "Why do I have to be careful?"

Shock and uncertainty made him glower. "Do you want to be a fucktoy for a dozen drunk bastards all trying to one-up their buddies?"

Few women would, but what she wanted was irrelevant. Tuck had taught her that. "Why would it matter?" she asked.

"What?"

"It wouldn't be number one on my list of life experiences, but what would it matter?"

"I don't understand what you're—"

"I'm not saving myself for anyone," she said. "I'm hardly a virgin, and to be humiliated you have to care or matter to someone, somewhere, or at the very least mean something."

"Kade, I—"

She couldn't have this conversation, not when the

outcome meant nothing. Being touched by strange men, being hurt by them, maybe even killed, it wouldn't be a choice she would make. But if it had happened, no one would've noticed.

Dempsey didn't know where she was, and Tuck had his own life to live. If she got herself killed then maybe there was a reason, maybe she deserved to be treated that way. With Tuck, she'd had a happy life for so long and given her history, her lack of family or affluence, she had been spoiled by the love in their relationship.

Maybe karma was just coming around to bring her all of the negative experiences she should've had in her twenties but was saved from by the cocoon of Tuck's protection. Which was a shield she no longer had the privilege of existing behind.

What she needed was a clean break. For a while after they'd broken up, she'd wanted to be back in the safe place he provided for her and would've done anything to have him back. But she had come to see that she couldn't take shelter there, not when it wouldn't last. That security wasn't assured, he'd shattered it once before when he dumped her. If she went back to that life, she'd have to live at his mercy, never knowing when he might cast her out again.

Kadie needed to remember where she came from, the rough nature of her early childhood. That meant learning again to have her wits about her, to be hard, and detached, and to never forget that she was on her own.

"You were leaving," she said, because if he was going to go then he had to go now. Once the effects of the drugs had worn off, she could return to the new life she was a part of and could think of this as a lucid dream. All she could hope was that it would fade with time, as dreams so often did. "I think you should do it now."

Hardening herself meant she had to ignore his offense. "Leave? You're not well—"

"That's not your responsibility," she said, shuttering all emotions behind her eyes, she'd gotten good at it. Tuck had given her a good example to follow.

"You don't expect me—"

"I don't expect anything from you," she said. "I

would like you to leave."

Blustering, he was solid and unmoving. "I'm not going anywhere."

"Okay," she said, and managed to draw in a long breath. Even not being at the top of her game, she wouldn't be forced to stay here with the man who had broken her heart and was now passing judgment on her. "Thank you for your time."

Pushing her fists into the bed, she slid past him to the end. The drugs made her head pound, but she'd recovered from their exploits on the bed. Now was no time for feeble indulgences of weakness, she had to get out of here. Confronting their relationship when there was no hope of rekindling the life they had was a waste of time.

"Where are you going?" he asked, snatching her wrist when she found her feet.

Her life couldn't be more different from the one she'd had with him, but it was her life, and he had no right to keep her from it. "I told you I have work to do," she said. "My clients aren't nearly as squeamish as you are."

She saw the moment that clarity hit him, his eyes widened and he leaned a fraction closer. "No," he murmured. "I don't believe you."

Childish notions of fairy-tale fantasy had no place in the kind of lives they led. "What does belief have to do with anything," she said, tugging on his grip. "Please let me go. Bruising will cost you extra."

It was funny how she'd never considered that he might understand what heartbreak was until this moment when she saw the pain her revelation caused him. But that was what she wanted, shock value, she wanted to disgust him, to send him back to the adventure of his life while she focused on salvaging what was left of hers, though that couldn't happen until she could get to Howie.

"Kade," he whispered. The gentleness of his tone made her shiver, somehow it was easier to remember the lover or the man than it was to remember her soulmate. The depth of emotion behind their love wasn't something she thought about, she couldn't or it would consume her.

"Why? Where? How?" he beseeched in that same intonation.

More questions. "I'll answer yours when you answer mine." His eyes shuttered. "That's what I thought."

Addressing the flaws in her character, in her life, that came easy to him and she believed he'd do everything in his power to "save" her, if he found out the truth. But she didn't want him on conditional terms, didn't want to be an inconvenience he had to swoop in and rescue on a sporadic basis, like she was a child getting herself into trouble just to get attention from a responsible adult.

"I won't let you go," he said, his hand becoming a vice on her wrist.

With a wry laugh, she relaxed her resistance. "You can't do that."

"You want to watch me?" he said. "I'll hogtie you if I have to."

"Rope, chain, or leather?" she asked, not at all intimidated by his assertion.

"What?"

If he wanted the truth, she'd slap him in the face with it. "Rope leaves a hell of a burn and it can splinter. The wounds have to be treated or they become infected. It can ruin the mood."

The flash of horror on his face made it seem like he was talking to a stranger. "What are you talking about, Kade? Jeez, Toots, don't tell me—"

"I wasn't telling you a thing. You brought up the bondage, I'm just telling you the rules… I don't have any tools here," she said, running her free fingers through her hair. "But I imagine you could afford the premium, so we could have them delivered."

"How could you…?" His eyes traveled down her body, scared by what they saw. "You're…"

"I'm what?" she asked. "I'm nothing, now let me go."

"I won't," he said, yanking her down to sit on the bed. "I can't. You can't."

The righteousness was probably obligation because if he really cared about her then he would never have left her in the first place. Accepting who he was had been part and parcel of being with him, now he was looking at her and didn't like what he saw, and he thought it was his right to change her.

Kadie wasn't so easily browbeaten. Tuck was bigger and stronger, no doubt about that, but his interest wouldn't hold long enough to break her.

"Oh, please," she said. "You don't have a conscience. Anything can be justified with the right argument. You taught me that. So don't you dare stand there and pretend this is against your moral code. What's good enough for you is good enough for me."

"I don't sell myself," he said, wrenching her against him.

"Don't you? You sell your skills," she said and enjoyed leering at him. "And you taught me plenty of ways to keep a man happy."

His jaw clenched and he shook her. "How did you get here? I can't believe that Dempsey—"

"Leave my cousin out of this," she said, sick of Tuck using Dempsey like some kind of surrogate babysitter. It might have made him feel better to leave her under the care of her cousin, but Kadie didn't appreciate being a burden to either of them. Her life was hers to lead and she was tired of being under the purview of men who believed her inferior. "You gave up your rights to care, or to reprimand me for my choices."

But he wouldn't relent, she shouldn't be surprised, Tuck was as stubborn as she was. "This isn't a choice. I know you. You wouldn't—"

"What wouldn't I, Tuck?" she asked, because it wasn't his place to assume what was in her mind. "I wouldn't… what? You'd be amazed at the dividends."

Confusion marred his squint. "Dividends?"

"Everything's a means to an end," she said, almost proud that she still had the ability to rile him and that he now understood how frustrating it was to be confronted by secrets and silence.

"What could you possibly gain—"

"I'm not answering your questions," she asserted.

"You'll never have to see me again. I promise. We can just forget about this whole sorry affair. Now let me go."

"I won't."

The tightness of his fingers around her arm grew and he lifted her limb higher to get even nearer. But it didn't matter, he had no choice, they couldn't sit like this forever. "You have to," she said.

"I don't have to do a damn thing."

Invincible he was not. People would have seen them together. He had his own crew who would come looking for him and she had her own explanations to give. "We left the bar together, did anyone see us?"

Making him see their predicament may get them out of it faster. "I don't give a shit—"

"Do I look like the type who stands on a street corner?" she murmured. "He'll come looking for me."

"He," Tuck said, springing to his feet. "Someone's forcing you into this? There's a guy—"

"He didn't force me to do anything," she said, observing how he went into combat mode now that he believed he had something, or rather someone, to fight against. "He looks after me."

Whipping around, his head tilted. "No," Tuck said, slowly shaking his head. "How can you…" Closing the space between them, he covered her cheek with his palm. "You're smarter than this, Kade. Can you hear yourself?"

"I know what he wants from me," she said. "I know how to make him happy. It's easy with him."

"Easy?"

She nodded. "Sex and money are his trade, they're his language. There's no misunderstanding. I know where I stand. I can't fail him… not like I failed you."

He froze again, still his eyes were locked to hers. "You didn't fail me," he said. "I failed you. I left to set you free. I left because… I didn't want this. You're more than this."

"Apparently not," she said. "If he finds me here and he's feeling charitable, he'll let you go. I couldn't bear to see what would happen if… When he's angry… you don't want to see him angry."

Nykiel Sikorski could turn on a dime and no one was safe around him. Even his closest, most trusted associates, could face his wrath if he was having a bad day. Most of the time he ignored the women he had under his purview, but if this was one of the times he chose to care, she'd be in trouble, they both would. Not because Sikorski cared for her, but because the insult would indicate disrespect and there was nothing he hated more.

"Does he hurt you?"

Hearing his concern was familiar, it was right that they should give a shit about each other after being part of each other's lives for so long. But she wasn't going to let herself be distracted by niceties, the danger in her life was still very real and she couldn't afford to let her guard down for a second. "No," she answered. "Never damage the merchandise, that's what he tells his men."

"The merchandise," Tuck repeated, followed by a stream of curses. "I told you not to get into trouble, didn't I?"

"I'm not in trouble," she said. "I'm still alive, aren't I?"

"Alive," Tuck said. "You think that's the measure for trouble?"

She shrugged. "I don't see what it matters. I'm okay, there's nothing wrong with it. We're careful, and he makes sure we're okay, we're always okay."

Crouching in front of her, he touched her legs. "How did this happen? Tell me how—"

"No," she said, trying to ignore how right it felt to have him touching and consoling her. "I'm going to leave now. Forget you ever saw me."

"I can't forget it," he said, holding his palm up for her to see. "Do you see that? Do you know how I did that?"

The gouge on his hand was scabbing over, but there was no mistaking the wound. "How?" she asked, touching it with her index finger.

"I smashed a glass in my fist—"

"Why would you—"

"Thinking of you with another man," he said. "The

idea popped into my head, and I… I can't forget."

She sighed. "This doesn't change anything. You're you, I'm me, and we're not a part of each other's worlds anymore."

"I want to know how; I want to know why."

"So did I," she said. "Nine months ago when you showed up just to cut out. I didn't have the answers then, and I can't give you them now."

"This is about me?" he asked, unsettled by the idea that the demise of their relationship might have landed her here. "Are you punishing me? Do you think this will—"

"I'm not doing this because of you," she said. "I admit my life took an… unexpected turn when you left me. But I didn't plan this. It just… happened."

"These things don't just happen," he said. "You don't wake up one day, and decide to…"

"No," she said. "I didn't go looking for him or for this. But I have my reasons for doing it."

Explaining how she'd ended up here and why she persisted in living the way she did, wouldn't adjust his opinion. She didn't need his judgment and the longer she sat here shooting the breeze, the more likely it was that someone would notice she was missing. The last thing she wanted was for Howie to hear she'd disappeared. Although his first thought would be concern for her, he'd also be scared because he'd feel alone.

"Why?" he said. "Did you need money? No, that can't be it. I signed everything over to you, the business, the property, the cars, the investments, everything is yours."

She shook her head. "I didn't sign any of it."

"You—"

"None of it was mine. I didn't sign the papers. I didn't give them to our lawyer, I… they're still in that envelope in the basement… unless Dempsey has already broken in."

This was serendipitous, she had the chance to tell him he was still responsible for all his assets and managed to divert his line of thought at the same time.

"You didn't… You fucking stupid, idiotic, insane—"

"Don't swear at me," she said. "None of it was mine,

and to accept it would have been… let's just say experience in my current line of work would have started a lot earlier."

"You think that was payment for your services? Five years together, and you thought I'd leave you with nothing?"

She didn't want stuff, she never had. Property, possessions, it meant nothing to her. Material things were a substitute that had never satisfied her. "You did leave me with nothing," she said. "If you thought for one second that any amount of money or goods would fix my broken heart then you're not the man I loved, and you don't know me at all."

"I knew I wasn't coming back," he said. "I couldn't give myself the excuse to come back. Leaving it for you was the coward's way of protecting myself. I wanted you to be happy, and that meant getting me out of your life."

Pragmatic to the end, to him cutting all ties meant severing every association. "I don't want to talk about this," she said, trying to twist her wrist free. "I have to leave. If I'm not back in—"

"What?" he demanded. "What happens if you're not back?"

Too many terrible things to contemplate. Until now, she'd avoided thinking about how many balls she had to juggle to keep her and Howie safe without raising suspicion. Taking a break, relaxing here, she was beginning to lose her grip and she needed to keep up the balancing act, she had no time to take a breath.

"He'll find me," she said. "And I'm not worth losing your life over."

"I'll be the judge of that," he said.

It would be such a pathetic waste if Sikorski tracked her to here and his men hurt Tuck just because she'd been waylaid by him. They wouldn't know who Tuck was to her or what he did beyond this room. A brilliant mind would be disconnected in a snap and she'd have to go back with Sikorski anyway.

"You have work to do too," she said. "You always have work to do, and your lady won't—"

"You're my lady," he snapped. "Did you really think there would be anyone but you? God, woman you are so dense."

"Lovely," she said. "So stupid that I have to get back to my pimp before I'm served up to his men for dessert."

His fingers curled tighter. "They touch you? Against your will?"

"What is will?" she said. The conditioning at the house, the way she and the other girls were treated was having an effect on her psyche. Sometimes she could see herself from outside her body, saying the things that she was expected to say, while her internal self was screaming the opposite. "My life means nothing, it is nothing. I'm nothing."

For a moment, he studied her. He didn't say a word. He scrutinized her with an intensity that made her shiver. Even while naked, she hadn't been this exposed. Resignation made him loosen. "Are you happy?" he asked her.

"No," she said without hesitation. "Are you?"

"No. But I never expected to be."

"Look at that," she said with a smile. "Even after all this time, we still have something in common. I would like to go to work now."

Charging the air with expectation, he ran a hand up her arm to the side of her neck. "Give it up," he said. "What will it take for you to never go back?"

"A miracle," she answered. "This is my life now."

A life that she didn't plan to keep. "Go home," he said. "Please, I'll give you the money, just—"

"No," she said, because she couldn't imagine anything worse than leaving Howie in danger and tucking herself into safety, alone and without purpose. "There's nothing there for me."

"I'll come back," he said. "I promise, but first I have to—"

"First," she interrupted, because that word was exactly what had made her rethink her desire to return to what they'd had. "Something else will always come first."

"I'll do whatever it takes," he said. "But don't ask me to walk away from the job, not today."

She understood him more than he knew. "We have something else in common then."

His pain could just be aggravation, but she couldn't let his motivation drive her. "You can't ask me to let you go, not to that. I can't imagine how it must feel—"

"Feel?" she snorted. "I don't feel anything. It's an easy trick to muster, to be numb. I was worried that I might be awkward, or uncomfortable the first time. I thought it would be strange and unpleasant because I'd been with the same single man for so long… but the other girls were right, it's like… you know it's happening but your mind, your soul is somewhere else."

"I won't let anyone touch you." Wringing her wrist, he marked her like sheer will could alter what would happen next. "No one."

"You're too late," she said. "What did you think would happen when you left me?"

"Not this, this never entered my mind."

It had never entered hers either. A series of unexpected events had maneuvered her into her current position, no conscious choice was made. None except to keep herself and her friend safe. "I'm full of surprises," she said, and this time when she tugged her wrist free from his grip and began to walk backward to the door, he didn't pursue her. "It was good seeing you again, Hotshot. You look… the same, exactly the same." She stopped with her hand on the door handle. "It seems I meant that little to you… Goodbye."

Without giving him any opportunity to respond, she opened the door and left. Once the door was closed, she squeezed her eyes shut and willed herself to forget the image of him. Returning her focus to what she had to do, and how she might explain this, she began to make tracks, fast, because Tuck would shirk his shock and be out of that motel room door in a matter of seconds and he'd already delayed her for too long.

EIGHT

"WE HAVE A serious problem."

Tuck didn't even know how to begin explaining his night to Brodie and Zara when he got back to the Kindred motel room they'd been using as their base. Brodie was cleaning out his rifle and Zara was reading something on the bed, but both of them stopped what they were doing after letting him into the room.

Brodie wiped his hands on a rag. "One cryptic call in the middle of the night to tell us that you're alive is not protocol."

Zara scoffed and shimmied to the edge of the bed. "Now you know what it's like, beau. What happened?"

"Kadie." On saying her name, he sank down into the chair next to the door and was pleased to see his colleagues immediately grow concerned. "She showed up at the bar last night, I had to yank her from a group of lowlifes."

"Oh my God," Zara said, crossing to crouch in front of him and take his hand.

"Any trouble?" Brodie asked, coming over to stand behind his woman.

Tuck shook his head. "Nothing I couldn't handle. They're not the type to follow up, though if I see them around—"

"We'll handle it," Brodie said.

It didn't occur to Tuck for a second not to confide in his kin. One of the best things about being part of the group was knowing that nothing happened to any single one of them, what happened to one, happened to them all.

"What was Kadie doing there? Where is she? Why didn't you bring her here?" Zara asked.

All valid questions. He had thought about bringing her straight back here last night but thought better of it because she'd already be off kilter by what happened. Waking up to one familiar face would be easier on her than waking up with strangers in the room.

Another factor in his decision was their present mission. If Kadie woke up here, she might see what they were up to and might want to be a part of it. Leaving her current situation just to get mixed up in his would endanger her and he wouldn't have that. Though now he was educated about exactly what she did, he wished he'd brought her to the Kindred.

"She split," Tuck said. "She wasn't real happy to see me."

"Well, of course not, you broke her heart," Zara said, standing up to put her hands on her hips and lean back on Brodie.

Kadie used to lean on him like that. He'd broken that trust when he broke her heart, he'd never considered that he'd need it back because he thought she'd move on to a happy life and curse him as a mistake she'd never make again. As it turned out, getting involved with him was one of the more sensible mistakes she'd made, if her life choices since leaving him were any measure.

"Where is she now?" Brodie asked. "Extracting her will be easy if we have a location."

He'd had her that day, she'd been in his reach, and he hadn't been able to make her stay. Letting her walk out of that motel room was the dumbest thing he'd ever done, but he was still reeling from what she'd revealed. Not only was she selling her body, but she was doing it for a man and believed the scum-sucker thought more of her for it.

"She's working for a pimp." Saying that was easier than saying she was selling her body to perverts.

"Sport," Brodie muttered, and Tuck guessed he had the same dark look when he'd heard that news.

He and Brodie had been in each other's lives for years, they had seen dark times together, and Tuck was as protective of Zara as he ever would be of his own woman. It didn't matter that Brodie and Kadie didn't know each other, Brodie understood—since getting with Zara—what it was to love a woman and be at the mercy of her happiness.

Zara sat in his lap and looped her arms around him, giving him a reassuring hug. Linking his hands at her waist, he kept his embrace loose. Although he appreciated what she was trying to do, it didn't make him feel much better when Kadie was out there alone.

"We'll get her back," Zara said to him. "Priority one applies, everything else can go to hell."

Exhaling a laugh, he eased her back. "Who are you and what have you done with Swallow?"

Since Kahlil Samara had died three and a half months ago, the Kindred had made it their mission to find out what really happened that day. There were loose ends and they hated those. Tracking Benedict Leatt and Nykiel Sikorski were their priorities because they wanted to assess every threat who knew about Game Time. Only if they were satisfied that the men's motivations were no longer of the mass destruction persuasion would they be let go, which was really Zara's order because in the old days he and Brodie would just have taken out the trash.

Seeing the transformation of his best buddy since he'd met Zara Bandini had been quite a journey for Tuck. The confident assassin gave orders and made decisions, but if Zara hesitated, Brodie did what it took to make her happy.

Zara was different too, her time with the Kindred had opened her eyes to the world and she was definitely more cynical than she had been in the early days. Yet, she was still the most optimistic member of the troupe, no doubt about that.

"Right, that's enough comfort," Brodie said, bending to snag her arm and pull her out of his lap.

Tuck was no threat to the couple and the trio knew that. Zara was more like a sister to him than a potential mate. It was his lack of sexual interest that allowed him to ignore the texture of her skin and the sight of it when he'd, more than once, walked in on her with Brodie or while she was getting changed. Working in such close quarters meant modesty was a luxury. If someone had to pee and someone else was in the shower, they dealt. It was as simple as that.

Brodie linked a hand around the back of Zara's neck and she folded her arms. "We need a plan," she said. "We find her. We eliminate the threat. Then we have pizza."

She smiled, but Tuck wasn't as encouraged. "I don't know if she wants to leave him."

"You and I have had this conversation," Zara said, nudging her knee on his. "You want her back, you'll get her. There isn't a better man than you, Swift." Brodie must have squeezed her neck because she tilted toward him. "You're taken, so you're not in consideration."

She winked at him and left her love to go over to a laptop on the table in the center of the room, they'd pushed the two beds against opposite walls to make the room for it. "What did she tell you about him?"

"Nothing," Tuck said, watching her open the laptop and begin to type. "All I know is that she showed up in the bar. I don't know where she went or who she's with."

"Then we start at the bar," Zara said, fixing a frown on the screen. "Did she have a vehicle?"

"Not that I'm aware of. I can ask Linc."

She nodded. "I'm going to check our surveillance feed from the parking lot, see if we have her going in. If she came from a vehicle or didn't arrive alone, we'll have more information to work from. Do you have a picture? Can you tell me what she was wearing?"

"Not much," Tuck said. "There are pictures in the personnel files in that terminal. There weren't many other women in the bar last night, we should be able to spot her."

That they were setup and monitoring the place gave

them a head start and might have been why he was able to let her walk and take some time to contemplate their unexpected reunion.

"Even better," Zara said.

"Swallow's on the hunt," Brodie said with a pride Tuck could admire. "You think we created a monster?"

"I think we'd be lost without her."

That was the God's honest truth. Before Zara came into their lives the Kindred had been a definite all-male affair. These days she mothered them all, took care of the manor, and kept their heads on straight. Sometimes he forgot what it was like when Art was in charge because Zara had slid so seamlessly into their ranks.

He'd take his turn checking out the feed if Zara came up blank. In the meantime, he'd go through the business she'd left and figure out what Dempsey had been up to. If Tuck could piece together when Kadie had left then he might be able to figure out what had been the catalyst for her leaving. Maybe a client had offered her a better job or something had caught her eye that would lead him to where she was now.

No matter what, Kadie was now the Kindred's primary mission. Their other work was important, but it would wait, because looking after their own was always bumped up to the top spot when the need arose. It didn't matter that he'd broken up with Kadie, she was still his, and he would do whatever was necessary to keep her safe, even if that meant overruling her life choices. Hate him or not, he wouldn't see her used and broken. She deserved happiness, and whatever it took, he'd make sure she'd find it.

***

LITTLE OF THE narrative of Kadie's life had been pieced together that day. Zara had located images of Kadie going into the bar and had watched right up until Tuck took her out. They confirmed that he hadn't been followed, so she wasn't any kind of plant meant to snare the Kindred. But she had been dropped off by a cab and had come inside alone, so they still didn't know what had brought her there.

In hope that it wasn't a one-time deal, they decided the best course of action was for Tuck to return to the bar. Doing so suited the Kindred needs too. Intelligence that Brodie and Zara had gathered indicated that their mark was going to show up there that night to complete the deal they'd been hearing whispers about.

If it came down to a choice, they'd go for Kadie and keep her safe. But there was nothing stopping Tuck from carrying on with business as usual, it was the best way to blend in. After how he'd dealt with saving Kadie, some people might be watching him.

Being as normal and benign as possible, he strolled into the bar as if nothing untoward had occurred there. "Surprised to see you tonight," Linc said to Tuck when he sat in his usual stool. The bartender filled the chipped glass then shoved it to him. "If you're gonna break this one, let me know and I'll switch you to plastic."

"I'm making no promises," Tuck said, slurping the welcome heat of whiskey. At least Linc wasn't asking him to pay for the damage, given this place's usual breakage, especially after a brawl, one glass wouldn't be too big of a deal.

"What happened to the broad?"

Answering questions about Kadie would be impossible without revealing his connection to her, and he couldn't leave either of them open to that avenue of manipulation. Once a person knew what was important, they knew exactly where to squeeze.

"Don't ask," Tuck said, dismissing last night's events as insignificant. "You seen him?"

Linc shook his head, then cast his eyes behind Tuck. "Couple of his boys are in though."

Tuck saw the group of quiet thugs chugging draft beer next to the pool tables. While checking them out, he took the chance to glance around at the other patrons but didn't recognize any of them as the men who had assaulted Kadie.

Tuck took his focus back to the men Linc had pointed out. "They been in long?"

"An hour maybe," Linc said. "You're not a cop, are you?"

"My answer hasn't changed since the first time you asked me that," he murmured, while still watching the group.

"Just with that lady last night, you seemed… I know men that do that to a woman are scum, but—"

"I had history," Tuck said, recognizing that he'd have to give Linc something of an explanation. He'd just have to keep it brief. "With that particular lady. But keep that under your hat."

"Ah," Linc said with a nod of understanding. "Doesn't hold her liquor well, does she?"

"No, she doesn't, never has. But I don't think it was the booze in her system that floored her, do you?"

"You hang around long enough you learn not to ask questions."

Seeing an opportunity, he took advantage of Linc's interest in the topic. "Have you seen her in here before?" Tuck asked.

"No," Linc said, wiping down the bar. "But doesn't mean much in here, one face looks just the same as another."

Linc was more observant than he let on, but turning a blind eye, forgetting details was what had kept him in business this long… and in oxygen too. "You've been coming in here every night for a week, what's so important? If you've got beef with this guy—"

"No beef," Tuck said. "I want to do a bit of business, that's all."

Linc knew who Tuck was looking for and that gave him excellent cover for coming in here to watch out for Kadie. But he wouldn't play this game forever, if she didn't show up tonight, he'd get more aggressive in tracking her down. "Hell of a lot of trouble to go to for business."

"This guy has what I need."

Zara had met the fucker face to face, so they'd be keeping her out of the field on this assignment. Having been such an integral part of their previous missions, she wasn't as thrilled with her passive role, though Brodie was more comfortable with it. Tuck wore a Kindred earpiece tonight, but they were maintaining radio silence while he was in here, the line was for emergencies only.

"He's not a guy to cross," Linc said. "Word to the wise."

"Thanks," Tuck said, tipping his glass to Linc then taking another sip. "But I know what I'm doing."

Linc only took a deep breath, then turned to serve another patron at the other end of the bar. Truth was, it was closer to two weeks that Tuck had been coming in here. But he'd do it for another two if it meant catching up with the guy. Without a clear signal on the mark's HQ, all they had to go on were the usual meeting places, of which this was one. A place for dodgy deals that he wouldn't want on his own doorstep. The Kindred had narrowed this down as the spot to watch.

As far as the Kindred mission was concerned, this was the slow number before the last dance. But things would get exciting yet, the real action came when the music was off, the lights dimmed, and the game was reduced to two. Except this time the action would be of the wits rather than the body.

The bar door opened with a rush of bitter air, one man entered, holding the door open, the patrons scowled at the introduction of cold air into their humid room, but the scowls dissolved in lieu of nervous fear. The reactions of the other patrons revealed to Tuck that he had his man.

Taking one step inside, the man he'd been looking for came into view. All of the Kindred work was paying off because he was finally in the vicinity of the villain they'd been tracking. Now all he had to do— Two women appeared at either side of him, beautiful smiling faces, their hands linked into his elbows. Why wasn't he surprised?

Nykiel Sikorski was evil personified, lower in the Russian mafia's chain of command than he'd let people know. He had much more to prove, which made him all the more dangerous. This maniac was the Kindred's mark and there he was, leading little Kadie Harris toward the occupied table Linc had pointed out to him.

If she'd noticed him, she didn't let on. Sikorski sat, Kadie and the other woman flanking him, standing next to his chair rather than being allowed to sit. The bodyguard who had entered in front of them stood with his back to the three at the table, protecting his master.

NINE

TWO BIRDS, one stone, Tuck could handle that. The Kindred mission wouldn't have to be sacrificed after all. Kadie couldn't have hooked up with a more dangerous man if she tried, the stakes got higher, but the end game was the same. He'd get his girl and find out what Sikorski knew before ending the guy. The original mission might have called for mercy, if the others had voted that way, but now that Tuck knew the Russian had had his hands on Kadie, there would be no mercy.

Letting Raven and Swallow know they'd found their mark, he didn't expect a response, but knew they'd be listening when he muttered, "Now we've got a party," before examining what he could see of the table.

Sikorski and his harem faced in to the table and the bodyguard faced out, observing the bar and patrons. Wise, maybe, but by keeping his back to the room Sikorski made himself an easy target, it wouldn't take much to take the bodyguard out.

And if Sikorski expected the women to slow Tuck down... usually two petite woman would be easy to ignore. This night was different, one of Sikorski's entourage would slow him down because he'd have to keep her out of harm's way and do his job at the same time.

He had his approach practiced, he'd used it enough time in various guises, but for the first time he second guessed himself. Could he trust Kadie not to blow his cover? How would his act and reactions change when she was observing him? Any variables introduced into the equation left it unbalanced, and he'd be a fool to believe he could play his usual act with her beside him. For starters, if she was anywhere near him he'd probably end up with the boner of the century, especially when she was dressed like she was and smiling so innocently. It was hard to keep a straight face when your libido was panting.

Tuck also had to take into consideration what success would mean. If he got in with Sikorski, he might be taken back to the Russian's lair and end up on the inside. From all immediate appearances that's where Kadie was. He wouldn't leave her. Taking her with him, when there was a chance she'd put up resistance, would raise suspicion.

Usually, he did what he came to do and blew out of the joint, with no responsibility to anyone, except the job and the Kindred, who were trained to know what their roles were and how to handle themselves. Kadie wasn't as experienced in subterfuge. If he was on the inside, he might have to see her, he might have to see her work, or the other men enjoying her. Could he do that without putting a bullet in the brain of any man who looked at her sideways?

Considering how she would change his plans, he took his eyes off the table to sip his drink and regroup. When he lowered it, he saw that Kadie was on her way to the bar, heading in his direction, although she didn't spare him a glance.

On reaching his side, she ensured no one was in their vicinity before she spoke with static lips. "What are you doing here?" she asked through a glowing, wide, vacant smile. Her eyes trailed to Linc, who was still serving at the other end of the bar.

"Working," he said. "What's your excuse?"

Pushing her tongue inside her upper lip, she plumped, and then salved the juicy flesh. "Me too."

"That's your client?" Tuck asked, swirling his liquid in the glass, doing his best to be just another patron, one who happened to be beside a beautiful woman who wasn't talking to him.

She was good at this, better than he'd thought she'd be. How had he never seen this side of her? Her character leaned over the bar, pushing her breasts together in the scrap of fabric that barely covered them, to give Linc a birds-eye view of her voluptuous cleavage. Suckered in, the bartender immediately began to approach.

Still smiling, she managed not to move her glistening lips. "That's my boss," she said. His focus was on that delicious mouth he'd sampled just that afternoon. All those times it had tormented his body, he'd taken it for granted. Being so close to it now, and being barred from enjoying it, he learned the true meaning of frustration.

"And my mark," Tuck muttered just before Linc got to them.

"What can I get you, sweet thing?" Linc asked.

"Champagne," she said.

Linc laughed, that wasn't a common request around here. "In this joint?"

"Oh," she said, blinking in absent ignorance, and paused her fidgeting figure. "Nicky will be disappointed if—"

Linc held up his hands, "Let me have a look."

She nodded and widened the smile to a grin. "Thank you," she purred.

The airhead act worked for her, only in that it amused him because the last thing she could be accused of was being a bimbo. But for some reason, she wanted Linc to think she was, maybe because Sikorski thought she was. It made a lot of sense for her to play down her intelligence and her sass, Sikorski didn't like to be undermined by anyone, much less a woman. Kadie was playing a part, he just had to figure out why.

Linc disappeared down the bar and kicked open the cellar. He glanced back at Tuck. "Keep an eye on things," he said.

"Me?" Tuck said, downing the rest of his drink.

"You certainly took care of business last night," Linc said on a half-smile, then disappeared down into the cellar.

Had Linc noticed that the primped woman at the bar was the same one he'd walked out with last night, and just admitted he had history with? He hoped for all their sakes he hadn't, but it was unlikely because Linc had the senses of a hawk, even though he liked to downplay them.

"Shit." Tuck sighed. This was getting more complicated by the second. So far his earpiece was silent, his colleagues had faith that he could handle the situation and he knew what words to use if he needed back-up. With Sikorski strolling in, Tuck decided to fall back on the Kindred plan and use that as a way to get close to Kadie, which might help him to figure out why she'd been so adamant to stay with Sikorski, rather than split with him from the motel room.

Some of her confidence wavered, though she didn't let it show on her face. "Sikorski's your target?" Kadie muttered, spreading manicured fingers across the bar.

"Are you gonna tell him?" If she was going to blow his cover before he made his move, the Kindred would need a new plan.

"He's dangerous, Tuck," she whispered, and the glitter of awareness touched her empty eyes when she glanced at him. "You'll get hurt if you—"

She was worried about him getting in over his head? That seemed unbelievable given her own predicament. "Are you telling me to back-off?"

"I'm telling you that he's volatile." The concern she showed now was an improvement over the indifference she'd left him with earlier.

Playing the Kindred mission through would prevent a scene from unfolding between them, and he had to see what she was capable of. If he grabbed her and dragged her out, he'd have Sikorski's people to deal with and the Kindred would never get the information they needed from the Russian.

She could be worried, he was okay with that, but she couldn't be a barrier, then he'd have no choice except to cart her out of here now, no matter the cost. "Are you going to get in my way, Toots?"

"I'd never put you in danger," she said, and he believed her. "Tell me what it is, and I'll get it."

That was an unexpected offer. She wanted him to clue her in on the mission he'd been running with his cohorts for months when they only had a few brief seconds together. Then she wanted him to sit here and watch her stroll out of the joint with one of the most dangerous men Tuck had ever heard of. No chance, that wasn't happening.

"And put you in danger? Not the way I operate." That was the truth. Putting any innocent person in danger wasn't his MO and it sure wasn't the Kindred's. If he even thought about it, Swallow would be waiting for him with a weapon at the end of the night. Swallow was getting tougher with every mission and as her confidence grew in her ability, so did his. "You can turn around and walk out of here right now."

"You think you can take on Nicky and his men by yourself?" she asked.

"Who said I'm by myself?" he asked, lifting his forearm off the bar to bring his drink up to his lips. "If you walk out that door right now there will be a woman waiting to take you to safety."

"A woman?" she asked, and he liked the tinge of jealousy in her voice. "I thought there was no 'she'."

If Kadie could still be interested in where he put his dick now, she could be interested in letting him put it in her again. Except he had to dismiss that thought as fast as he'd had it. Kadie still had the ability to turn him on, but that muddied things that were already boggy enough. They had to get out of here clean before he thought about what was next for their relationship.

"She doesn't belong to me," he said. "I've told you that before."

"Swallow?"

Well at least she'd been paying attention, although he kind of wished that she hadn't been because knowing what little she did could put her in danger. "What did I tell you about saying those names?"

That question went unanswered. "So I walk out with her and what? Rave and the chief come charging in to back you up and there's a huge scene that could cause people to get hurt."

Always worried about what would happen to other people, Kadie was a mother hen, even if she didn't admit it. Looking after him, his business, and whoever else strayed into their lives, she was always protecting someone, and usually neglecting herself in the process, as this situation reiterated.

Raven would come in to back him up if the need arose. Between them they could clear the room. Both were trained and they'd fought together enough times before to know how the other worked. Training together helped them to learn their weaknesses and how to use their own strengths to offset those vulnerabilities.

One thing was for sure, the chief wouldn't be coming in. He wouldn't have back in the day either, not unless things got really grim. Art recognized that his athletic skills were inferior to the younger, fitter members of the team and preferred to direct from afar. That was the irony, during the first field assignment he'd participated in for years, he was killed. No, the chief wouldn't be coming in to save the day, but Kadie couldn't know that.

Now wasn't the time to explain who the chief was or what had happened to him. The last thing he needed to do was remind Kadie of the mortality rate in his chosen line of work. "Raven and I will handle it," he said.

"I'm surprised you ever came back to me if this is how reckless you are."

He'd come back to her because she was the light at the end of his tunnel. Some missions depended on him thinking of her and dreaming about their reunion. Any time the situation was touch and go, or he got himself hurt, Kadie was the image he emblazoned in his mind's eye because he'd promised to go back to her. Once he'd made a promise to Kadie, he stuck to it. She'd put up with enough bullshit from him, she didn't need to worry about his honesty too.

"I'm not reckless," he said. "I know how to play this game. I've been doing it for a long time."

Apathy seemed to prevent her from fighting harder, or maybe she was just aware of their audience and was playing the game too, because she accepted his words. "Okay," she said. "Whatever it is that you have to do, do it quickly."

So she thought he took orders from her? In bed, sure. Dinner plans? Whatever. When it came to life, death, and Nykiel Sikorski, Tuck called the shots. "When I leave, I'm taking you with me," he said despite having not consciously made the decision on how to do it.

The Kindred didn't like to make a scene. They kept their missions low-key and avoided drawing attention to themselves, it was how they'd remained so successful and so mysterious, which contributed to their formidable reputation. The Kindred were a myth, no one had tangible evidence that they existed. Most of what people knew were half-truths and whispered stories.

Still, if Tuck told Raven and Swallow that he wanted to storm in with guns blazing and blow the place to kingdom come, they'd do it without hesitation. Having each other meant Raven and Swallow understood the depth of passion that came with love and as hard as they'd fight for each other, they'd fight for Kadie the same amount.

"I won't go," she said. Putting up resistance to his suggestions was always her opening gambit, all he'd have to do was counter until she had no valid argument left. Force she might oppose, logic she couldn't combat. "I have my own motives for being here."

"Motives," Tuck said, glad that she was giving him information, even if it was in a trickle. "Apart from the money?"

The glow of blank happiness on her face was beginning to loosen. "I don't see the green. I made that up," she admitted. "We stay at the mansion and see clients on his property... for now."

"For now?" Tuck asked, "What does that mean?"

He knew more about the sex trade than he ever wanted to. While he and Raven had never gone after those in the trafficking game as part of their own vendetta, the Kindred had plenty of experience with it through their members.

Taking apart that industry, one pervert at a time, was what Falcon and Wren dedicated their time to. It put the Kindred's two more academic members into harm's way on several occasions.

Falcon, also known as Zave, was good at talking himself out of trouble. With his superior intelligence, he could argue any angle. Wren, the good doctor, whose real name was Thad, was a more nervous sort and so didn't maintain a convincing poker face. He'd bailed them out many times and his skills were invaluable to the team. But if Zave needed back up for anything that might get physical, he and Raven were called in.

"It means that he'll eventually get bored with me," she said. "When that happens we…"

"What?" he said through gritted teeth. The options were selling her on or killing her. Neither would happen now that he'd found her. But if he hadn't, she'd have been alone out here. When she needed him more than she ever had, he'd have been oblivious. Finding out what she thought came next would allow him to gauge if she understood how serious this was. "What happens when he's bored with you?"

"We get shipped out of the country," she said.

Selling her on, marginally better than killing her, but she was beautiful and her body would fetch a high price. "To what?"

"Stand on street corners," she said, turning her head toward him, and when their eyes touched a jolt of venom burst in his gut.

His gorgeous, innocent Kadie was in up to her neck. She didn't deserve this and he couldn't imagine how she'd gotten herself here. He couldn't let her go back to Sikorski, to the life she'd stumbled into. To hell with the Kindred and their mission, if Tuck had to do this himself then he would. Kadie might not argue with logic, but for some reason, he couldn't hold onto it.

Grabbing her and forcing her out of the bar now wouldn't end well. Acting on impulse would give Raven and Swallow no time to mobilize either.

But that didn't matter. Sickness and hot rage roiled

and burst within him. Kadie couldn't be here, couldn't be a part of this existence, she was pure, innocent of the evil he fought to protect her from. Seeing her this way proved to him that he'd failed her and if he was failing her, he didn't know what he or his life was about anymore.

"I'm taking you with me."

"No," she whispered. "He'll kill you if you interfere. No kidding, Tuck, he won't hesitate… Of course, he'll kill me first, let you watch while they gut me—"

"Do you think for a second—"

"I've seen it, Hotshot," she murmured. Stabilizing her vacant grin before she turned to look at the table, Kadie offered a finger wave to one of the men Sikorski was meeting with. While glancing at him, she noticed Linc returning from the cellar. Her next words were hurried, she wanted to get them out before Linc reached them. "We'll be leaving within five minutes," she said. "Nicky doesn't like this place. He won't stay here long."

Their time was up, their secret meeting over, Linc was only two paces away. "What's the meeting about?" Tuck asked, but she had no opportunity to answer, not unless she wanted to clue Linc in on what their conversation had been about.

"Look what I found," Linc said, dusting off a bottle that had clearly been hidden somewhere deep in the recesses of the cellar.

Kadie didn't miss a beat and slipped straight back into the bimbo persona. "Aren't you a peach," she said, pulling a hundred from her bra and sliding it toward Linc. "Don't worry about glasses, we'll drink it in the car from the crystal."

Taking the bottle, she bobbed her shoulders and was about to turn and leave when Tuck's hand shot out to grab her wrist. "How much?" he growled.

Linc didn't take the time to look at them, he turned and walked away. "Excuse me?" Kadie drawled.

"How much?" Tuck asked her, no longer hiding his attention.

If she walked away with Sikorski now, the Kindred still wouldn't have a lead on where he was based. Interrupting

Sikorski's meeting was always part of the plan, Kadie had just given him a prime opportunity to do it by proxy. In spite of that, mission or not, he wouldn't let her go back over there and saunter out of this disgusting place with that repulsive man, just to get drunk with him in his garish car.

The uneasiness in her eyes told him she wasn't sure how to handle his outburst. Should she keep going as the dumb slut or was he about to blow her cover after she'd promised to maintain the secret of his?

"We don't work for money," she said in a low enough tone that he recognized she was talking to him as herself rather than the character. "We're traded for favors; you have to have something that he wants."

Wanting Sikorski's attention, he gave her body a lurid once over, examining her goods as a stranger, not a former lover. "What about you," he said. "What if I have something you want?"

The connection was made and her sultry eyes narrowed in feigned innocence. "Are you flirting with me?" she laughed, descending into character. He'd never heard that giggle before so to him it was a dead giveaway, others would buy it though.

"I have something your boss wants."

"Saffy!" A shrill female voice drew the attention of them both, and they saw that a woman was approaching, the one who Kadie had entered with. Sikorski was on his feet, getting ready to leave the table.

"Saffy?" Tuck muttered, assuming Kadie had her own alias for her own reasons.

"Sapphire," she replied, looking at her counterpart with eager ignorance. "Because—"

"Your eyes," he said, needing no further explanation.

"Yes," she said, glancing back at him, and for a second, she was his again.

The actual bimbo interrupted them. "We're leaving!"

"Right," Kadie said, stepping toward the woman. Tuck snatched her again, unwilling and in actual fact, unable, to let her go into the clutches of that evil bastard.

"Let me talk to him," Tuck demanded, making no

secret of his intention to touch her and get an audience with her boss.

He could play it that Kadie was a stranger to him, a beautiful woman who had his attention, that maybe he wanted to spend some intimate time with. If she stayed at the mansion, as she'd said, then he doubted she picked up clients in random bars. The show was a means to an end. All he needed was Sikorski's attention for a few seconds, and once he said what he had to, Tuck would have his in.

The bodyguard made his way toward them while Sikorski stayed behind his hired-human-shield like the well-dressed coward that he was. "Do we have a problem?" Sikorski drawled in his Eastern European accent.

"He wants to talk," Kadie said, pouting at the lusting honcho whose job it was to protect Sikorski. Tuck was impressed, she was protecting him by distracting the bodyguard and managing to do it in a way that raised no suspicions. "He says he has something you want."

"Is that right?" Sikorski said with an intent look, like he was trying to place the stranger. He and Tuck had never met, but he couldn't discount that he might have crossed Sikorski's radar. Sikorski was in deep and met all kinds of people. It was no surprise that he didn't have instant recall on the names and faces of every person he'd ever met. "What on earth could a… being like you have for me?" Clearly, he wasn't impressed by what he saw.

TEN

TUCK LEFT HIS stool. Kadie knew this man inside out; she knew everything about him. Maybe not about his work and his colleagues, but she knew his personality, his motivations, and recognized his moods.

Yet, looking at him now, there was something scary about the menace in his unyielding form and grim scowl. Tucker Holt was terrifying, and until today she'd never seen this side of him. Choosing not to look directly at him, she felt him loom beside her like an immovable force, an intimidating reckoning that saw the world and everything in it all at once.

He knew everything, feared nothing, and just like that she got it. The man she loved, the man she had been with for years and trusted with her heart, the man she had saved herself and her world for, was dangerous and capable of anything, absolutely anything. Sikorski didn't move, his expression didn't change. For the first time, she saw him actually intimidated, something she'd thought was impossible. Sikorski owned everyone and everything, but she read fear in his gaze and for some odd reason her pride in Tuck grew.

Sikorski started, but Tuck didn't let him finish. "I'm bored of—"

"Game Time," Tuck said, shutting Sikorski up with

two words. Sikorski's default was to ridicule and patronize, to put people in their place. Tuck didn't even have to blink. With those two words, he'd shaken Sikorski's core, which was something else she'd never seen.

Sikorski's expression relaxed a miniscule fraction, but it was enough to tell her that Tuck had his attention. "What is that?" Star, her female companion, piped up. "It's a game? You want to play a game? I love games. What kind of—"

"Quiet," Sikorski demanded. Immediately, Star silenced, and shrank back, though her eyes danced with curiosity at this new colleague. Tuck was attractive, his defined features and muscular body were impossible to ignore. Kadie didn't like it when other women checked him out, but she tolerated it while they were together because she trusted his fidelity. That safety net didn't exist anymore.

"You have it?" Sikorski asked.

"Is that a trick question?" Tuck said. "It doesn't exist... does it?"

Sikorski's lips curled up slowly. "You have my attention Mr....?"

"Swift," Tuck said, using the name she'd heard before.

Kadie didn't flinch. Tuck had to be able to trust her and registering anything she knew to be a lie in front of these people might get him hurt. If he had a choice, she wouldn't be here at all, she didn't need him to spell it out. Having her in this situation would terrify him, maybe because he thought she'd cause him trouble, or maybe just because these people they were with were dangerous. This was Tuck's job, lying, getting close to dangerous people, he was practiced. Kadie had to prove that she could approach this as a professional too and put her own fears aside.

"Swift..." Sikorski prompted. "Is that a first or last name?"

"Just Swift for now," Tuck said.

Sikorski was still going to vie for superiority, he had to find a way to adopt a lofty position over this stranger who, to all external parties, appeared to be the commanding power. "I've concluded my business for the evening—"

"I can take my business elsewhere," Tuck said.

"No one said that," Sikorski said. Uncertain about this development, her boss hid his intrigue under indifference. "This is hardly the place to talk of such a… delicate matter."

"You gotta take these lovely ladies somewhere," Tuck said, eyeing the blonde, Star, with great interest even though Kadie stood closer.

"Yes," Sikorski said. "Somewhere, but nowhere you are welcome."

Using her to get himself close to Sikorski conflicted her. It was odd, but warming, to be accepted as part of his work and she was glad to be of help to him. Except she knew it would never be as simple as that. Tuck had his reasons for wanting to be near Sikorski and one of those reasons was to get her away from the Russian, he'd been explicit about removing her from her pimp.

Kadie didn't want to stay with Sikorski forever, just for long enough to make an extraction of her own. Being a novice, she hadn't figured out how to do it yet, but she wouldn't give up just because the situation was difficult. Her whole reason for being in this bar alone the other night was to meet Howie, they'd managed to come up with a plan that was supposed to give them an out. Howie hadn't shown up and she hadn't seen him since. Urgency was making her anxious.

Tuck wasn't dissuaded by Sikorski's condescension. His persistence might have pissed Sikorski off, if he hadn't already made it clear he was useful. "I've come a long way—"

"You'd have had to," Sikorski said, sneering at their surroundings. "What if I don't like what you have to tell me?"

"We part as friends," Tuck said. "But I hear you're the man to talk to about this, and I guarantee what I have to say is worth it."

Sikorski considered him for a moment, then looked at his own bodyguard to size up who would triumph if things came to blows. The Russian cast a look at her, and although the exchange was brief, its subtlety wasn't missed by Tuck who was invested in the villain and his interest in Kadie.

This wasn't the first time she'd checked someone out

for Sikorski, so she knew what to do and how to play it. She was just pleased that he'd chosen her for the task, not only because she didn't want Star to put her hands all over Tuck, but because her main concern was Tuck getting out of this alive. So if he had any weapons or contraband, she couldn't let anyone else find them.

Damn him for coming into her life now when she needed to be prioritizing elsewhere. She was only here, only knew who Sikorski was, because of her former lover. But she couldn't blame him for the mess she was in.

In this moment, she had a role to play, one that she was more used to than she'd ever wanted to be. Widening her smile, she pushed out her chest. Tuck knew how to read her eyes and they would reveal more to him than her breasts, but he dutifully looked at her chest, understanding that was the point of her presenting her cleavage. Any man that saw him miss that invitation would be suspicious.

"Do you work out?" she whimpered. Flirting with him, as she would any other person Sikorski wanted her to frisk, she had to make their exchange look good.

Touching his abs, their physical connection fizzled, scorching her skin. Now wasn't the time to be thinking about his dick, but her instinct was to get closer to it. Sliding her hands around his ribs to his back under his jacket, her splayed fingers slid up, down, under his arms, then out of his jacket to his wrists. Linking her fingers in his to draw his arms around her, she checked his pockets while he held her.

She was here to frisk him. Plastering her body against his was meant to be a distraction that would lower his guard. Men were happier to be touched by barely clothed women than the club-fingered oaf of a bodyguard.

The distraction would work for any other man, but probably not for Tuck who had been inside her many times, as close as a man could get to his woman. His heat reassured her, pushing her on, giving her the confidence to feel safe, even with her back to Sikorski and his bodyguard. This mission would have to be completed quickly by both of them. Haste could lead to mistakes, but with each other in the mix there was too much at stake.

"Well, Sugar, you sure know how to introduce yourself," he drawled, her foot left her shoe, and touched his ankle, sliding up to his calf, and around his shin as her hands dipped into his jean's pockets. Her other foot did the same on the other leg. This time when she went to lower it, he snatched her knee, and pulled it up to his hip. She gasped, but he caught her waist to keep her balance.

Kadie worked hard to maintain her façade. When he touched her, took control of her, it made her forget that there was any act to uphold. "You didn't say please," she said with a twinkle in her eyes.

He had to realize that she would feel his erection as she searched him. This move told her that he wasn't shy about his physical reaction to her proximity and wandering hands. Tuck wanted her to know it was there, to feel it.

To the world he was tough, thorough, and harsh. Life pulled no punches, and neither did he. But he wasn't ashamed of being under her spell. When she'd been his girl, she'd known it, known his body was a slave to hers, just as hers reciprocated.

Almost a year had passed since they'd been intimate, yet the time melted away to nothing when she was here, breathing the same air as him.

"Put the girl down," the bodyguard barked.

Still twined around him, she was in no hurry to retreat. "It talks," Tuck said, scrutinizing her every nuance as she tried not to squirm against him.

Her back was to the others, but they might catch a glimpse of her expression in the mirror if he didn't keep his body in the way. Yes, Kadie's reaction was as strong as the one in his pants. Despite the odds, they were both tempted to shatter the illusion, it was written in the intensity of his gaze. If she pushed up, let him kiss her, then that would be it, they'd both lose their cover.

Inviting as the temptation of tasting him was, she couldn't take the risk and had to prove her loyalty to Sikorski while not leaving Tuck vulnerable. "It also packs heat," she said. Keeping her tone dry and impatient, perhaps even annoyed, her eyes held a warning. "Long, hot, throbbing heat."

If he hadn't known already that she would protect him then she confirmed it by blatantly ignoring the knife strapped to his ankle. While they were together, she'd known it was there, because he always carried it. Not only had he told her that in words, but she'd removed it for him during their bedroom activities and had watched him strap it on several times before he left for a job. Kadie knew it was there all right, and she hadn't told her new friends, she'd chosen to support him instead. That was her way of letting him know that she wouldn't leave him swinging in the wind.

Pressing into the sheath with her foot when she'd searched him, she didn't allow any flicker of recognition to cross her expression. She wanted him to have a weapon. A way to protect himself and maybe even protect her if they were found out. For however long he was planning to hang around, she would have a split loyalty and she had no idea how that would play out to all of their advantages. Tuck had more experience and if it came to it, she would confide in him and maybe he could help her find a way out for all of them.

All he had to do at the moment was to make sure that no one else found the blade, because if she was suspected of helping him then they would both be in trouble and both of their missions would fail. Unexpected, and somewhat unwelcome as it was, she had an ally on the inside. Tuck might be the person she trusted more than any other, but he was also the one she cared about most. Having him involved in this risky game increased her need for success.

She would rather that her ally wasn't the other half of her whole. If anything happened to him, it would be happening to her not long after. If not at the hands of the villain, then at her own hand. Sikorski would kill them both if he uncovered their association. But if Tuck lost his life in this game, she wouldn't be able to go on without him, the guilt would eat her up.

Tuck released her leg, and she spun on the spot to face Sikorski again, her shoulder blades wavering against Tuck's chest. "He's fine on the weapon front," she said.

"Fine," Sikorski said, giving her body a full, carnal

perusal before looking over her head at Tuck. "Come for a ride in the car and we'll talk."

"In a car?" Tuck said. "So you can drive me out to the middle of nowhere, and put a bullet in me for my knowledge?"

Kadie wouldn't have thought of that. Tuck's previous associates must have been real treats to work with. "What would you rather?" Sikorski said. "My girls fuck it out of you?"

Fucking Tuck for information, Kadie could handle that. Except her former lover glanced past her to fixate on Star instead. "Maybe."

"Star has your interest? You must be a man of the earth," Sikorski said.

Tuck leered. "Something like that."

Kadie didn't know what that meant, except that Star was somewhat simple most of the time. That Tuck had dismissed her as an option infuriated her and made her wonder what the erection had been for if Star was the one he wanted to get close to.

"You may come with us," Sikorski said, and the bodyguard retrieved something from his back pocket. "But you must agree to our terms."

Tuck watched the bodyguard approach with a blindfold. Kadie had seen this before too. New associates would get into the car, but wouldn't know where they were, or how to get out again.

Proving his experience, Tuck didn't flinch. "Paranoid motherfucker, aren't you?"

"Careful," Sikorski said. "My patience is renowned for being thin. If you please me, and give me what I want, you will reap rewards and this discomfort will be long forgotten."

"I could be a one-trick pony," Tuck said, testing the boundaries. Most men would just be grateful to have what they sought, a way in, Tuck was still battling for dominance against a man who'd always fight back.

"A man who speaks of Game Time has broad associations, sinister knowledge, or both. But if I do not like what you say, this discomfort will be the least of your worries."

Without breaking a sweat, Tuck maintained his aloof pose. "I wouldn't put myself at risk if I didn't know it would pay off."

"Which begs the question," Sikorski said. "What is it you want for this knowledge?"

Tuck snatched the blindfold before the bodyguard could reach him. "Let's get where we're going. Like you said, this is hardly the place to talk about such a delicate matter."

"So you agree?" Sikorski asked.

"Let's get out of here," Tuck said with a single nod.

His unwavering confidence awed her. He might be jumping into the fire, but he didn't appear to feel the heat. And after leaving Hells Waiting Room for the last time, the fire was the only place left to go.

ELEVEN

THEY AT LEAST let him get into the car before Warta, Sikorski's personal bodyguard, tried to take the blindfold from Tuck's hand. Tuck snatched it out of Warta's reach.

"The pretty girls can touch whatever they like," Tuck snarled at the man holding open the back door of the limo. "You're not my type."

The rear seats faced each other and Kadie found herself next to Sikorski, sitting with her back to the sealed privacy panel. Tuck was diagonally opposite her, next to Star, and was the last to get in. Star took the blindfold from Tuck, and leaned in close, pressing her breasts to his arm as she reached around him to put it over his eyes.

Sure that her breathing had stilled, Kadie looked straight at him in the clutches of a wave of panic. Her usually casual Tuck was tense, not because of the blindfold, but because Sikorski's hand was resting on her upper thigh. His eyes flashed from it up at hers to sear his fury into her skin before Star covered his eyes and fastened the blindfold.

Warta closed the door and went to sit up front with the driver where he always traveled. After they heard the front passenger door closing, the vehicle started to move.

"Are you a nervous traveler?" Star purred into Tuck's

ear. Her hand slid up his leg and covered his package with caressing fingers.

Tuck slid down the seat a few inches to better Star's access and Kadie nearly growled aloud at his barefaced acceptance of the advance. "Are you offering a little relief, Sugar?" he asked, turning his head in Star's direction. She was plastered the length of his side, allowing no light to penetrate. Star had a great body, one of the best. Men favored her over most of the other girls at the mansion. Star's leg twisted over one of Tuck's, and she drew his earlobe into her mouth.

"That could certainly be arranged," Star hummed in his ear.

Kadie could've forgiven him being the passive party, but when his hand slid to Star's hip and up her waist to her breast, Kadie was certain fire was ready to burst from her nose. There in front of her was the man who had refused sex with her that very day in the motel room. He couldn't have any hard and fast rules about taking care of his needs during a mission because his hand covered Star's breast, clearly sampling the density of the flesh.

Sikorski took a stack of papers from a pouch next to him and began to read, indifferent to Star's display. Kadie's equivalent was pressing kisses to Tuck's face, his jaw, his neck. When he tipped his face toward Star, the hussy didn't hesitate to take his mouth in a clamor of tongues that fueled Kadie's ire.

"You don't know where he's been, Star," Kadie said to her colleague, trying her best to sound disgusted instead of indignant.

The couple ceased kissing, and Star giggled while burying her head against his neck. One of her hands began to unbuckle his belt, and the other slid under his tee shirt onto those stone-solid abs.

"Don't worry, Sugar," Tuck drawled, wearing a swaggering smile under his still covered eyes. "There's plenty of me to go around."

"In your dreams, Swift," she said, spitting out his false name.

Star reached for the top button of his jeans, and the

space they all occupied got smaller. Pressure on her chest left Kadie desperate to gasp for air. She couldn't, he couldn't, surely—she couldn't breathe, couldn't stop her hands from shaking, was this panic? Or shock, or—

A sharp splintering sound stopped Star. Tuck sat up straight. Sikorski looked from side to side, the papers falling from his limp hand. A shout from the front seat was silenced by another crack. The car lurched to the side and gathered pace.

"Get down!" Tuck demanded, leaping off his seat and snatching Kadie from hers in the same stroke he used to push Star to the floor.

"What—"

"Stay," Tuck said, ripping the blindfold off.

The whole car shook. The smooth road was no longer beneath them. They bumped and banged along uneven ground, surrounded by the sound of wheels trundling faster on grass, whipping plant life out of the way.

Tuck was up in a crouch, holding the button to open the privacy screen. "What was that sound?" Sikorski demanded. "What is—"

"Gunshots," Tuck said, without looking at the immigrant. Instead, his eyes touched hers and something went unsaid before he shoved her toward the floor and jumped into the seat she'd vacated. Rolling through the privacy screen, he clambered into the front of the car. "Hold on!"

"We're going to die!" Star screamed. "We're gonna die! We're—"

"No!" Kadie said, snatching the blonde's hand. Sikorski was forgotten on the floor, protecting himself and no one else.

Star wasn't placated, tears of fear streamed through her mascara. "But we're gonna—"

"Do not panic," Kadie said, speaking as slowly and calmly as she could while imparting her vehement confidence. "He will get us out of this."

The car lurched to one side. The back spun out on the grass and they were thrown to the left wall of the car. On another bump, and a choice curse from the front, the car skidded, unable to get purchase on the slick surface.

"Three," Tuck murmured from the front. They hit a deep divot, bouncing them from the floor to the ceiling of the vehicle.

"Two," he said in an eerily serene whisper.

The car was decelerating, she could feel it. Deliberately slowing her breathing, she closed her eyes and prayed for salvation. Tuck was in the front, if they hit something head-on—

"One," he said just as the car heaved to a stop, shoving them all toward the front in a bundle of bodies.

No one moved for a moment. Sikorski lifted his head first. Star started babbling. Raising her focus, Kadie saw the steady movement of Tuck's shoulders as he breathed out some of the adrenaline. In a blaze of sudden movement, he threw open the door beside him and left the car. She could hear him moving outside, slowly, deliberately.

It took him a while, but eventually the back passenger door opened an inch. It stuck in its frame, clearly bent out of shape. Accompanied by a roar from Tuck, the door was yanked from the frame, and he stuck his head inside to look at them all. Grabbing Star, he hauled her out, and shoved her to the dirt beside the door.

"Stay there," he demanded of Star.

Returning to the car, he reached in and lifted Kadie completely off her feet. Taking her out, he stayed low as he carried her around the door and put her on the ground by the front wheel. "Are you hurt?" he growled. She shook her head, but that didn't stop him from running his hands over her, through her hair, checking her scalp, her joints, her face.

"I'm okay," she said, taking his hand from her skin. "Are you?"

"That's the most interesting car journey I've had in a while," he said, locking his eyes on hers, their hands were joined, and she didn't want to let him go, even when Sikorski came out of the car.

"Where are my men?" Sikorski demanded.

"Front seat," Tuck said still crouched in front of her, he didn't let go of her hand. "Dead."

Sikorski blustered. "Dead, I don't—"

"Check for yourself," Tuck said. "One head wound each. Two bullet holes in the front windshield. Sniper, and a damn good one, clear kill shot to a moving vehicle, we had to be going forty miles an hour."

"How do you know that?" Sikorski questioned.

"I've ridden in a car before and I pay attention," Tuck said. "Unless you know who the shooter was, and what they wanted, you should be careful up there."

Sikorski was frowning, pissed off and probably calculating ways to retaliate against whoever their assailant was. "What, I—"

"Why do you think the women are in the dirt?" Tuck asked, still crouched, sandwiching her between him and the car. The car door shielded one side while there was a group of trees on the other. Protecting her was his motivation for the position and their lack of altitude. Fixing her attention on him, she was humbled by his instinct to cover her from every angle, although one of the shields was him. A sniper wouldn't get her, deliberately, or by accident.

"Then we should be in the car," Sikorski said, opening the front door to look at his men. Star crawled around behind him.

"You saved us," Star said to Tuck, who was stroking Kadie's finger with his thumb.

Averse to praise, he didn't look happy to be labelled a hero. "I saved myself," Tuck said. "You folks came along for the ride."

"Where…" Star looked up to examine the car and where it had been headed. "What's over there?"

"I wouldn't look over there."

Star didn't hear him. She crawled to the trees they would have hit if the car had gone another ten feet. As soon as she got there, she screamed and scrambled backward until she got to them. "It's a drop," she shrieked. "A dead drop."

Kadie didn't look at Star, her panic was obvious and well-founded. Tuck's thumb moved faster over her hand. The slight impatience in that maneuver betrayed to her that he'd known exactly what was beyond those trees.

"Lucky break then," he mumbled.

Star was in the midst of her own emotional outburst and didn't see, or care, that Tuck was uncomfortable. "You… You're our hero! You saved our lives! Without you, we'd…!" Star's tears dropped to her cheeks, and she launched herself at Tuck, wrapping her arms around him, and sobbing against him.

"What do we do now?" Kadie asked, unmoved by her colleagues clambering actions.

Tuck held on to her hand, and although Star had her arms tight around his neck, and her body against his, their simple connection was much deeper.

"How far are we from our destination?" he asked her.

Kadie shrugged. "Two miles, maybe three from the road we were on, but I don't know how far off-road we are."

He nodded. "We won't get the car out of this," he said. "Not a car like this, on this terrain."

"Can we walk it?"

Glancing down at the spike heels she wore, the corner of his mouth curled upward. "The heels might kill you before the sniper does, I suppose. Is this the first of these?"

"There is always someone trying to kill me," Sikorski said from behind them. "It's the price of being the best."

Tuck wasn't startled by Sikorski's interjection, but Kadie hadn't even known he was there. "You might have told me I'd be a target," Tuck said, acting like this was an inconvenience that could've been foreseen.

The Russian was unapologetic. "You are not," Sikorski said. "I am the target."

Anger tightened Tuck's expression. "Except I was next to you. Those guys in the front weren't the target either, how did that work out for them?"

Being shot at would shake anyone up, it had hit her hard, she was still trembling. Sikorski showed no remorse for what he probably considered collateral damage. "Feel free to walk away if you can't handle—"

Star leaped to her feet. "He saved our lives!"

Sikorski didn't look at the emotional woman, but his hand moved in a blur through the night, to backhand Star in response to her insolence. The blow sent her back to her knees. Tuck was about to leap to her defense but Kadie pulled his hand to her chest. This was not the place to start a fight, not with two dead bodies already on the scene.

"I shall call for transport," Sikorski said, retrieving his phone from his pocket.

Star was already forgotten, she sat in a daze a good six feet away, her hand covering her cheek. Sikorski walked away from them toward the back of the car, then kept on going, and for a blessed moment they were alone.

"What were you trying to prove?" Kadie muttered, squeezing her fingers between his. "What were you thinking?"

"That you were in trouble," he answered.

Lifting her eyes to his, she saw the truth there. "You were in trouble too."

"Never entered my mind."

She believed that he prioritized her wellbeing over his. Their push and pull games became insignificant in view of how close they'd come to losing each other just now. "What good are you to me dead?" she asked, covering their joined hands with her other one, and pulling it toward her hammering heart.

"I'm not much good to you alive," he said, casting his eyes to Sikorski who was at the rear of the car.

How he could still be thinking about her association with Sikorski when they'd just nearly lost their lives, Kadie was astounded. But he'd proved himself. If nothing else, she knew he had skills and instincts that would keep them alive. "There are things you don't understand," she whispered.

"Have you been with him?" Tuck asked, snapping his attention back to her. "Have you?"

Worse than thinking about her connection to Sikorski, he was thinking about her bed and who had been in it. Thoughts like that seemed out of place right now, but he was adamant. "Tuck," she said on the quietest breath.

"I'm going to kill him."

"That's not what you do," she said, dipping her head toward their hands.

"It will be today," he growled.

"No," she said. "You're better than that."

"You can't tell me you wanted his hands on you."

After seeing him kiss Star, she could imagine what it would feel like to think of him being intimate with another woman, his anger was understandable. At the start she'd wanted to hurt him for hurting her, now she wanted that pain to go away. "Not everything is as it seems," she said.

His eyes narrowed. "What? What's going on?"

"There's no time," she said, watching Star crawl in Sikorski's direction, probably with the goal of apologizing as she'd been conditioned to bow down to the Russian's will. "I can't explain everything here, he'll be off the phone soon. It won't take his people long to get here."

"When?" he asked. "When will you explain it to me?"

"The house, it's bugged, everywhere. Cameras, audio, you have to be careful."

He exhaled. "That's nothing." He touched his ear and glanced toward Sikorski who was still on the phone. "Are you guys with me?"

Frowning, Kadie realized that he wasn't talking to her, he was using her as cover, again. "Who are you talking to?" she asked.

"Yeah," Tuck said. "Two down. Our people are fine. Objective achieved." He smiled, just a brief flicker, but it was there. "You didn't really doubt me, did you, Swallow?"

Horror made her squeeze his hand. His people were in his ear. "Did you plan that?"

He made eye contact with her but didn't answer her. "You did good, Rave. Took out both guys, one shot each. I owe you a hundred bucks."

"Tuck," she hissed, smacking his chest. They'd almost died and the whole thing was a ruse perpetuated by his people. "You nearly got us killed."

He caught her hand on his chest. "Don't call me that again, not out here, we have rules."

"I don't care about your damn rules, what did that achieve?"

"I just saved the fucker's life," Tuck said, nodding toward Sikorski who was dealing with a weeping Star. "I have his respect and now he owes me. A threat to his life that endangered mine, means I have a favor to call in."

"What the hell kind of favor?" she asked.

Whatever her mission entailed it was nothing to what he and his people wanted to achieve. It was her goal to save a life, not take them. Swift was part of a team who were capable of murder, he was smiling and chatting about a bet to the man who had just murdered two people and she couldn't imagine that was the first time something like that had happened.

Raven was his best friend, that's what he'd told her once. He'd never told her that the man was a killer. Never told her that he was a sniper capable of taking almost superhuman kill shots. Tuck had told her that Raven and Swallow were together. She couldn't picture a woman who would want to be with a man who had such lethal skills.

Yet, Tuck had just pulled his own crazy stuntman maneuvers to get them out of a moving vehicle that was dangerously out of control. He'd trusted his colleagues to kill the bodyguards, just as they'd trusted him to get the car pulled to a halt. If they needed something from Sikorski, and had chosen not to kill him, then his death wasn't their ultimate goal. She needed to know their objective.

This kind of exploit terrified her, but Tuck hadn't broken a sweat. "We're going to talk, tonight," Tuck said to her, stroking her hand again. "You're going to tell me everything about what you're doing here and if I'm satisfied, I'll reciprocate."

"If you're satisfied?" she asked, widening her eyes at his audacity. "Your friend almost killed me."

"The privacy screen is bulletproof and Rave knows his angles, he'd never have taken the shot if he thought it might hit you."

He knows his angles, a man she'd never met had pulled the trigger and risked her life. "What if he missed?" she asked.

Tuck smiled again. "I'll let you ask him that when you meet him."

That took some of the wind out of her sails. She couldn't bluster about a man who she might have to face-off against soon. Tuck had never so much as hinted about these people while they were in a relationship and here he was suggesting that she was going to meet them.

"I don't want to meet him."

"I'm taking you out of Sikorski's place as soon as I can, and when I do, you'll meet the Kindred. Those of them who are here anyway." His head tilted and she guessed he was listening. "Yeah, Swallow, I guess she will need her own codename… But it won't be one she uses for long."

So he wanted her to meet these crazy, killer people, but wanted her out of his life as quickly as possible too. Maybe he hoped that by meeting his cohorts, she'd be terrified enough to tuck tail and run. Maybe she would be. If the Kindred were as lethal as she'd seen tonight, she wasn't sure that she wanted to be a part of their ranks. Though that had once been her greatest wish.

But there was no time to argue. Sikorski was heading back toward them and Tuck noticed, so his frown blended his features. "How long have you been here? With him."

The numbness returned to her soul because she didn't need to be reminded of what she'd been through. "Too long."

Sikorski came to the front of the car, Star dragged herself along behind him. "A vehicle will be here to get us momentarily," he said, then looked at Tuck. "Then we have business to conduct."

"Yes, I think we do," Tuck said. Both men were as sure, and as arrogant, as each other.

With all the parties suspicious and angry, Kadie couldn't imagine what they hoped to achieve tonight. Anyone else would want time to recover from this trauma. Not these men. Eventually, the vehicle would get here to take them back to the mansion where Sikorski had been staying with his people. But then what?

TWELVE

TUCK TOOK THE heavy crystal tumbler that Sikorski had just filled with a generous measure from the Waterford. He watched Sikorski drink before he took a sip. There hadn't been much chance to see the house so far.

When the off-road vehicle had arrived, within ten minutes of Sikorski's call, they had all been bundled inside. Sikorski still requested that he be blindfolded. By then, he was too fed up to argue and put the thing on without objection. Raven and Swallow would have caught up and been watching the route anyway, so he was secure that he had backup.

His saving grace in the vehicle on the way to the mansion was that Kadie had been at his side. She wasn't as forthcoming with the advances as Star had been and he'd been grateful of that. By then, he'd been wound so tight that he'd have taken her up on the offer just to fuck out some of his frustration, and to remind himself that she was really here, alive, and that if nothing else, he was better positioned to keep her safe.

As the engine had started, Kadie made a comment about seatbelts and he heard everyone click in. Despite the fact that he hadn't moved, he wasn't exempt from her instruction. Kadie's body covered his as she reached over him for his belt and clicked him in, and just like that he was rock hard.

Both women had guided him into the house when they arrived. He was brought to this room, pushed onto a leather couch, and then left alone. When the door closed, he took off the blindfold to see he was in an office lined with high bookcases. Two couches faced each other in the center of the room, and a huge carved desk stood under the imposing bay window on the wall opposite the door.

Sikorski had entered moments later and headed straight for the decanter. Now he sipped high quality whiskey with the man responsible for Kadie's predicament.

"We have business," Sikorski said.

Eliminating the driver and bodyguard had three goals. The first was divide and conquer. Sikorski liked to be safe, but he didn't trust many people, which meant the number of guards he kept around was low. Picking them off in minimal numbers, so as not to arouse suspicion, kept their options open for future moves they might have to make that could lead to more obvious confrontation.

The second purpose was to give Sikorski a scare, to remind him that there were people out there capable of hurting him when he least expected it. The Kindred needed information about some of those people, not because they wanted to protect Sikorski, but because they wanted to protect themselves and the general population.

Some of Sikorski's enemies were their enemies too and some of those people wanted power, which they planned to get by hurting others. The Kindred had no intention of letting that happen, especially not with the device they'd been keeping out of circulation for months.

As he'd told Kadie outside the limo, the third reason was to put Sikorski in a position of debt. Tuck had risked his life before, so often that he thought nothing of letting his friend and colleague kill the man driving the vehicle he was riding in. The suggestion was so mundane that he hadn't given it much thought. He hadn't factored in just how difficult it would be to see Kadie scared or how his own adrenaline would react in his desire to protect her.

If they'd thought Sikorski would be slowed by an attempt on his life, they were wrong. He was sitting in the office, with his newest associate, drinking liquor like nothing had happened and he didn't have a care in the world.

"You want to do this tonight?" Tuck asked, appreciating that he was capable of conducting business.

"I think tonight's events prove that there is no time like the present."

Fair point, and one Tuck wouldn't refute. It wasn't like he enjoyed being in the company of this man, so anything that would get him out of it sooner was fine by him. "Okay," Tuck said, discarding the glass on a side table. "You have something I want."

Sikorski wasn't moved, in fact, he scoffed. "You think you can make demands of me?"

Sikorski was still acting like he had the upper hand. If he wasn't so used to arrogance like this, Tuck would be amazed. The mansion that they were in didn't belong to Sikorski, Swallow had whispered that in his ear not long after he'd arrived.

Knowing that his people were on the periphery, doing the background and still close enough to check in with him, was reassuring and meant that his own confidence wouldn't take any kind of knock just because Sikorski acted like he was the big man.

"I think I saved your life tonight," Tuck said. Sikorski had frozen when the car went out of control. Tuck assumed that was what came with always expecting someone else to pick up after you. Sikorski had a staff that he liked to order around. Without them, he was paralyzed and didn't know how to act for himself. "I think you might owe me one."

"You did," Sikorski said. Tuck gave him a point for not arguing or trying to rewrite what had happened by implying he'd somehow had it under control himself. "How do I know it wasn't orchestrated by you?"

"You think I want to kill myself? I was in that car too and I work alone," Tuck said. In their industry, everyone was suspicious of everyone else because almost everything was a setup. What it came down to was who played the game better, and Tuck planned on that being him. "Except in circumstances of mutual benefit."

"And this is one of those occasions?"

If Sikorski gave him what he wanted then Tuck would let the Russian believe he'd get something back. "It might be," Tuck said.

Since being a part of the Kindred, he hadn't ever had to work alone. When dealing with legitimate business, he'd had Kadie and her cousin there with him. When doing his not-so-legitimate work he had Brodie and Art with him, and now Zara too. Working without a net didn't scare him and he always pulled his weight on the team. But all of them had to be able to walk into any scenario and bluff, Tuck knew how to play whatever role was required of him.

"Very well," Sikorski said. "I will see that you are compensated for your actions tonight. But that is separate to our deal."

Sikorski didn't like to be indebted to anyone, few men did. Tuck would take the guy's money, if that was what he was talking about, but he didn't care about financial compensation. What he wanted was information. It made sense to let Sikorski take the lead so that Tuck could feel out his opponent's expectations. Tipping his hand first would be a mistake. "What deal?"

"Game Time," Sikorski said. "What do you know about it?"

Definitely eager, which played into the Kindred's hands, Tuck noted how Sikorski tried to quell his desperation. For months the man had been trying to get his hands on the device created by Cormack Industries, a company connected to the Kindred. Just when Sikorski had probably given up hope of ever obtaining the tech, here was Tuck, just in time to dangle it in front of him again.

Superiority felt good, but he had to be careful about being too cocky. To get what he wanted from Sikorski, he had to portray himself as a worthy associate, which meant he had to be confident, a man Sikorski wanted to deal with through respect. That would make the whole process easier. But if he took it too far, Sikorski would push back and they'd never get out of this pissing contest.

"What do you want to know?" Tuck asked, stretching his arms the length of the couch.

Sikorski took his time, he must have sensed his own zeal and been trying to pull it back. "Where is it? Do you have it?"

The Kindred had had it since the day Art died. They'd been protecting it and trying to erase evidence of it from everywhere it still existed. But Sikorski didn't know about his links to the Kindred. If he believed that Tuck was a third party with access, maybe to steal or rebuild the device, then they'd be in business and the Russian wouldn't see the long-term agenda that put his remaining days of mortality on a countdown timer.

Tuck got comfortable on the couch. "I know where it is, and yes, I do have it… in a manner of speaking."

"You better know who you're dealing with," Sikorski snapped, slamming his own glass down. "Give it to me."

"You're not the only one who wants it."

Except, he sort of was. All of the original Game Time bidders were dead, sort of. But there were two people still out there in the world who did know about it. Two beyond the Kindred. One, Griffin Caine, couldn't care less about the device or its capabilities. The other, Benedict Leatt, they weren't too sure about and it was him that kept the Kindred on edge because he was a wild card.

"It's a myth," Sikorski said, perhaps testing Tuck's knowledge. "Everyone wants it, no one has it. No one's seen it."

"I have," Tuck said, glancing toward the window.

Though he couldn't blame Sikorski for being skeptical. Anyone who had contact with Game Time tended to end up dead, which left any concrete proof of its capabilities as nothing more than stories. Being one of the few people to have deconstructed the device, Tuck knew more about it than most and if his hand was forced, he could throw something together that could get the Game Time job done.

But his hand wasn't being forced and he wouldn't allow it to be. The Kindred wanted Game Time erased from the face of the earth because their key founding member had died to keep it from falling into nefarious hands. Game Time wouldn't take a life, they couldn't let it, or Art would have given up his life in vain.

"Why should I believe you? I don't know a thing about you. You can't expect me to believe that scum like you would have witnessed such a thing."

Sikorski should know better than to make assumptions. His willingness to do so, however, worked in Tuck's favor. That was the thing about haughty men surrounded by money and sycophants, they grew to believe themselves superior and invincible. Both qualities that the Kindred could exploit.

"Scum like me," Tuck said, looking back at his host. "You don't know what I am." Raising that question mark would play with the Russian's head.

His opponent wasn't so easily dissuaded from his presumptive assertion. "You hang out in that disgusting, repulsive hole of a—"

"I was looking for you," he said.

The bar they'd met in might be disgusting, he wouldn't argue against that point, but it had been the place Sikorski chose to do business for that very reason. No one would look for people like them in that pit, and the people there had so little credibility that no one would believe stories of what they said went on if they ever did choose to speak out.

"Why?"

Tuck wouldn't give out too much before making it clear that his offer was conditional. "You have something I want."

Sikorski was trying again to temper his mood. "So you've said. But you get nothing from me. Nothing. This is baseless information, nothing but vague references, hearsay and—"

"No hearsay," Tuck said. "I've seen it."

"How? How could you have seen it? It doesn't exist, you said it yourself."

"It exists."

"How do you know that?" Sikorski asked.

The corner of Tuck's mouth turned upward knowing he was about to deliver the body blow Sikorski would never have suspected in a million years. "Because I have built it," Tuck murmured.

Sikorski blinked, absorbing this news and the possibilities it revealed to him. "You've been that close to it?"

"Close as you can get," Tuck said, and although Sikorski would never say it, he was excited.

Tuck didn't get it. Something about being close to powerful things got a lot of men off. He could identify with a good piece of hardware as much as the next guy. But people like this, who were aroused by mass destruction, he didn't get it.

From their background checks, they knew that Sikorski was working alone in his quest to acquire Game Time. His goal was to get the device, cause havoc, and impress his bosses back home. Maybe that would work and get him the respect he wanted from others in his organizations. Still, Tuck didn't get it. Anyone who placed that high a premium on destroying innocent lives was a mystery to him.

"If you have it, if you have those skills, why deliver them to me? Why not use them for your own gain?"

Typical that this man would think that way. "I don't have the drive for it," Tuck shrugged. "Why would I need something like that?"

"So why get involved? Why build the device?"

"Professional curiosity," he said and in part, that was the truth.

Taking something apart to figure out how it worked had been a favorite pastime of his since he was a kid. By his teenage years he'd gravitated more toward software, and computers were his comfort zone now.

Working with the Kindred meant working with Xavier Knight, who was one of the smartest inventors on the planet and had been heading into the stratosphere of innovation when his parents were killed and his whole life changed. Little got the reticent billionaire excited and fewer people got to see him when he was. Tuck was one of the lucky ones.

Any problem that cropped up, it was their job to solve, Zave built and Tuck programmed. They'd been doing it for so long now that they knew each other's quirks and building or reverse engineering was their idea of a good time on a Saturday night. Few understood it and Tuck might not have been so exuberant about it if working with Zave hadn't been so inspiring.

It took time for both of them to relax with each other, to trust each other. These days, they discussed every minute technicality and brainstormed any time one had a glimmer of an idea. Zave was so stand-offish that they could go months without hearing from him. Then Tuck would get a call at three in the morning that would pull him out of his bed and they'd be speculating and taking notes on how they might overcome a technical hitch. Zave had taught him a lot about hardware and he was proud to say he'd returned the favor on the software side.

"What do you want?" Sikorski asked. "What do you need from me?"

Given that this opportunity had fallen into Sikorski's lap, it was no surprise that the Russian wanted to close the deal as quickly as possible. Tuck might have tried to conclude their business tonight, except with Kadie somewhere on the premises, somewhere he didn't know, he couldn't rush this through too quickly.

"A couple of things," Tuck said, reaching for his glass again. "First thing is, this meeting never happened. This exchange never took place. If we do this, that's it, no further contact and you never mention me to anyone." That was a kind of standard Kindred contract. "Because I don't exist either."

"If you have these skills then I must have heard of you."

"You'll have heard of my work, just as I've heard of yours. Software is my day job, I can get into any system. This was sort of a… side project. Sport."

"Software," Sikorski said, raising a brow. "You're a hacker?"

"Well that's crude," Tuck said with a slight side nod.

"But, yeah, I guess you could call it that." Now he got to tell another secret, one he'd wanted to boast about for a while. "I'm the guy who zeroed your bosses' bank accounts back in the day." That had been about two years ago and man was it fun to watch the carnage as the Bratva began to implode. They recovered too quickly, many crooks lost their lives, while more lost their livelihoods. But that's what happened when the Kindred got pissed off.

Sikorski froze, he frowned and rocked back in his seat before flying to his feet. "You... you're..."

His work was known to many people. Some of it because of the Kindred, some because of the business, and another group were aware of other jobs he did on his own time. Keeping himself free moving, never sticking to one handle or IP, he did his best to hide his signature, especially when he was working under his own steam.

But when he did reveal himself to people, they were always so amazed, he was used to extreme reactions from people who were impressed or angered by what he did to them or their associates.

"Let the chips fall where they may," Tuck muttered because now that Sikorski knew not only did Tuck have his respect, but he had his undivided attention.

"You're The Anomaly."

"Also known as... Also known as," Tuck said. More often than not, it was the victims of his work that gave him a title. The only ones he recognized were his real name and his Kindred moniker.

Sikorski wasn't done educating him on his own identity. The shock of the revelation erased the Russian's perfected game face. It was funny to see just how disconnected he'd become from the game they'd been playing a few minutes ago. "The Prodigy, The Marvel. The Creator... I don't believe it."

With stupid names like that neither did he. "Believe what you want," Tuck said, sipping his liquor. "I couldn't care less if you know my resume. It means nothing to this deal."

In opposition to what he had just said, Sikorski carried on in a way that implied he did in fact believe that Tuck was who he said he was. "The Poet," Sikorski said, edging closer. "They call you that too."

Most of the names he ignored, but he'd been stumped the times he'd heard that one. Brodie still needled him about it when the chance arose. "That one always confused me," Tuck said. "There's no brevity in what I do."

"You're a myth," Sikorski said, drifting toward him and sitting on the couch beside him staring like a child in wonder at a mist that would disappear at any moment. Everything was a myth because leaving a trail got people in their line killed or arrested. Too quickly, Sikorski snapped from his daze. "This is… with this new information—"

"Let me stop you there," Tuck said, having heard the spiel from others before. "You're going to make an offer to put me on your payroll. I'm not interested. Not in the long-term."

"And in the short-term?"

Until he had what he wanted, he'd dance with this bastard, but not for a second longer than he had to. "That's what we have to discuss," Tuck said.

"Yes," Sikorski said. "Yes, we should. But it's late we should continue this discussion tomorrow."

Spinning on a dime, suddenly Sikorski wanted him to hang around. Tuck had seen this play before too. Crooks who wanted to exploit his skills, especially ones with means, like to flaunt a lavish lifestyle in their attempt to tempt Tuck onto payroll, meaning they'd have access to him and his brain on demand. With his skills, he could have gotten a legit job and made a ton of money. But he did what he did because it was important and he could affect change that others couldn't.

The Kindred had been there for him when he needed a crutch. Art had pulled him from drunken brawls and week-long parties and got his head screwed on. The Kindred were the only family he'd ever known and nothing would seduce him into turning his back on them.

Trying not to sneer or ridicule, Tuck wanted to point out the shift in power without being explicit. "Minutes ago you wanted to talk it out, get it over with."

"Yes," Sikorski said, now glowing in the ecstasy of his

discovery. "But I think a friendship could be mutually beneficial to us, and your actions tonight demand our gratitude."

"Now you're rolling out the red carpet?"

Until Tuck agreed to be Sikorski's employee, he'd get the special treatment. If he did agree to work for Sikorski all of that would go away in a hurry and he'd be treated the same as every other scum-sucking lowlife around here, it didn't matter that he had a tangible ability that would aid Sikorski's organization, the man wouldn't have anyone rising above him in the ranks and so Tuck would be reminded of where he was on the food chain.

But the seduction was relevant, needed to make him believe that he would be important and revered around here. Maybe he would be in lower ranks, if it came to it, but he'd never be allowed to get ideas above his station, which was another reason he'd avoided joining any kind of criminal enterprise. The Kindred allowed him freedom to pursue his own interests, any of them were allowed to say no if they disagreed with the plan of action, and everyone was encouraged to participate in decision making.

The Kindred was built on mutual respect. Sikorski just wanted people to fear him, he wanted to be better than other people, more powerful. Tuck squinted at the man sitting beside him, wondering if he truly believed he might tempt Tuck into working for him. Why an independent contractor such as himself would sign on when he had no debts or addictions that needed to be tended, he couldn't figure out. Still, if Sikorski wanted to treat him like a king, he'd take it. It would make putting a bullet in the guy so much more satisfying. Taking advantage of him only to screw him over was no less than the perverted tyrant deserved.

The drama in the car had been discounted by Sikorski when he didn't want to be grateful. The situation had flipped and Sikorski wanted Tuck to think that he was valued. Tuck wasn't falling for it and from the faint feminine giggle in his ear, neither were Zara or Brodie. Either that or his friends were getting busy, but he doubted they would when he was in the thicket of enemy territory.

"I'm eager to witness your talent," Sikorski said, as though that was an explanation for why he'd suddenly decided Tuck needed a party to celebrate his bravery in averting disaster in the limo. "Tomorrow will allow us maximum time to explore this union."

Tuck heard what he said but read between the lines. Staying the night here would be followed by a test, one that would be designed to test his patience before his talent—there hadn't been a test compiled that he hadn't aced. Sikorski would want to see what he was capable of, so at some point, Tuck expected a computer to be wheeled out and a command to be given. Except he wasn't here to hack for the criminal, he was here to tease him with Game Time.

There was no indication that Sikorski understood how apathetic Tuck was to the seeming hospitality. But he'd let the guy go on for as long as he wanted to. Staying here had been discussed by him and his people, he'd rather have walked away, but with Kadie around, he didn't mind sticking close.

Sikorski was still blathering. "You will have a suite here. Our cook will prepare you anything you wish to eat. I'll have personal effects brought to your room to make you most comfortable. And, of course, female companionship will be provided."

He said this like he was offering him a toothbrush. "I prefer my women willing," Tuck said, because he wasn't interested in Sikorski's whole harem, one sole female was his only fascination.

"They will be," Sikorski said, "willing to do whatever you wish. They will please you, that is guaranteed. We have various women on the grounds tonight, I can have them rounded up while you eat and you can select—"

He didn't need to see a parade. Staying near Kadie wasn't as appealing as staying on her and that was what Sikorski was offering tonight. They needed a chance to talk to each other and if she was in his bed then she couldn't be in anyone else's. "What about the women with us tonight?" Tuck asked, because if it took being direct then that's what he'd be.

During their brief interaction tonight, he and Kadie had played it cool. As far as he knew, no one knew they were connected, no one had picked up on their chemistry. Given that she was the first one to approach him at the bar, he could use that initial contact as cover for his specific interest in her.

"Two of my newer additions," Sikorski said, showing no suspicion on why Tuck had brought them up. "My more experienced—"

Tuck shook his head. "I'm not interested in the bottom of the barrel." More experienced women, women who had been here longer, had been passed around to every employee and guest. While he wouldn't be interested in them anyway, he dismissed the offer of women who had more experience under the guise that they were more damaged than fresher merchandise would be.

A grimace crossed Sikorski's face. "Star speaks with a common tongue," Sikorski said. "She's sloppy, and shrill—"

"What about the other one?" Tuck asked, acutely aware that he was playing a dangerous game.

Singling Kadie out gave him the chance to protect her by proximity. But it also betrayed to Sikorski that he had a type, and if his interest in Kadie was used against him, it wouldn't be a casual fuck they'd be exploiting, it would be the woman he loved. Know it or not, Sikorski already had the weapon in his arsenal that would persuade Tuck to do anything asked of him. Because to save Kadie pain, he would relent in a heartbeat.

"She's… um…" Sikorski drifted from his sentence and looked past Tuck while he tried to find a single word to explain Kadie. There wasn't one. Kadie was as complex as a woman could be and it was her ability to throw him a curve ball that kept him interested from the start.

"That's the one for me," Tuck said, happy to make it seem he wanted a puzzle. "I want exclusive rights for the duration of our business." Confident that this wouldn't be suspicious, Tuck knew that a lot of men didn't like to share the women they were sampling. Some would get bored and move on to a new one after a few nights, but for those few nights, they wanted to be the woman's only master.

"She has a temper," Sikorski said.

Tuck didn't want to know how Sikorski knew that, or

what Kadie had to use her temper for. He also didn't have to be told about her volatility. Riling Kadie was easy because her fuse was so short. That explosive passion had been his companion for years and throughout them all it had never diminished.

"I like my women to have some fire." Being more specific, he liked his woman to have fire. Just one. He guessed that tonight he'd get burned by some of her heat, he could pray for it in bed, but it would more likely be her temper he'd test on this night.

"She'll be prepared, and brought to you," Sikorski said.

One thing taken care of, he needed another. "I'll need a computer," Tuck said, sliding to the front of the couch and watching wariness overcome Sikorski. Him with a computer, after what he'd just confessed to being capable of, Tuck didn't blame the guy for being reluctant.

"I don't—"

"I can't offer you reassurances," Tuck said, being honest, but not backing down. "It doesn't matter what condition the thing is in. I'll admit if I wanted to, I could do damage." Because it would insult both of their intelligences for Tuck to play down his ability, he was direct. "But right now that wouldn't serve either of us. Attacking you from inside when I'm alone is beyond risky. I can do my work from a thousand miles away, why would I attack you from your own house?" He wasn't alone and it might be fun to poke the guy from inside his safe, little bubble. But he wouldn't, Kadie's presence made him more careful. "You can have it back tomorrow."

Sikorski wasn't convinced. "I really don't think…"

It didn't matter what Sikorski gave him, so long as he gave him something. "Fine," Tuck said. "Have you got a phone? A tablet? Anything with Wi-Fi or a hard line?"

"Who do you need to contact?"

Tuck stood up and straightened his jeans. "My computer," he said. "Do you think a man like me wouldn't have a dozen contingencies? If it doesn't receive my signal…"

"What?" Sikorski said, leaping to his feet.

It wasn't like him, but Tuck enjoyed panicking the man who was exploiting his ex. "Why don't we wait and find out?" Tuck said with steel in his voice to remind Sikorski that he was still dangerous, even if he was playing nice in this minute.

Sikorski conceded a nod. "I'll have it brought to you."

"I also want all recording devices removed from my room," Tuck said.

Insult made the Russian's mouth fall open, but Tuck wasn't fooled by the innocent act. "I don't know what—"

"I've been in this game a long time," Tuck said. "I wasn't born yesterday."

In the technology age, everyone was monitored almost everywhere they went. Even McCormack Manor, the Kindred base, one of the most secure and mysterious buildings on the planet, was covered from various angles by cameras and recording equipment. He knew because he'd placed most of them himself. "Yes, but—"

"I'll find them if you don't," Tuck said, making his opponent believe that he had nothing to lose and no patience for being dicked around. "Then I'll take my business elsewhere. Don't insult me."

His expression cleared. "I'll see to it."

"Make sure that you do."

Sikorski nodded again and went for the door, he disappeared and Tuck was left alone. He had been at this game a long time, all of this was going through the motions, posturing, the same old song and dance. Except his woman was in this house somewhere, hurt, possibly being subjected to… it didn't bear thinking about.

Keeping Kadie out of the Kindred and away from this part of his life protected her, but it protected him too. The stakes had never been higher and so much about Raven's relationship with Swallow became clearer. Having your woman in the field clouded your vision.

All the training in the world didn't prepare him for this and planning was impossible when he had no idea how the scenario would play out if anyone ever found out what she meant to him. If Kadie ended up in the line of fire, all bets were off and that could mean disappointing the Kindred, something he'd vowed to never do.

Until she was in his arms, he'd be tense. Coercing her into playing along might be difficult if he had to withhold some of his own answers. Whatever he did, it would be to protect her. He just had to pray she'd be willing to see it that way because whatever had happened between their break-up and now, Kadie wasn't as pliant as she once was, nor as forgiving, but he only had himself to blame for making her what she was and putting her here, and it was his job to get her out, no matter what it cost him.

THIRTEEN

KADIE DIDN'T KNOW how he had swung it, she didn't even know why he had bothered, but she found herself being escorted to the suite that Tuck was apparently in. When they reached the wide double doors, the guard knocked and opened the door, stopping just short of shoving her inside.

The room was dominated by the huge four poster bed on the facing wall. A long desk stood under the side window next to the door for the large ensuite. Another two doors led off on the other side of the room. Tuck stood beside the window and looked up when she entered. Clocking her, he tossed the black device he was fiddling with to the desk, then strode to the end of the bed with the audacity to be wearing a faint smile.

"What do you want?" she asked his sock clad feet, clutching her bag in front of her.

Trussed up like a Barbie, her hair had been teased and fluffed into a high up-do. Uncomfortable bones from the corset she wore dug into her ribs but they succeeded in spilling her breasts over the top of the siren-red, strapless leather dress she wore.

She felt like an idiot. She'd never dressed up for Tuck like this. Throughout their relationship there were times they played games and she had plenty of nice lingerie, but he'd never asked her to don anything like this and she was disgusted that he might have requested her to gussy up like this through Sikorski.

"If I told you to stand on one leg and bark like a dog, would you do it?"

Glaring up at him, she quelled her desire to scream. "I might," she snapped, resenting his enjoyment of her embarrassment. "But you'd only enjoy it long enough for me to come over there and bash in your skull."

"Temper, temper," he tutted, how could he be enjoying this? He didn't even want to have sex with her, he'd refused her in the motel and not much had changed since then. She couldn't fathom his motive for calling her here to his room, dressed like some Vegas hooker, just to jeer her. "Come here."

Narrowing her eyes, she tried to see into him because he was softer and the smile was gone. "Why?"

"Come on, Toots," he murmured, so quietly it was almost like he was talking to himself, as if she wasn't actually here. Pleading with a gentle whisper meant to soothe her and convince him that they were actually together here. "Please."

Tossing her bag down, she took a step toward him. "I'm here for whatever you need," she said. "Nic—"

"Don't say his name," Tuck interrupted. "This is us, just us here. If I'd lost you tonight—"

"You saved me tonight," she said. "You saved us all."

It was difficult to be too grateful given that his people were the ones who had endangered them. But she couldn't' ignore the risk he'd taken by allowing himself to be put into that position and no matter how they got there, he had been the one to get them out of the situation.

The tick in his jaw reminded her of how he hated to be dubbed a hero. Changing the subject was his way of preventing her from gushing too much about his bravery. "This is a dangerous place. You keep very dangerous company."

"How did you do this?" she asked, taking another step.

His ability with computers was undoubtable, but she'd had no idea that he and his crew were capable of subterfuge like this. By working together, they'd orchestrated the limo accident, which got Tuck here and by another miracle, he'd managed to persuade Sikorski into letting her stay the night with him. She supposed Tuck might have been honest and just said that he wanted to keep her away from danger, which was the only reason she could guess as to why she was here.

"It wasn't that difficult," Tuck said, uncomfortable in a way that made her want to ask more questions.

"Why am I here?" she asked, curious about what else she didn't know he could do. "I mean what... how did you...?"

"Shh," he said, holding his hand out to her. "Come here."

Moistening her lips, she crossed to eliminate the last of the space between them. He took her face in his hands to lift her gaze from his chest to his eyes. "I want to hold you," he said. "For a minute, or the rest of the night, your choice. I want to just start over, can we do that?"

Erase the last six years of their life, no they couldn't do that. Forgetting the last couple of days might be easier, but it wouldn't change anything. "No," she said. "You can't erase this, not any of it. Our history is what makes us who we are."

Tuck might have been through trauma of his own and his meeting with Sikorski couldn't be easy, but she couldn't be picked up and put down, not anymore. "I don't want to erase us," he said. "I want to forget all the shit for a minute, forget that you're here in trouble and that I have no idea how to persuade you to come with me. I want to forget the fear on your face in that car. Will you let me hold you?"

So it was comfort he wanted and she had to admit that she wasn't averse to the idea of a little TLC herself. "He'll be watching," she whispered.

They had to be aware of eyes everywhere in this place. The building itself wasn't that old, but it felt haunted, like someone was always looking over shoulders and listening in. The hallways were monitored, even bedrooms were bugged.

There was no privacy in this place.

Though his smile should be familiar to her, his confidence made her cautious. Her uneasiness wasn't mirrored by his. Feeling vulnerable while under surveillance must be foreign to him. "Me? With my gadgets? Do you think I'd share you?"

Reminded of the device he'd been fiddling with when she came in, she guessed he'd already checked the place for bugs. He wouldn't appreciate her questioning how thorough he was, but he wasn't the one who would have to stick around here when this was over.

"I don't know what—"

He sank a hand against her styled hair. "You're mine," he said. "Exclusively. We can talk freely, I told him to take out the bugs and the cameras. I checked it out myself too."

"If you're wrong..." The potential information Sikorski could gather about them and their relationship could damage them both.

"I'm never wrong," he said. "And I don't care if he watches. I don't care if he knows. You're mine."

Getting Sikorski to agree to that must have taken some negotiation. Only the most influential of associates got to pick a girl and tag them as their own, according to what the other girls had told her. So far, she'd been spared that particular pleasure, but keeping to herself had kept her safe.

If Tuck had to give something up for Sikorski in order to get her here, Kadie had to know what it was. "How did you get him to agree to—"

"I'm not talking about any agreement," Tuck said, opening his fingers to drive them deeper. "This is me talking to you and I'm telling you. You're mine."

He'd said that several times already and she still didn't get what he meant by it. Had Sikorski sold her to Tuck? If he had then she'd have to fight it, not because she wanted to be here with Sikorski or away from Tuck, but because she hadn't done what she came here to do. "I don't understand what you mean."

He took a breath and widened his stance which

nestled their hips closer. "When I left, I thought I was saving you from me."

Addressing their relationship breakdown here was either very smart or very stupid. They couldn't row like a long-term couple and she couldn't storm out on the man she was supposed to be pleasing for her boss. But for nine months she'd wanted to know what had caused him to turn his back on her and now she was getting the chance to find out. "Saving me?"

"Except," he said. "That left no one to save you from yourself."

Oh, that made her feel like a burden again, like the naughty child who'd gone too far. True as that might be, she didn't want to be deadweight around his neck slowing him down. "I don't need saving," she said, trying to move away but he kept hold of her and wouldn't let her go.

"You have a story," he said, and she read how calm he was. "I don't know what you've been through. But I want to know."

"Will that make you feel better?" she asked.

If she was simply satisfying his idle curiosity then she wouldn't waste her time. Yet, if he needed this, needed to hear every word before he could move on with his life then she would have to accommodate him.

What she really wanted was for him to trust her, to let her in and share his experiences with her. He might believe himself to be impervious to trauma, but ignoring difficult incidents only compounded their effect and she didn't want him to be numb to what made him human.

Emotions might make him feel weak, maybe that was why he'd walked away from her. But Tuck, when he was alive and feeling, was the most incredible person who deserved to be happy. She wanted to know all of the things about the man she loved, the things she'd ignored because she'd thought that's what he wanted her to do. Instead of trying to be what he wanted her to be, Kadie wanted to be herself, and that meant satisfying her curiosity about the man she'd shared her life with for half a decade.

She'd be lying if she said she didn't still love him. Mad

as she was about the way he'd abandoned her and as scared as she was in her current situation, she couldn't deny that having him near to her, in her life again, even if it was just for a short time, bolstered her and reminded her of what it was to be human, what it was to matter to another person. Tuck could deny his feelings for her all he liked, and maybe they weren't as deep as they once were or as intimate, but he still cared about her. If he didn't, he wouldn't have orchestrated this moment, this night, just to keep her safe.

"No," he said. "I'll probably hate every minute of it. I've done a lot of things in my life that I should be ashamed of. But I only have one regret. Something about tonight made me see that walking away from you like I did was the dumbest thing I've ever done."

"I'm not buying it," she said, taking his wrists to pull his hands from her face and hair. "You did fine without me before this."

Believing him and falling into his embrace would be too easy. Losing him had been the hardest thing she'd ever endured and she'd been completely open, unprepared for it. If she had to watch him walk away again and experience the panic that had consumed her when she discovered he wasn't in the basement, she would lose her last glimmer of hope.

"Do you think I would use you?" he asked.

Not in any way that would hurt her directly. But she'd learned a lot about her former lover in the past couple of days, proving that she didn't know as much about him as she'd thought. "I don't know what this is," she said. "But I know you well enough to know that you have an ulterior motive. You always have one."

"Do I?"

"Yes," she said. Tuck had a great mind and was a natural problem-solver, she wasn't so great at seeing the big picture. Somehow, she knew that she factored into his mental calculations, she just didn't know how vital a variable she was in the equation. "You didn't want anything to do with me when I threw myself at you in that motel room."

"This isn't about sex," he said. "Keep your virtue, I don't want it."

She wasn't reassured by his declaration that although he regretted walking away from her, he wasn't interested in her body anymore. Women were supposed to be the conundrum, but Tuck wasn't making it easy to figure him out. "My virtue is long gone," Kadie said. "But if it's not sex you want…, what is it?"

"I want to have sex with you," he said.

Another one-eighty. Hadn't he just said that he didn't? It wasn't easy to draw any conclusions, especially when he'd started the conversation by asking to hold her. "No you don't," she replied, because he'd refused her body and stated after that he didn't want it.

"Sure about that?" he asked, grabbing her hand and forcing it against his erection.

When their bodies had been together, she'd felt his arousal, but something like that was easy to conjure with the right thoughts and stimulation. That he could have that kind of reaction while she was trussed up in the way she was, didn't encourage her to believe its sincerity.

"You can control that," she said, arching a brow.

"Can I?" he asked.

"Yes, you can," she replied. "It's not much of an achievement or a compliment to me given you were just as happy with Star in the back of the limo. What was that about by the way? Just a little game to keep yourself entertained?" Declaring her as his on the back of making out with another woman put his claim deeper into question.

Without shame, he shrugged. "I was playing a part. She was there and refusing her would've been suspicious," he said.

Understanding his point intellectually didn't relieve her of the memory of watching it. "We're not together," she said. "You don't owe me anything." She didn't like seeing him kissing Star, and she wanted to slap him for doing it in front of her, but it wasn't her right to punish him for enjoying a beautiful woman.

Snatching for her when she tried to retreat, he didn't let her withdraw. "It's a part I won't have to play again. I claimed you. While you're mine, I'm yours, as far as Sikorski is concerned."

"Am I supposed to be grateful?"

"If it was so easy for me to control my dick, why was it hard as fuck when we were together earlier? And in the bar when you frisked me, I know you noticed."

"I…" she started, glancing down and back up when words didn't immediately follow her opening her mouth. "I don't know, you're teasing me." But Tuck wasn't cruel, at least the Tuck she loved wasn't.

"It happens around you," he said. "Only you."

"Am I supposed to believe you've been celibate for nine months? You boasted about being with other women when you…" Split up with her. "Why am I doing this? I'm leaving."

Reliving what he'd said on the night they broke up only brought the truth to the forefront. What they'd had was no more.

Spinning around she sought the door but didn't get two steps when he snatched her up from the floor. She kicked, and shouted, but he didn't pay any attention, he threw her to the bed, and was on top of her before she could get up.

"God damn it, Kadie," he roared.

"Don't use my name," she whispered, going limp when he pinned her wrists with his fists.

Using the fake name protected her from more than just having her past uncovered.

"The room's clean," he said. "I checked it myself. I have the compact scanner in my—"

"No," she said. This wasn't about who was listening, this was about how she could look at herself in the mirror while she was here. "I don't want to be her, here in this place. I…" Kadie needed distance, something that put a line between the real her and the things she'd witnessed here in this horrible place.

Some of his anger waned, but not all of it. "How long have you been here? Why did you leave home?"

Fighting his questions was getting too hard, she wasn't strong enough to stand up against so many people at once. Tuck was supposed to be safe; he was supposed to be a sanctuary. Exhaustion made her heart beat slower until she could only whisper. "When this is over, when you've got what you want, you'll leave me. Please don't ask me to lose you again."

Honesty had always been her go-to position and lying didn't come easily, that's why it was easier for her to keep secrets than make something up. Tuck was stronger and she had to concede that he'd win, he wouldn't give up until he knew everything he wanted to. Before she surrendered, she had to beg for his mercy, to reveal her fears, and hope he'd be gentle when he walked away.

Her pain reflected in his eyes and she saw the truth of how deep this man was in her psyche. Tuck might have walked away from her, but her existence was still on pause, waiting for him to return to her so it could resume. Their paths had crossed, sort of by accident, either fate wanted them together or it wanted to play a last cruel joke by tearing them apart once more.

"I wasn't serious about the other women," he said, soothing her. "I said it to hurt you, because I thought if you hated me, it would be easier for you to move on. I only wanted your happiness, that's all I ever wanted."

The masks fell away and they became each other's again. Truth, vulnerability, it was what he needed from her before he'd give it back. Despite his strength, he needed her reassurance, needed her commitment. Someone had to take the first steps back to trust, Kadie wasn't strong enough to resist. "I was happy with you."

"No, you weren't," he said. "You said it yourself." After having sex in the office, she'd told him that they couldn't keep doing this. That hadn't meant she wasn't happy or that she wanted their relationship to be over. "I thought it was what you wanted, to be free of me."

Nothing could be further from the truth. The only time she ever felt free was when he was with her. "I was never under any illusions," she said, part of Tuck's allure was his adventurous, fearless nature. "I knew our life together wouldn't be the picture perfect fairy tale."

"That's what you deserve," he said. "You deserve

perfection."

"Perfection doesn't exist and I don't know what you think that would look like for me. I wanted you to let me in. Marriage and kids, without ever knowing what you did every day, would never have worked. And a dozen children ruining our sex life? That life would bore me, I thought you knew me well enough to know—"

"The things that you don't know about me, Toots. It could be too much for you to hear," he said.

Except, how would they ever know unless he trusted her? Protecting her was an excuse. Nothing would make her turn him over to the authorities, but maybe he didn't know that. If this Raven guy was a killer, it stood to reason that Tuck could be too, maybe this Swallow woman was a murderer as well. Keeping her in the dark protected their liberty.

"This has been a bad year. I can't let you back in unless you tell me what you've been through." She wasn't getting through to him. "I want to let you back in, Hotshot."

Instead of being forthcoming, he deflected. "I don't understand why Dempsey would let you go off alone. Why he would let you walk away from the company. He was supposed to look out for you like he always did, why did he let you leave now? Is he looking for you?"

She shook her head. "No, he thinks I'm safe."

Accusing him of double standards became ridiculous when she realized she was as reluctant to confess her mistakes as he seemed to be. Sharing the adoration that they did, or that they had, gave them something valuable to lose. If she told Tuck the truth, he would probably feel betrayed and he'd be mad as hell. The last thing she wanted was to see him lose respect for her.

"You're anything but safe," Tuck said. "You're supposed to have someone looking out for you."

And just like he'd said about setting up the business to keep her occupied, he made her feel two inches tall. Being coddled didn't make her feel valued, not anymore, it made her feel weak. Resentment for the idea that she might be unable to look after herself built. Yes, she'd made mistakes, everyone did, but she'd fought on, she hadn't given up.

If either of them could be accused of quitting, it was him. Tuck hadn't fought for her or their relationship. The minute things got tough, he bailed.

"I do have someone looking out for me," she said. "You."

Because the only way her cousin would let her venture into the world on her own was if he thought she had her capable lover with her.

"I'm here now," he said. "But for the last year—"She shook her head. "What?"

"We left together," she said, watching her finger trace the neck of his tee shirt because she couldn't look him in the eye.

While he was scowling at her, she didn't want to reveal that she'd lied. "I don't—"

"Dempsey thinks we left together. I didn't tell him that we did, but he assumed when I left that I was going with you."

FOURTEEN

HER FINGER STOPPED, and her head fell back to the bed when she noticed he was in the midst of one of his crashes. Closing her eyes to fully appreciate his weight on her, Kadie needed the chance to regroup too and understood the virtue of shutting down her senses to just process.

Tuck hadn't been a part of her life a few days ago and now he was back. Not only was he back, but he was lying on top of her, in a bed. It didn't take them long to return to old habits. Griping at each other, vying for power, and being unable to resist the magnetic pull of their bodies, they'd always been this way.

Feelings or not, love or not, it was possible that they just didn't know how to be around each other without being sexually involved. Choosing to dismiss that idea, Kadie couldn't believe that this was just learned behavior when it felt so good to have the anchoring weight of the only man she'd ever loved with her now. Try as she might to hate him for walking away from her, this was the sole person who had the ability to refocus her.

One blink brought him back to her and she tried not to tense because if he was mad, the blow out could be epic. "You didn't tell them what happened at the birthday party?"

She shook her head again. "They think we're together."

She couldn't work out if he was pissed off or just incredulous. It wasn't exactly a direct lie, she'd just failed to be completely honest. His indignation was tougher to swallow because he lived a life filled with half-truths. Being judgmental of her reluctance to confess she'd just been dumped was more than a little bit rich. "Is that so unbelievable?"

"Are you stupid?" he barked.

Intense, immediate anger jolted her. Expecting a comment on her deceiving Dempsey when she prided herself on always being honest, she didn't expect him to berate her. Arguing was their forte, and she wasn't going to back down and let him feel superior. If anyone should be judged for making stupid, snap decisions, it should be him.

"In comparison to you—"

"No," he said, leaping from the bed. "You don't do that! What if something had happened? What if you needed me? You needed them? What would you have done…? Wait, this… is this, here, your idea of getting yourself out of trouble?"

"I don't need you," she replied. "And I don't need Dempsey."

"Everyone needs someone."

"You don't."

What was becoming obvious to her was that Tuck did actually have a support system, she just hadn't been a part of it. While she'd thought herself the most important person in his life, as the woman he loved, she saw now that she was just incidental. A warm body that he could call his.

Sitting up, she watched him turn back to her. Fury wasn't the only emotion surging through him. Shouting at her wasn't about getting her into trouble, it wasn't about feeling superior either. His concern was for her safety.

Something could have happened to her and Tuck would never have known. One day, probably far in the future, the two men, Tuck and Dempsey, may have met each other, maybe by accident. It would only have been then that they'd have realized her deception. By then, it could've been too late.

"I had you. I thought you were at home. I thought

you were safe—that's what I fight for."

So he had considered her integral to his life. Raven and Swallow, they were his colleagues, his friends, but she had been his lover. Despite his assertions that he hadn't gone without sex while they were apart, Kadie couldn't bring herself to believe that he'd been unfaithful when they were together.

In light of the dangerous things she'd discovered he did, it flattered her to consider that she might have gotten him through, that she might have entered his mind and given him something to keep fighting for. "You thought about me?"

"Every second of the day," he said at the end of his rope. "You know that."

Beseeching her with his narrowed eyes, she wanted to believe that and saw how it hurt him that she might have doubted it. Tuck had made assumptions. She could understand that it was hard to keep track of what she knew and what she deduced from when he came home and when he left again. But he knew everything, she didn't. Tuck wanted to believe that she understood the depth of his love, how he depended on her, but because he'd never told her, she couldn't have ever known.

"How could I know that?" she asked. This had to be the break-through moment where he realized honesty was going to bring them together.

He couldn't protect her forever if he wanted them to be connected on every level. They were too old now for games and going with the flow. He had to decide if he wanted her in his life and if he did, it would have to be all the way. Kadie would have to learn about his past, and she may hear things that she didn't like. Once the stories were told, they'd have to decide to be together or walk away for good.

"What if I'd needed you," he said. "What if I had come home and you weren't there?"

She doubted he knew how revealing his question was, but it confirmed what she'd thought about being a motivator for him. "You'd have told Demps the truth and you could all blame me." Because that's exactly what would've happened if he'd gone home to find her gone. The first thing Dempsey would've asked was where she was.

"I'd have been pissed as hell. But fuck that," he said. "How would we have found you?"

"I left thinking that I could find you," she said. "I thought if we could put the pieces back together that it would be all right again, that… that we could pretend you still loved me and forget that conversation out behind Gwen's party ever happened."

It had been cowardice, but losing Tuck was difficult enough, the idea of standing up in front of Dempsey and telling him that her relationship was over, it broke her. Not long after coming to that conclusion, she figured out that she couldn't go about business as usual either. Working in the offices of her former lover, in the same rooms they'd made love in, laughed in, argued in, it would've been impossible.

Tuck had told her to move on and staying in his building while trying to do that would've been ridiculous. Losing Tuck was a catalyst for moving on, it made sense to her then as it still did now. Except she didn't leave the business to move on with her life, she left it to chase her old one, hoping that if she found Tuck and persuaded him that it was insanity for them to break up, she'd never have to tell Dempsey the truth. She'd believed for months that if she'd tracked him down, they would have an emotional reunion and she would get what she wanted from Tuck, the truth. Man, had she been wrong.

"Pretend," he said on a breath of laughter. "You stupid woman."

The decisions she'd made were driven by emotion, as she so often was, but it wasn't her fault she'd been unable to read Tuck's mind. He put too much of the blame on her and didn't own up to his own failings. If he'd told her how vital she was, beyond using the word "love", maybe she'd have made different choices.

"Thanks," she said. Twisting to roll in an attempt to get off the opposite side of the bed from where he stood, she didn't succeed in her departure. Tuck launched himself toward her and pulled her to her previous place, flattening her on her back, with his body on hers again.

"I fucking love you, and you know it," he whispered

against her lips.

Her body sagged into the mattress, hearing the words broke her, it snapped the hold she'd had on her grief and it all came spilling out in one gush. Filling her body and squeezing her heart, her soul left her body and she drifted, looking down on herself like a spirit unable to cope with the weight of devastation she'd been damming.

"You don't love me," she said as tears seeped from the corner of her eyes. "You left me. You promised you would never… you left me, Tuck."

His arms tightened around her and he pulled her with him when he shifted to his side. His lips touched her scalp, pressing so deep she felt his imprint with the heat of a branding iron. "To save you from me. You were unhappy, what was I supposed to do?"

"Take me with you," she said. "You were supposed to take me with you."

He quit rocking her wriggling body and she caught a glimpse of his frown. "You wanted to come with me?"

"I told you that you weren't the one that had to change. I wanted to be with you. You did have some safe contracts."

"I had no idea."

Rating him on his openness had brought him up short by her measure. Being pissed off that she couldn't read his mind went both ways. In her defense, there had been no time to finish the conversation they'd started after screwing in the office. If he'd stuck around long enough then she could have told him what she meant. Except she hadn't and he'd taken off believing that she'd have a better life without him, without actually consulting her on what she wanted.

"No," she said. "And you didn't ask me. You went ahead and made a decision for both of us on your own."

"You didn't fight me, you told me to go."

She did, in a moment of insane arrogance when she was sure he'd come to his senses before he got back to their apartment. "I came after you," she said. "I thought you would be at home, I wanted to make-up somewhere near our bedroom. You weren't there so I went to the basement… and found your envelope. I couldn't believe that you'd gone so fast, I thought we still had time, that we'd have time to talk it out and I would be able to make you see that I could be trusted."

"I wanted to protect you, to keep you safe. Concealing the details of what we do, it's meant to protect people like you, people we care about."

"I stayed in the basement for a week," she said. "Surrounded by that deafening silence. I lay in the sheets we'd made love in and tried to remember what it was like to be in your arms. I knew you were gone the minute I opened the door and saw that the lab was dead. A part of me died right there."

"Kadie—"

"Don't call me that," she snapped, and tried to push at him. Opening herself to him was making her forget their peril, forget how she'd ended up here and what she was trying to salvage. He hadn't heard her when she said she didn't want to be herself here, he ignored her request not to use her real name. Hearing that word, being in his embrace, it was too familiar and she couldn't afford to be complacent. "Get off me. Let me go, let me—"

"Stop," he said, grabbing her wrists and pinning her down when she tried to break free of him. "We're in this together now… When I go, you're coming with me."

"No," she sobbed, and shook her head against the sheets. "No, I can't."

Stern and determined, Tuck wasn't messing around. "I didn't ask you a question," he said. "You're coming with me."

"He'll kill you if you undermine him."

Sikorski didn't care about playing fair, he cared about winning. His victory was sweetened by how bitter the defeat of his opponent was. If Tuck showed her too much favor, Sikorski would use her to destroy him.

With an answer for everything, he didn't waver. "I'll make sure you're part of the deal."

"Me for Game Time?" she asked. She hadn't forgotten what had been said in the bar and what had gotten

Sikorski so interested.

"Among other things," he muttered.

"What is it? Game Time?"

For a second, he said nothing. If he lied to her, that would be it, the proof that she couldn't forgive him. "A device designed to kill people in a horrible way."

Knowing the truth made her feel better about her relationship with Tuck, it didn't make her feel better about what Sikorski was capable of. "Oh."

"It can disseminate viruses in public places, making innocent people very ill. Tracking the source would be near impossible for authorities if the right diseases were used."

Steeling herself, she didn't break-down or whimper. Tuck was giving her trust, she had to prove she could handle whatever he told her. "Something like that in his hands—"

"Trust me," he said.

Saving lives and taking down maniacs, she trusted him to do that. Until now, she might not have realized just what it was he did and she still didn't understand exactly how he did it, but something told her this kind of task was up his alley.

She nodded; he skimmed a hand up to her face. "Why would you want this for yourself?" he asked. "This life?"

"I didn't come here to be a whore for this man," she said. "Approaching him was a mistake, then it got away from me. I can't leave, not yet."

Stroking her, he brushed a kiss to her head. "Why not, Toots?"

Telling him the whole truth could damage him. Chasing Sikorski with the belief he'd bring her to Tuck seemed crazy now, but she'd been so sure at the time. Explaining to him that Howie had gotten mixed up in the scenario too would just be another layer of guilt to add. Too much uncertainty existed about what they were to each other, she still couldn't trust him all the way.

"I'd never be able to live with myself if I ran away. And what's the alternative anyway? I have nowhere to be, I have nothing."

"You have me."

Adrenaline and emotion made it difficult for her to muster an expression to go with her words. "Once upon a time, not anymore."

"You've always had me," he said. "Just because I wasn't beside you didn't mean that every fiber of my being didn't belong to you. You're my reason, and that hasn't changed, not for a second. I want to make the world safer and happier for you. I do it for you, not for anyone, or anything else."

Tuck was good at selling what he said and after what she'd seen in the bar, she knew he was good at acting. "How can I believe you?"

"Everyone told you I was bad news," he said. "Everyone. You trusted me."

Yes, she had. Tuck was an enigma, but too mysterious for most women to take a chance on. Kadie had fallen hard and fast, no one could have convinced her not to be with Tuck. "I was a kid," she said. "I didn't know what was good for me."

"Did I ever deny loving you? Did I?" She took a deep breath and shook her head because that was one thing he hadn't declared out back of the nightclub. "We're here together, this whole thing stinks, we're both in danger." He rolled away from her, freeing her from his prison. "If you'd rather go to his bed, go, I won't stop you."

Sitting up, she looked down at him. Without any expectation on his face, she wanted to know what was going through his head. After a pause, she shuffled off the bed, and started for the door, lifting her bag on the way. Doing what she needed to do and getting out, that had been her plan before Tuck appeared in her life. There was no reason for her to change that plan now.

FIFTEEN

UPON REACHING THE door, she grabbed for the handle, but froze without pushing it down. The man on that bed was the only one capable of hurting her, he destroyed her once, and there was a good chance he would do it again. Sense told her to leave, to forget any of this happened, to have another girl sent up in her place to really put a period at the end of her association with Tuck. But, if he was telling the truth, he wouldn't want anyone else.

If anyone found out they were in cahoots, both of their lives would be over. Leaving him here didn't eliminate that as a possibility. When the car had stopped after their dramatic accident and he had lifted her from the stationary vehicle, his world narrowed to her. She'd been with this man for half a decade, he was the love of her life, and he always would be.

If she left him now, she could be giving up her last chance to feel again. But with feeling came fear, and that was it. In the back of that limo, when his eyes had touched hers as the vehicle was careening out of control, fear flashed in his eyes. It wasn't fear for himself, it was fear for her. Deluding herself that this, and everything they'd shared, had been a ruse was a defense mechanism and one that wouldn't hold up for long.

He could make her feel, and she was the only one capable of showing him that he was human and therefore vulnerable. Without her he had no vulnerabilities, he didn't care about himself, and that made him reckless.

Who would look out for him when she turned her back on him? Would there be another woman capable of giving him the reason he attributed to her? Did she want to give him the chance to find out?

Dropping her bag, she turned and went to the bed without looking at him. Instead, she climbed onto the mattress and twisted her body onto his. Sliding a hand around to the back of his neck, she closed her eyes and pressed their mouths together.

"Be sure," she whispered on his lips. "I'll hurt you one day."

His lips curled up under hers because they were the words he'd said to her on their first night together. "I look forward to it," he said. "Give it your best shot because you won't see me going anywhere without you. Never again."

"Anywhere?" she asked, lifting her mouth to look at him.

"Anywhere," he replied, and swept her under him. "Can I hold you?"

She nodded. Asking to hold her was his way of being respectful, which made sense being that he was the one who'd been a prick and dumped her. But she hadn't come back to be held. Reassurance would wait, as would explanations. What she wanted was to put her mark on the man who'd thought he could escape from her.

"After three or four orgasms," she said, matching her smile to his.

Nine months was the longest she'd gone without indulging in his body since they'd met. With proverbial guns pointed at both of their heads, being cautious about her desire could end up being her major regret. "Yours or mine?" he asked.

"I was sent to this room to please you," she said, grabbing his tee shirt in her fists.

"Maybe," he said. "But I have some apologizing to do."

Lifting his lips to hers, he began to kiss and taste her skin, her neck, even that soft spot by her throat he remembered made her weak and receptive to his every want and need.

For a man with his talents, he could probably tempt any woman he wanted. This man could do anything he turned his hand to. Six years ago, he'd picked her to be his mate. For some unfathomable reason, his adaptive mind that could make an argument for any eventuality had locked onto her. Separating hadn't been what he wanted, not if she believed what he'd said tonight. He'd given her up, sacrificed his own happiness, because he thought it would ensure hers.

Tuck had confessed to wanting her. Had told her that he planned to help her, to stick by her, and rescue her from this awful place. Making love with him again had been a fantasy she feared she'd never fulfill. Before they got to it, she had to make it clear to him that she wouldn't submit to his instructions if it meant abandoning what she was doing here. Abandoning Howie.

"I have to tell you something," she whispered as he unzipped her dress.

"Tell me," he said, sitting up to pull off his tee shirt and tug down her dress. Throwing both to the floor, he frowned at her corset. "And I thought your labored breathing was a reaction to being in my presence."

She smiled because he could still make her laugh. With one hand on her waist, he deftly flipped her onto her front and began unlacing her. "I've been here for three weeks," she said, propping her chin on her hands, one was flattened on the other. "And I have my reasons for being here."

"Which are?" he asked. Rolling her to her back, he slid an arm around her waist to lift her torso from the bed. She unclipped the suspenders at her thighs and he pulled the corset up over her head with the other hand. He undressed her like she was a mannequin, his to contort and display as he best saw fit.

For the longest time, he scrutinized her figure, which was clad in nothing more than her stockings and a wisp of a thong. "I can undress myself," she said when he didn't touch the apparel on her body.

"No more," he murmured, leaning down to kiss the red gouges left in her skin by the offending corset. "I want you naked." When he kissed the underside of each of her breasts, she rested her hands on the back of his head, savoring the sensation that she never thought she'd have again. "I want my girl."

Pressing his thumbs to her lips, he tried to scrub the lipstick from her mouth. He kissed each of her eyes and she knew he was wishing away the garish makeup. She might have offered to wash her face before they made love, but she was reluctant to leave this bed and anticipated their reunion with a fervor that kept her in place.

"I'm here," she said, running her hands into his hair.

This bed and building were foreign, leaving them disjointed in their ability to sink into the moment. Questions dampened desire. "Do you want to tell me your reasons?" he asked, sliding down her body to lick around her belly button.

At some point, her shoes had fallen from her feet and when Tuck kneeled, she wriggled up the bed, opening her legs on either side of his. Curling his fingertips around the top of each stocking in turn, he took his time peeling each one off, his fingers sending shivers to her dampness.

Her reasons for being here required a greater time allotment than they had because she needed him inside her, the craving was growing like a lead weight pressing down on her core from inside. But there was one thing she should be straight about since she'd misled him.

"Are you sure he can't hear us?" she asked, looking around the room.

Given all that they'd already shared with each other, if Tuck had been wrong then Sikorski would probably be in here by now, pulling them apart and accusing them of consorting. On the off chance that Sikorski was being nice by allowing them to bond, or collecting more surveillance, she had to make sure that Tuck had no doubts before she revealed something that would make Sikorski lose any notions he may have held on showing them mercy.

He paused, his fingers under the lace strip over her hips that held up her thong. "Yes," he said as his drowsy eyes flashed with awareness. Some of his desire receded and she was amazed by how quickly he could turn on his brilliant mind. "What is it?"

"Don't panic," she said, sitting up to touch his naked chest. She'd forgotten just how perfect this man was, hard, unyielding… hers. "I just… in the interests of honesty you should know…"

"Tell me," he said, releasing her thong and folding his arms. His stance told her that sex could wait and she almost wished she'd kept her mouth shut. He sat with one knee on either side of her thighs, half-naked to her almost complete nakedness, and his expression was serious, possessive, entitled. Sex was on his mind; he was just better at side-lining it than she was.

"I'm not allowed to tell anyone," she whispered. "If he finds out I told—"

"What?" he snapped, grabbing her arms to pull her half-up off the bed. "Did he hurt you? If he fucking touched you without permission—"

"No," she said, curling her fingers up to his shoulders. "He likes to… sample each of the women before they go on… general release."

A shiver of disgust went through him that filled her with shame, despite what she was about to reveal. "You should've—you should—"

Touching her fingertips to his lips, she smiled. "For the first couple of weeks after I arrived, nothing happened. I was fed, exercised, and our Madame told me how everything worked. I helped in the process, had to watch a couple of times, you know, watch the girls with some of Sikorski's men, so I would know what they liked. I watched through monitors, you know, not in person…"

Tuck ground his teeth together, and she was sure steam seeped from his ears. "Is this going somewhere?" he growled.

Pissed off as he was now, she hoped what she was going to tell him would make him feel better about what they were about to do. "I'm trying to tell you," she said. "Nicky didn't call for me until this week."

"You've been with him this—"

"No," she said, pushing closer, using his strength to hold herself up when she clutched his upper arms. "No, he… can't—or he couldn't… Madame says it happens sometimes. He's okay for the first week or so, just blames the girl but… he's been known to get violent, and—"

"He can't," Tuck frowned. "Are you telling me you haven't been with him?"

"I haven't," she said. Squirming, she wasn't sure if she should share the rumors or if they'd get her into more trouble. Over the last few weeks, she'd gotten close to some of the girls and they'd confided in her that there was more to Sikorski than met the eye. "Some of the girls, they say that he… that we're sort of a prop."

"A prop?" he asked, and his loose expression tightened then relaxed as he tried to figure out what she meant.

"He touches the girls and screws some of them, sometimes, but… the girls say there's a couple of his men, young men, very young men who—"

"He's gay?" Tuck asked and when the surprise cleared, his whole body seemed lighter.

That was what had been implied to her, though the girls who told her that were quick to make sure she knew not to share that piece of information with clients. The girls were here for entertainment and Sikorski did like to throw lavish parties where anything went and the girls were expected to do anything asked of them, anything at all.

Since she'd been here, there hadn't been any large parties. The few gatherings that there had been were deemed too intimate and important for a novice like her to get involved and she'd been in no rush to put herself at the front of the queue. A couple of the new girls were eager because they thought they could win the interest of influential men who might bail them out of this terrible situation. Kadie knew better than to expect that.

There were girls who had been here for years. Girls who lasted a few weeks or months and were shipped off to various clubs and brothels around the country. The least fortunate ones were sent to auctions and once they left for those, they were never heard from again.

Talking was about the only thing they could do while they sat around waiting to be called upon. All of the women were expected to keep themselves in shape, so they worked out. They were expected to be groomed too and so they taught each other how to preen for maximum benefit to the customer Sikorski put in front of them.

"Bi maybe," she said. "He has had sex with women, according to what I've heard. I just think maybe he… leans more toward the male persuasion." Which was fine with her and she didn't really understand why a guy who commanded so much power and respect couldn't be honest about which gender he liked to stick his dick in. "I want you to understand, he's had me in his bed and he's touched me—"

"Stop," Tuck said, closing his eyes. "Gay or not, I'm not capable of hearing it, Toots. I can't think about—"

"The great and powerful Oz," she murmured, touching her lips to his chest in an effort to soothe the tension building in his taut muscles.

"Don't tease me," he said. "The thought of you with anyone—"

"That's what I'm saying, there hasn't been anyone."

Everything she'd said in the motel was meant to hurt him, well, most of it was. Being realistic about what might be expected of her here had forced her to contemplate giving up her body to a man she didn't know or want to be intimate with. If Tuck hadn't shown up when he had then there was a good chance that she would've whored herself. She'd struggled to care about what happened to her when she thought her love had given up on her.

Experiencing pain, punishing herself, was the best way to make herself feel something, anything. Now that she had him back, she wanted to take back the things she'd said and the fear she'd instilled in him.

"Anyone?" he asked, grabbing her arms, hauling her up to his eye level.

"No," she said.

After Tuck she wasn't interested in going to bars or dating, she left to track him down and that's how she'd ended up here. What other man could gratify her body after it had been spoiled by Tuck's love for so many years?

Finding herself here with Sikorski, on her own mission, she had to adjust her priorities and make decisions about how far she'd go. Risks were easier to take when she didn't have to consider Tuck's feelings and reactions, so she switched off the part of her heart dedicated to loving him.

Having him back in her life made her revert to an earlier state and it became important again to factor him into her decision-making. Honesty came first and he had to know what her mind-set had been.

Admitting her intentions wasn't easy. "But I would've done it. I want you to know I haven't been with him, but… if it had come to it, I would've let him be with me. What I'm doing here is important enough for me to make that sacrifice."

"You'll tell me all about it," he said. "Everything. Whatever you're here to do we're going to get it done, together. We have a lot of talking to do, but I have a claim to stake first."

So maybe it wasn't so easy for him to ignore his desire for her. Kadie could live with that and it would make talking easier if they didn't have their hormones clouding them. "There are condoms in my bag," she said.

Every girl in the mansion had a bag that was prepared by Madame before they were dispatched when it came to one-on-one encounters like this. They carried condoms, breath-mints, restraints. There was lubricant in there, body paint, and massage oils. A lot was crammed into one small pouch and extras were added as per the john's request.

Sikorski wanted his women to provide every service. Toys could be provided, costumes, paddles, clamps, anything at all and no woman was allowed to say no.

Just because she hadn't been with any other man didn't mean that Tuck had been celibate and she was too afraid to ask about who he might have been with. Now she could understand why he'd silenced her so abruptly when she mentioned being in Sikorski's bed. She didn't want to remember the sickness that came with watching him kiss Star in the limo—act or not.

"You're not on the pill?"

That's what she'd said in the motel, but it was another untruth. "I am," she said. "But I kept it hidden. I didn't want him to have the excuse of not using protection."

Keeping anything hidden in the close quarters they lived in below the kitchen was difficult. Some of the women made it a point of prying, and snitching too, if they thought it would earn them brownie points. But Kadie wasn't the only woman who took birth control pills in secret. They were contraband, rather than sneaking in heroine or other illegal drugs, the women here coveted contraception.

"Since me," he said. "Since that time in the office, how many?" She shook her head. "No other man has—"

"No," she said. "No one."

"I love you," he said, his whole face relaxing into pleasure.

It made her feel good that he wanted her body to be his own again, but she had to prod at him a little for being so cocky. "Stop strutting, and get on with it," she said, laughing at his swagger. He dropped onto his side against her, their legs twined together and his arm around her shoulders.

Yes, she was his, and there was no way to deny it. Allowing Sikorski to touch her, to get close enough to kiss her, it hadn't been easy and she'd fought nausea throughout. Lying beside him, with his hands on her, she'd really thought that he might have sex with her. But his touch never got too amorous, she could close her eyes and separate herself from what was happening because it never got too intense. Sikorski's hand had slid up her inner thigh and she'd thought that was it, the moment she'd be penetrated by someone other than Tuck. She'd almost screamed. Then he stopped, moved onto his back, and told her to leave. She'd never fled a scene so fast in her life.

Thinking about Sikorski while she was lying in bed

with Tuck was like remembering a nightmare and one she hoped that she'd never have to live through again. Whatever Tuck had done with other women, he wouldn't put her at risk. So in an inadvertent way, she could find out who he'd been with, without having to ask for details.

Before she even said the words, her lips began to dry. "You're allowed to—you don't need to use the condom, but I won't be offended if you do, if you don't believe me."

Her heart was beating at a thousand miles a minute. "Why wouldn't I believe you?" he asked, wearing a scowl though he began to stroke her belly, up over her breast, down to the heat between her thighs. Cupping her sex, she held her breath in anticipation of his fingers, but they never ventured into her, he skimmed his hand up, slowly exploring all of her, her ribs, her abs, her chest "You didn't even ask me if I could be putting you at risk—"

She recoiled as though someone had slapped her. "You wouldn't endanger me," she said, tracing her fingernail down his abdomen. "You didn't perform for Star... not beyond that kiss."

"My body responds to yours," he said. "Only to yours."

Good. That was just what she wanted. Loyalty was important to him, it was a part of who he was. While they hadn't been together before, they were now and she'd make sure he knew that their exclusivity was back on the first chance she got. "It's the way you programed yourself, and your programs always work."

His ego was healthy enough, but it was enjoying this teasing. "Let's get to work on programing yours."

"It's still under the influence of the last one you infected me with," she said, because her body had never forgotten what it felt like to submit to him. Even under the influence of drugs in that motel room, her instinct had been to seduce and pleasure him.

Rolling onto his back, he shoved his jeans and underwear down his legs and kicked them off the bed, nothing was going to get in the way of them being joined again. Flipping over to settle unimpeded between her thighs, both of them relaxed. Draping her arms up around his neck, the bed dipped when his fists landed on either side of her to prop himself up.

"Damn glad to hear it, Toots," he said. "But it's time to install the upgrades."

Tossing her head back, she arched closer to him, but her laughter echoed against the walls. Bringing her attention back to him, she linked her fingers behind his head. "Mm," she teased. "Geek hot talk, somebody save me from the sizzle."

Teasing felt good, being light in this place of darkness was refreshing, and it was what she needed. Tuck kissed her, soft at first, he let her want grow. When she started to move, to rub herself on him and strengthen her arms to bring him closer, his mouth slid away.

This man knew how to make love to her and despite her need to be joined with him, it was obvious he planned to take his time. Biting her nipple, he let the nub grow taut beneath his tongue. His attention on her breasts was something she'd taken for granted back in the day. During her daydreams after they had split, she struggled to remember how he tormented her body. Foreplay became a blur when her focus returned to his dick so frequently.

Tuck liked to take things slow. He pressed and squeezed and rubbed everywhere. His whole body could stimulate her in the way he moved up and down on top of her, kissing her mouth then her belly, her breast then her clit. Alternating routes and stopping at new sensitized spots along the way, no part of her body was neglected.

"Hotshot," she whispered, stroking his thick shoulders and the length of his arms, right down to his deft fingers that were trailing over her hips now. "I don't want to be pampered. I want to be fucked."

Meeting her eye, he curved his arm to slip his fingertips to her moist opening. Without going inside her, he circled and massaged the O he'd be plundering in such a short while.

"Prepare yourself for the upload," he said with a wiggle of his eyebrows.

Sometimes he could be a real geek, and he wasn't often one to crack too many jokes. His ease betrayed how ready he was to forget the negative experiences they'd had since being apart. Getting this chance to be together again was a gift they might easily have missed out on.

"You'll make me lose control before the action," she taunted. "Less of the talking… your mouth is far better at other things."

With that, she looped both arms around him and pulled his weight up, bringing his mouth down to hers, and with the docking almost complete she steeled herself for the transfer. It was long overdue. If she could kiss him just right and just long enough, he'd forget all about teasing her body or learning her shape again.

His dick knew its way home and she was right, it didn't take long for the thick head to push against the circle he'd teased with his fingertips. Lifting her hips, she welcomed the sating pressure that made her tongue still in his mouth. After nine months of celibacy, she needed some time to adjust to the invader that was intent on reaching its destination.

Tuck surged forward and even when she gasped, he just pulled back and plunged in deeper. "Keep breathing, Toots," he said, his lips curling away to show his gritted teeth.

Tuck could be gentle, until he lost his senses, and then he was a man who got what he wanted. Forgetting the burn that hampered her pleasure, it didn't take long for the friction to become gratification. Kissing her while fucking her might be easy for him, but she struggled to maintain focus on what his mouth was doing with hers when the heavy weight of orgasm made her pelvis buck then sag.

She was spent, ready to cry and laugh, and sleep, but Tuck kept on going, and it felt so good to watch the determination grow in his gaze. She knew what he looked like when he came, knew what his body felt like when it exploded inside hers. But she wasn't prepared for the overwhelming heat of relief that flooded her when he injected his seed into her again.

No condom. Just them. Their bodies merging and sharing fluids the other had thirsted for, for far too long. Tuck drove in to hold himself inside her and while still staring into her, he bowed to kiss her once, then again.

The world already felt like a better place and all they'd done was have sex. The next part of their bonding might not be so easy, but they were moving forward and the struggle would be worth it in the end.

SIXTEEN

"HOW DID YOU do it?" she asked, drying her hands on the hand towel while loitering in the ensuite doorway. They'd made love again and she was sure that they weren't done for the night. But this interlude gave them the chance to wash up and hopefully exchange some information.

"Well," he said, linking his fingers behind his head, his gloriously naked form on full display for hers in the center of the bed. "It all starts with proximity to your delicious self…"

"Hilarious," she said, tossing the towel over his face as she approached the bed. "I'm serious, tell me."

"I can't reveal trade secrets," he said, throwing the towel aside and snatching her wrist with one precise maneuver that saw him lift, twist, and lunge for her, all at the same time.

Playing it innocent, she knew he'd see through her pout. "You can tell little me," she said, stroking the hair on his chest.

Relaxing on his back, he tucked her head on his shoulder and kept an arm around her to hold her in place. "How did I do what?" he asked, kissing her hair.

"How did you convince him to let you have sex with your secret girlfriend?" she asked, imagining it took some serious skills to manipulate Sikorski into something like that in such a short meeting.

"You're my girlfriend now?" he asked, she tipped her head back and scowled at his slick expression.

It didn't take him long to get back to the teasing that had once defined their relationship. "Ex-girlfriend then," Kadie said.

"Ex as from three minutes ago?"

Twisting the hair on his chest, she pinched his flesh causing him to whimper and wince. "Ex as in forever," she said, "if you don't stop changing the subject."

"I'm notorious," he said, covering a yawn while his body contracted in a stretch.

"What does that mean?" she asked, sitting up beside him to frown down.

Tuck didn't want her going far. "I'm well-known," he said, trying to urge her back down but she resisted. "I've done jobs that people have heard of."

"You didn't…" Tilting her head, she peered into him. He'd told her not to use his real name or even the aliases of his associates. It seemed counterproductive to put that command to her only to ignore it himself. "You weren't insane enough to tell him who you are… were you?"

Whatever he and his friends did, they had to have pissed off some serious people in their time. It seemed impossible to work in their small band murdering people and hacking their whatever without gaining a few enemies.

"Got me some nookie, didn't it?" he shrugged.

"Tuck," she whispered, unable to believe that he was being so nonchalant about revealing himself to a man who could definitely not be trusted.

"There are a dozen versions of me," he said. "Don't worry about it. I didn't out the Kindred. I didn't give up any Circle secrets."

She didn't know about the Kindred or about any Circle, but she knew what made Nykiel Sikorski tick and he wouldn't let a man of Tuck's skills just saunter out of here. Just like Howie. Sikorski would seduce him with wealth and trap him before he realized he'd been snared. Tuck spoke about taking her away from here, but somehow failed to see that by revealing his abilities to Sikorski, he guaranteed that he would be the one in need of saving.

"He'll never let you go now," she said, gripping the hair at her temples because the impulse of stress made her want to tear it out. "You have to go now, tonight, don't wait—"

"I'm not going anywhere," he said, sitting up and taking his turn to glower. "I know what I'm doing. I've done it before. This is what I do and I'm not afraid of Nykiel Sikorski. The guy is insane and unpredictable, but I wouldn't be here if we weren't sure I could take him on."

This wasn't about who had the bigger balls, this was about his life. Tuck was supposed to be smart and sensible, not ruled by dumb male testosterone. "You can't take him on," she said. "He'll kill you if you piss him off. And he hates women. If you even hint that you might give a fuck about me… You can't, okay? You cannot show him that you care about me. Do you hear me?"

"I care about who I want," he said, choosing, in her opinion, the completely wrong thing to get pissy about.

"No." She shook her head. This wasn't just about him and his mission, and it wasn't about their relationship either. If the last few months had taught her anything, it was that she didn't need him to stand in front of her holding a huge placard telling anyone who approached to back off. "I'm a whore—"

"Hey!" he cut her off. "Don't you dare—"

"Not to you," she said.

He didn't get it, she had to make him see that she wasn't making a judgment on herself or what they'd just done. Since finding Sikorski in that club, she'd known that she would have to hide her identity and her personality. Getting what she wanted from Sikorski relied on it.

Back then, she'd thought she'd only have to spend one evening with him. When it all went wrong at the end of that night, she'd been sucked in too deep to walk away. The image of herself that she'd cultivated, that's what she'd been relying on since that night, not only to protect those she cared about, but to protect her own sanity. Thinking of herself as the lowlifes here thought of her put a line between who she was and what she had to do here.

"I would never think of you that way."

"But he would… he can't know we have history." Sikorski hadn't even given a single thought to her personality, the first thing he'd done when they met was name her like she hadn't existed before he picked her up. "We'll limit our contact outside of this room, which shouldn't be hard. We're not allowed to eat together, or socialize for anything but business—"

"If I want you there—"

Frustration made her exhale in a growl, he still didn't get it. "Want me, yes," she said. "If you decide you want to screw me at lunchtime then I'll be summoned, but we can't—"

"I don't want you leaving my sight, not for a second."

"It doesn't work like that," she said, grabbing one of his hands with both of hers. "You walk out of this room alone and you enter alone. We can only be together if you tell them you want sex."

"You're spending the night," he said, wearing a scowl. Endearing as it was to see her man be affronted by the idea that they might be separated again, they couldn't lose sight of where they were or why they'd ended up here.

She shook her head. "Madame says we're not allowed to form relationships," Kadie said. Following her training, doing exactly what she was told and what was expected of her, would be the best way to buy them time to do what needed to be done. "Unless it's for business purposes."

"So you can tell them you have the ability to manipulate me. I'm cool with being manipulated by you and I'll do whatever it takes to satisfy—"

"I don't care about that," she said. Although he was right, that Sikorski did ask the women in his harem to manipulate or spy on the men they slept with, she hadn't been asked to do that with Tuck. Yet. "I can't believe you told him what you were capable of."

When she was just a one-night indulgence for Tuck, her masters probably didn't believe she would have the time to figure him out. Their concern with her inexperience already made them doubt her. If Tuck took a specific interest in her and maintained that interest, her Master or Madame may ask her to gather information or tempt him into working for Sikorski.

Her loyalty to Tuck might be steadfast, but those she worked for here didn't know that. With each second that passed, the situation was getting more complicated. Would she have to agree to spy on her lover for her boss? If she did, what information should she return? It would be information that she and Tuck agreed to share, but if he asked her to provide false information to benefit his mission, would she have to sacrifice her own?

"No one knows what I'm capable of, including me," he said. "I know what I'm not capable of, and that's leaving you behind."

She assumed his abandonment of her nine months ago didn't count by his reckoning. "If you show weakness, the tiniest, slightest opening, then he'll exploit it. If he suspects your interest in me is anything other than sexual, he'll use it to make you… I don't even know what, Tuck. But neither of us will leave here again. He'll find a way to…" Use her to hurt Tuck, to force him into taking actions that he didn't want to take. "You do what you need to do, walk away, and do it fast. I'll… I'll find a way out, I'll think of something—"

"You're leaving with me," he said.

"I can't," she said. "This is already unprecedented. Madame checked twice when the order came down for me. I'm too new to be trusted with a client as important as you, that's what she said. I haven't even been… out, you know?"

Women were trained, conditioned, by the Madame in the basement and by Sikorski's men so that they wouldn't make fools of themselves in front of people that Sikorski was trying to impress. The Russian used sex to manipulate and impress the men he wanted to work with. Having never been an attraction at a party, or even in the bed of his men, Kadie was viewed as too inexperienced to be given responsibility.

It wasn't about sexual experience, it didn't matter if a woman was a virgin or a whore in that regard, they were taught how to manipulate and how to bow down even when presented with something, or someone, they didn't want to respond to.

In the first few days of being here, she'd gotten herself into trouble by speaking out when she shouldn't, which got her a reputation as a loose cannon. Seeing what some of the women went through, especially the younger ones, tore out her heart and it was difficult to see these things happening without reacting in any way. But she'd learned to keep her mouth shut.

"I'm special."

"Yes, you are. Already that scares me. It shows he'll do anything to get you working for him." The fancy suite, the stripping of the bugs, the free whore for the night, all of it indicated Sikorski wanted to impress Tuck into staying. "What would he do if he realized all he had to do was threaten me to have you nuke Tokyo?"

"Tokyo?" he asked. "What interest does he have in—"

"You know what I'm saying."

Everything was computerized these days. With Tuck's skills he could access banks, governments, weapons systems. Without leaving his chair, he could order executions, dismantle governments, and commandeer the media. Sikorski could achieve everything he'd dreamed of with Tuck under his command.

"I do," he said. "And you're right, that is a possibility because I would never put you in danger. But I've factored that in, I'm not gonna ask him for your hand in marriage. I plan to be as derogatory about you as I can be in his company."

"Did you plan on telling me that?"

Maintaining one character had proved to be challenging enough. Sitting silently while the man who loved to tease her spoke down about her might be more than she could handle.

"I'm telling you now," he said. "But I knew you would know I didn't mean it. It's a performance, like theatre, you have to play your part well. Which, by the way, you do like a pro, why didn't I know that?"

Compliments always made her feel good, this one was sweetened because it set her up for the chance to chastise him. "You've never trusted me before. And by the way," she mocked. "You wouldn't be trusting me now unless I'd forced you into it."

"Course not," he said, pulling her into his arms and lying down with her again. "You're only good for sex. What use would a feeble woman like you be otherwise?"

This might be too much fun for him. "Getting into character?" she asked, kissing his chest.

"What character?" he teased, and she slapped his abdomen. "Stay here a minute." He kissed her head, then pounced off the bed to go over to the desk where there was a laptop and the device he'd been fiddling with when she came in.

Propping the heel of her hand on her hair, she watched him pick it up. "What is that?"

"My phone," he said, unclicking the back of the device and ignoring her confused frown.

The computer didn't look familiar and she hadn't seen him with any kind of bag or backpack that might have been carrying hardware in the bar or in the car. "Where did the computer come from?"

"Your boss," he said, putting the back of the phone on the desk. "Told him I needed it to check in or hell would rain down."

She could see him saying it, she couldn't see it being true. "If you have your own phone, why did you need Nicky's computer?" she asked.

"Because it's on his network," Tuck said, taking out the long metal wand he needed that had been secreted in the back of the handset.

She sighed. "I don't understand you. You have the skills to get into his network from the outside, why would you need to be here to get into it? That's a stupid risk just for a look into—"

"I've been in his network, plenty of times, stuck in my own bugs. My people know what he's up to. But we still don't have what we need."

"Which is what?"

He didn't reply and turned to sit down at the computer, he began to fiddle around with something, so she lay on her back and waited. "I have to contact the Kindred," Tuck mumbled and she was sure he was giving her commentary, but he was too distracted to provide details. "It will take me a few minutes, I'll have to secure the link, scramble his trackers. This little baby will work its magic, sever his link and copy everything on his network in seconds."

Maybe she was supposed to be awed, he must have forgotten that she'd seen him do all kinds of magical things once upon a time with the businesses they partnered with in their legitimate work.

"I better get going." Making the mistake of climbing off the bed at the side he was seated on, it didn't take him long to spin the chair and grab her wrist to tug her into his lap.

Turned out he was paying closer attention than she'd thought. "You're not going anywhere," he said. "This will take five minutes tops. I'm not taking the risk of direct communication, this is all passive, information gathering. My signal will ping and the guys will know I'm safe." Flicking a transparent bud that she hadn't noticed on the desk until now, she peered at it. "It's an earpiece, two-way communication. I took it out when I knew you were coming. I didn't want my people listening to what I knew would happen between us."

So he'd known before she even got up here that they'd have sex or was he referring to what they might say? It stood to reason that if he was private with her then he was private with the Kindred members too, which left her curious about what he'd told them about her.

Those were irrelevant at this moment, in this house, she had rules to follow and she'd tried to tell him that, apparently his mind had been elsewhere. "Have you been listening to me? I'm not allowed to stay—"

"I want sex," he said. "More sex, lots of sex… I could get used to this lifestyle you know."

Having her sent to his room to service him whenever he commanded it, yeah, she believed that he could get used to it. "They only have to think we're having sex," she said, making sure he knew that this illusion was still going to operate under her terms. Coercion had never been a part of their sex life and she wasn't going to let Sikorski change that dynamic. "You said this room was clean, so they'll never know—"

"It gives you a chance to flesh out your character."

Answers for everything, they'd reverted back to their typical teasing and flirting without skipping much of a beat. "My character's supposed to be having lots of sex with you," she said. Her role in Sikorski's household was to provide her body to whoever wanted it.

"Exactly," he gloated. "Practice, practice."

She loved that he thought he was winning this fight because it made disproving that he was a lot more enjoyable. "I've had lots of sex with you," she said, tipping her chin up to smirk at him. "I've had years of it in fact."

That truth killed his swagger, quick. "But…"

Righting her posture, she was happy to pick her hands up to his shoulders and rub her lips on his jaw. "We don't need to actually have more sex for you to be convincing. If you want to boast about my body, or criticize my technique in front of Nicky, mentally reference any of the other four billion times we had sex."

His eyebrow slid up. "Four billion? That might be an exaggeration."

"Not by much," she said, adopting a smile that matched the slight one curling his lips. "We have a lot of fun sex stories."

Given how long they'd been together, and how amorous they were after periods apart, they had a long list of sexual memories. "Do you remember the time we were screwing in a car behind that ancient movie theater?"

"When we missed the fact that there was a raid on the building behind it? And missed the police showing up with the SWAT team?" he asked, stroking her arm. "Yeah, I remember."

"The first we knew they were there was when they interrupted us."

"For witness statements," he said, pulling her body up when he stood to carry her back to the bed. "That was awkward."

Awkward didn't begin to describe it. The surprise of the bang on the window was one thing, Tuck got so mad that someone had thought to disturb them. When the parties on each side of the glass realized what the other was doing, there were a lot of stutters and averted eyes. The cops thought they had valuable witnesses when all they had was a sated woman and a guy whose mouth had been occupied by her pussy.

After recovering from the initial contact, the men were polite, but she and Tuck couldn't offer much in the way of observations. "For the world's most observant guy—"

"Ha. Ha. I never claimed that title."

Lying against him, she didn't know if he'd finished what he'd started on the computer, or if he'd put it aside to placate her. That he didn't miss anything was sort of an inside joke between them that she couldn't believe he'd forgotten. Kadie was happy to remind him of how far his insanity had once gone. "One time when I lost half a pound, you took my blood to your lab to test for weird tropical diseases."

"I look after you."

"It was half a pound," she said. "I missed lunch and you could tell just by looking at me, from a distance, too."

"I know your body," he said. "I love your body."

That was undeniable. "How do you think that made me feel when I put on half a pound? Instantly a heifer."

She wasn't actually offended when he'd approached to stroke his hands over her like he was searching for clues to a mystery. That he did notice and cared enough to question her health was better than the alternative of not giving a rat's ass.

"Never," he said, urging her head back down with his chin when she tried to look at him. "I don't care what you weigh. I wanted to make sure that you were okay. Anything could've happened to you while I was away. It doesn't hurt to be vigilant. Hence taking the blood, if that had been infected—"

"With what?" she asked on a gasp. "Never mind, I

don't want to know… Are you going to seduce me now?"

Everything would change between them. Even admitting that they wanted to be together again wouldn't put things back to the way they were before. For one thing, she couldn't sit at home and wait without protest when she knew he could be in danger, like he was here.

Kadie wanted to be a part of it, ugly or not, this was Tuck's world. Sticking by him, helping him, consulting him, what she planned to do while they were in this situation was prove that she could be trusted and that she could be an asset to him and to his team. If they were interested in accepting her.

"You're a sure thing, Toots," he said, pulling her closer. "Let's lie here for a while. I'll let you know when I'm ready."

Delaying their intimacy was a way of prolonging the time they could spend together. As long as he said that he wanted it, she had to stay here, but she couldn't stay once they'd finished having sex for the night. Staying overnight in a client's bed was a massive no-no and one she couldn't afford to ignore when she was still trying to make an impression. Errors for a newbie would be inexcusable. Perfection was what she needed to portray to maintain her place here.

Sliding her leg up his, her thigh covered his erection. "Uh, don't look now—"

"Ignore that," he said. "If we have sex every time that appears we'll be here for months."

Turning her smile against his skin, she drew in a long breath. "This is real, isn't it? If I close my eyes, will you be here when I open them?"

Taking a nap should be okay and lying in his arms was no hardship. He'd asked when she came in if he could hold her, she could hardly deny him that right now when they'd confessed the truth of their feelings for each other.

"Every time," he said, kissing her hair again, then releasing his own deep breath. "Just relax, you're safe with me."

"And happy," she muttered, letting her eyes close and her breathing even out. She could relax, sleep, just for a few minutes. He'd be ready again soon.

SEVENTEEN

EXCEPT HE WASN'T, or if he was, he chose to ignore his desire in deference to letting her sleep because the next time she opened her eyes he'd made the decision for both of them. Darkness greeted her. Darkness that shouldn't have been there because she wasn't supposed to spend the night. Her job was to pleasure the man her Madame pointed at and then return to her bed in the basement with the others.

The comfort of his arms made her forget their predicament as she was transported to a time gone by and it took her a minute to reorient. The sheets around them were foreign, they felt different and smelled different to the ones they'd had on the bed in their apartment. The curtains were drawn around the four posts of the bed and they hadn't been before she closed her eyes. Tuck must have chosen to close them for increased privacy.

Opposite to her instinct, Kadie couldn't stay. Fear of what Madame's punishment might be clinched her body in a tightening vice. Trying to slide down his body to get out from under the arms he held her in only brought her face to face with his solid dick, right there beneath the covers.

The possibilities tantalized her. For a second, she evicted thoughts of the Madame who was waiting in the basement for her. Nuzzling into him, his groan made her part her lips to lick the length of him. If she woke him up, they'd have more sex, and that would delay her arrival back in her quarters where the Madame would already be pacing.

Her slumbering lover grabbed her up and closed his arms around her in a bear hug so tight that she had to hold her breath. Thinking that tasting him had been too much, she expected his eyes to be open and for him to be ready to play with her again. They weren't. His need to hold on to her had come from instinct, not desire.

Taking that into account, she doubted she'd get away clean if she tried to struggle away. Experience gave her the inside track. Kadie knew how to work this man, how to manipulate him, even when he was sleeping. Pushing herself up as opposed to down, she kissed her way to his mouth. Each touch of her lips to his skin relaxed the ferocity of his gripping arms. The irony was, Tuck could be so alert and on edge that there had been times he'd woken up in an instant if a breeze moved a curtain in their bedroom, yet she could do this with him for hours without bringing him to full consciousness. She'd made love to him in the past, enjoyed fellatio, the works, and he'd remained in his sleep throughout.

Easing onto him, she stretched out on top of him using the small amount of room she'd created for herself. As soon as her full body was pressed into him, his arms loosened so that his hands could slide down to her ass, which he squeezed when she kissed him.

Tracing her tongue over his lips, she elevated her hips. The temptation to impale herself on his erection almost too great to ignore. Leaving him, having just got him back, was not going to be easy for her, but it had to be done to protect them both.

Spoiling herself one last time, she slid her clit down the length of his thick shaft and closed her eyes to savor the frisson of pleasure it caused. Kissing him once more, she rolled away to get off the bed, letting the curtain glance off her. She had to be quick, he'd register the breeze her absence caused, though with the curtains over the bed, she might have bought herself a little more leeway.

Grabbing her apparel, she crawled to the door without trying to put anything on until she crept into the hallway. The security guards at either end of the corridor got a full view of her climbing into her dress but modesty was a distant luxury that wasn't worth clinging to here. Having had a crash course in intimate availability, the women here had poked and prodded her, groomed her, commented on her body.

They washed together, dressed together, slept together, it was like being at whore camp in the basement rooms they were relegated to. Teaching her how to ignore the sickness caused by violation was lesson number one and the one that would probably have served her best had she ever had to do what was expected of her.

The house was quite eerie at this time of the night, so she didn't meander. She got back to the basement to see Madame still awake, as was her custom to be until all of her girls were accounted for. The woman was in her forties, but as beautiful and groomed as the teenagers they had around here.

The cynical woman was harsh with the girls when they didn't comply with direct orders. Though, part of the way they got the women to be so compliant was to manipulate them with kindness. Punishments were strict, but coercion was subtle. Madame was a pro who would tease and flirt better than the rest of them combined, and those skills didn't only work with the men they encountered.

Madame stood from her reclining chair and took Kadie's things from her to put them aside.

"You should not form an attachment," Madame said, turning Kadie around to check for bruising.

On coming back from any liaison, the girls were always checked. Madame had to know if there were any marks left that could put other men off and if there were any wounds that might need to be treated. Sick girls weren't working girls, they were a drain on resources, and Madame was proactive about ensuring that didn't happen. Kadie often wondered if they'd be treated like racehorses if they broke a leg on a jump. If it was deemed too expensive or tiresome, would they just be shot on the spot to save time?

"I know," Kadie said. "I fell asleep, he told me he wasn't finished. "

"We're there for their pleasure," Madame said, stopping Kadie on her twirl to look her in the eye. "We have our rules for a reason. You wait until he falls asleep then you leave. We don't sleep in the embrace of a stranger. I taught you better than that."

Madame was tall and elegant. Her years showed in her face when Kadie was this up close. She carried herself with severity, but Kadie believed that she cared for the girls who worked under her. Exhaustion hung around her, a weariness that living this life for too long had brought.

"Yes," Kadie said. "I apologize. It won't happen again." Still proving herself able to be of use, Kadie had to be apologetic and defer to the woman before her.

Kadie was about to walk past, back toward her bunk, but Madame kept a hold of her. "You must tell me everything that you know about this gentleman," Madame said.

It was customary for Madame to keep a book on each client so the girls always knew how to maintain their pleasure. Intimate antics weren't the only thing noted down and if she'd picked up on any useful intelligence, she'd be expected to share that too.

Tired herself, Kadie wanted to get some sleep before she started to talk about Tuck because she'd have to be careful of her words and how she delivered them. Madame knew people, she knew sex, and men, and whores, all of the things that Kadie would have to lie about in order to protect Tuck.

"Yes, but—"

"It will wait," Madame said, still not allowing Kadie to leave her or to request rest. "The Master wants you in his room."

Shock startled her and she almost pulled away. "What? But I thought—"

"It's not our job to think, we do. Our game is about action. We don't ask why, we do as we're told."

It had to be difficult to get to Madame's age and still consider yourself inferior to men. Madame was tough and capable enough to rule over the dozens of women that Sikorski kept on the premises. It could be that when she and Sikorski were alone, the dynamic wasn't so clear cut. But Kadie had never heard of them having private meetings alone and if what was rumored about Sikorski's sexuality was true, then it was possible that the two weren't intimate.

Sikorski saw everyone as beneath him, so it was unlikely he'd give the head of the whores any respect.

"Swift said—"

"I believe the Master is asleep," Madame said. "But he wants you to sleep in his bed."

Madame's implication that Sikorski didn't want sex was odd. They were expected to deliver pleasure on demand. She shouldn't be telling Kadie that she didn't have to do that now as though the idea might be understandably abhorrent.

Being the new girl, maybe Madame was just reassuring her about expectations. As far as Madame was concerned, Kadie had been broken in by her first client tonight. Some women were more emotional after that experience, though they'd try to hide any volatility because this was what they were trained for.

Detachment, rule number one, it separated them from their bodies and the hideous things they'd be asked to do with them.

Kadie knew she couldn't get out of this. She had no viable reason to object. Tuck would tomorrow, but that fight was for the men. She couldn't very well rush back up the stairs and wake her boyfriend just to cause a war they'd never win. For one thing, she'd never get up there in a mad dash, security would take her down before she got off the first floor.

Kadie's job was to obey orders, Sikorski's orders. With a nod she turned to go and dragged her feet every step of the way. Tomorrow Tuck would be angry but by then it would be too late.

***

WAKING UP ALONE pissed him off, but it did speed up his morning shower. Kadie had told him she'd leave, but he hadn't thought that she would, not after he got her to sleep. She was a heavy sleeper, and usually when she was out, it was for the night. He could understand how being in a place like this would put her on edge. Sleeping through the night was something she did when she was happy and content, neither was really possible here, no matter how he tried to soothe her.

On opening the door of his suite, there were security guys standing ready to take him down to the same office he'd been in last night. Spending the night here wasn't something he wanted to do again, it might make Sikorski feel better to have him under his roof, but Tuck didn't like to be in enemy territory.

Last night had proved to him that he had no influence over Kadie while she was here. Whatever drove her to remain here, it compelled her to comply with the orders given to her by Sikorski. He gathered that she hadn't been here for long, so it couldn't be conditioning that kicked in to drive her out of his bed.

Coffee was poured and he was offered food by a woman wearing far too much make up for the hour in the day. Women here were treated as robots, employees meant to serve. It didn't matter the time or who was around, they were supposed to glitter and the woman who served him did. In the light of day though, it seemed forced and although she had plenty of skin on show, there was nothing sexy about a woman performing for him under orders to tempt and seduce.

The coffee wasn't that good. It was probably expensive and carefully prepared, but he wouldn't relax until Kadie was beside him again. The books were incidental and he didn't see anything on the desk that would be worth scrutinizing or stealing. He'd guess that this room was a stage and wasn't actually functional. The absence of a computer was a good indicator of that. Most working offices, or any productive room in a home, contained a computer. Of course, it could just be a nod to his skills that they were too scared to leave anything lying around that he might be able to manipulate. It was sad that they were deluded enough to think he hadn't already been through their whole network and taken every bit of data.

Going over to the large window, he noted a guard walking the tree line. Because they were set on a hill, he could see down to the perimeter wall. If he got his timings right, he could get him and Kadie out of here without being seen, he just had to do the math. Straightening his arm, he freed his watch from his jacket sleeve and began to count. Being stuck in here didn't have to be a chore, it could give him an advantage.

Sikorski kept him waiting. If Kadie hadn't been stuck here, Tuck would've taken off after figuring out the guards' schedule just to show the fucker how little he was willing to be played with. It didn't help his mood when Sikorski came in wearing a smug smile.

"Sleep well?"

Coming away from the bookcase he'd been examining, Tuck walked away from the window side of the desk. "Better before my woman left me," Tuck said. "The deal was she stayed with me."

"Is the woman more important than the business we have?" Sikorski asked. Opening his arms as he sank down onto the couch, he nodded toward the one opposite his, where Tuck had sat last night. "I want the device."

If he hadn't been sure of that, this plan would never have worked. "I know," Tuck said, taking a seat.

"What do you want in return?"

"Before we talk money, I've gotta know if you can handle it."

Sikorski snickered. "You think I don't know how to utilize the device?"

"By all accounts, you wimped out of the deal the last time."

That erased his conceit. Tuck lifted one ankle to the opposite knee. Sikorski might think he was a formidable force and by the way he had women simpering around him and men bowing down, Tuck guessed he had an overinflated sense of his own importance and capability.

"Who told you that?"

The most unlikely of Kindred allies had told him that. But the name he gave wasn't the true source. "Kahlil Samara."

Sikorski's sneer grew. "Impossible. He's dead."

"Sure about that?"

Samara was dead. That was fact. But Sikorski could only be sure of that if he'd seen the body himself. "The man was weak. Incapable of simple tasks."

"Like killing you," Tuck said. "That was what he planned to do, you know that, right? You were the money. He was going to use your money to obtain the device for himself. Is that why you cut and run?"

An exhale of a laugh joined a half-shake of his head. If Tuck wasn't mistaken, there was a glimmer of admiration on Sikorski's face. "You are far more connected than I gave you credit for."

Tuck took his turn to sneer. "I'm the fucking internet, you prick. I'm everything and everywhere."

"You don't know why I backed out of that deal though, you don't know everything. If you did, you wouldn't be here." Unable to deny that Tuck didn't speak. "The deal was on. We made all the arrangements for the exchange."

"So what happened? Because when that fucker showed up, he was penniless."

"That he went to the meet proves what an idiot he was," Sikorski said, relaxing after a slow blink. "Those people, the ones he was dealing with. They are ruthless."

"Are they?" Tuck always enjoyed hearing about the Kindred myth.

"What were you doing? Lying in wait to steal the device when the hand-over was done? Taking it from Kahlil would be the best strategy, he was the weakest link."

"I'm not going to tell you how I know what I know."

Sikorski wouldn't expect him to, but he was allowed to speculate. The web of criminality across the world was vast, but somehow there was always someone who knew what someone else wanted to know. Secrets were tough to keep, which was why the Kindred Circle had been kept so small.

"If you know Game Time… If you know Kahlil Samara…" Sikorski was playing with him. "Then you know Zara Bandini."

"Maybe." Swallow. Yes, he knew Zara, better than

any other person in this building, that was for sure. Raven was the only man who knew her better. The only living man anyway.

"Women always screw up the deal," Sikorski said, glancing at the liquor decanter in the corner. Tuck suppressed a smile. Zara would be pleased to know she could drive this maniac to drink at breakfast time. Raven would be so proud. The woman was the only one with the ability to drive his best friend to the bottle too. "I met her once. She fooled me, so innocent and open, at least that's what she wants the world to think. All of this is her fault."

Uh oh, so this lunatic had an agenda against their Swallow. Oh well, Tuck wanted the guy dead for what he had done to Kadie. Soon as Raven heard Sikorski's opinion of Zara, they'd have to hide Maverick's ammunition. Once Raven's trigger finger was itchy, the mission slid into a precarious position. Tuck would have to work fast.

"Her fault?" Tuck asked.

This wasn't why he was here, but it was interesting to hear outside perspectives on the Kindred members. If Zara was gaining a rep, they needed to know what it was in case they had to capitalize on it further down the line.

"She manipulated Grant McCormack. He was the man at the helm of Cormack Industries, the creators of the device."

Tuck knew that wasn't the case. Zara hadn't even known the device existed before the Kindred told her and everything she did in relation to the initial negotiations was directed by the Kindred Circle. Zara probably got the blame either because Grant had implied it or because Sikorski found it easier to think he'd been thwarted by a woman using her feminine wiles than by a weakling like Grant McCormack.

Though, it later transpired Grant wasn't as benign as they'd all thought. He'd paid the ultimate price for betraying Zara and the Kindred. If Benedict Leatt hadn't put a bullet in him then Raven would have, of that Tuck was sure. Even though he himself wasn't the assassin of the group, he had been tempted to eliminate Grant McCormack plenty of times, none more so than after the loss of Art, the Kindred chief. At that time, it wouldn't have made strategic sense, but it would've made him feel better.

"You lost out on the initial bidding," Tuck said. "Albert Sutcliffe was the successful party."

"He's dead."

On that, they could both agree. Raven had been responsible for that shot and it was an overdue one. Zara had commented that Game Time cursed anyone who came into contact with it. Tim Sutcliffe had been the first direct casualty after the McCormack parents, but he wasn't the last. Art was gone. Albert Sutcliffe. Grant McCormack. Kahlil Samara. Mischa Corvi. All dead. If Zara was right, Game Time wasn't finished claiming victims.

"How'd you find that out?" Tuck asked, they'd never had confirmation on how Kahlil and Sikorski became allies.

"Samara," Sikorski said. "His employer terminated him after they too lost out on the deal. The man was in a rage, he came to me, told me he could get the device that he had information that could give us an advantage."

The story of Future's Hope, the boat that had floundered, taking the McCormack parents with it. "Did he give you the information?"

Sikorski shook his head. "I tried to extract it. But he insisted on keeping the information private. I suppose as leverage. If he gave me the information, I would have had no use for him."

Smart for Kahlil and perfect for the Kindred. Kahlil had known Raven's true identity. The fewer people who had that information, the better. Discovering that Sikorski was in the dark about that and about Raven's history was a point in their favor.

"So you told him to get to the device?"

"After being unsuccessful through Grant McCormack, I moved onto other interests. I didn't bother to follow what happened to the Game Time device. Kahlil said he knew who had it."

Kahlil had seen Art's death at the Atlas warehouse when the Kindred had taken control of Game Time, commandeering it before the injured Albert Sutcliffe could make off with it. The story Sikorski told was the same one Kahlil had fed Zara. All they needed was the confirmation that Sikorski didn't know details of the Kindred.

"Yet, you backed out. Lose your nerve? Don't want that happening to me."

"I told you," Sikorski said, enjoying his smirk. "A woman always screws up the deal."

"You think it was Zara Bandini's fault?"

"I know it was, but she wasn't the woman I was referring to." Now he was lost and his squint must have conveyed that. "After the death of Grant McCormack, Mischa Corvi was brought in to take over at Cormack Industries."

Tuck was aware of that and the friction it had caused in Raven's relationship with Swallow. "So?"

The door opened, interrupting them before Sikorski could respond. Kadie came in and from the way she came up short, he'd say she wasn't expecting them to be here. The rush of color to her cheeks wasn't caused by him, not by what they'd done last night anyway. Reading her tension and her reluctance to look at him, Tuck frowned. Something was wrong.

Sikorski was smiling, but Kadie didn't want to look at him either. "You wanted to see me?" she asked Sikorski, holding the door handle, and using the wood as a shield for everything but her head and shoulders.

"Yes, I thought you should join us," Sikorski said. "Our new friend has taken an interest in you. You won't mind her sitting with us while we talk business. Will you, Swift?"

Clenching his jaw, he could only shake his head. "No," he said, though his head was screaming yes. Whatever Kadie heard might change her opinion on him and with this audience, he couldn't offer explanations. In the bar, she'd proved that she could play a part and keep her cool when she had to. Whether her acceptance would carry beyond this room, he couldn't yet tell.

EIGHTEEN

SIKORSKI COULDN'T POSSIBLY understand what he'd done by bringing Kadie into the room. Tuck didn't know why she had to bear witness to this conversation, she had no choice except to comply with what Sikorski ordered her to do and Tuck couldn't object. Although he didn't want her to hear the gory details of the Kindred's past dealings in this setting, he had to look on the bright side. As long as she was in the room with him, he could protect her.

Sikorski gestured for her to sit on the same couch that he occupied and she tiptoed forward, closing the office door, and sitting at the end, as far away from her boss as she could. Warning bells began to fade up in his hearing. Although Sikorski didn't seem to notice that she was reluctant to be near him because the Russian was more interested in examining his newest business associate, Tuck saw it.

A flare of dismay colored her face when she caught Tuck frowning at her. Her reluctance to have his attention betrayed that she'd choose to be invisible in this moment if she could wish it. Except she should know better than to assume he'd ignore her when he could tell that she was unsettled.

Concern for the Kindred and moving forward

lessened in light of Kadie's meek expression and awkward body language. Something was wrong and he had to know what it was before he could fix it.

"Mischa Corvi," Sikorski said, and Tuck drew his attention around to the other man in the room. "We were not acquainted as such, but I'd heard of her, of course. She is famed in Europe for her resilience in business."

Tuck wasn't saying anything, his scowl was chiseled so deep that he began to get a headache. It amazed him how affected he was by seeing Kadie so close to this man he despised. Laughing with the warm, relaxed woman she was last night was a brutal contrast to the tense, nervous woman he was watching now. This woman was keeping to herself, trying to make her body as small as she could, desperate to be excused.

"I know who she is," Tuck said. "And I know she was involved with CI, briefly." Not anymore, Zara drove Corvi out before she got too cozy.

"Something happened," Sikorski said. "I don't know what it was, I didn't care. She called me on the morning the deal was about to go down. Told me that she could get the device to me and it wouldn't cost me a penny."

Damn, Cuckoo. Sikorski had pulled out, leaving Kahlil exposed, because Cuckoo had told him she could deliver the device. Without her connections to CI, she couldn't do it legitimately. He'd already shut down Winter Chill by then, the project that built the Game Time devices. Game Time only existed in the Kindred arsenal and the way she'd chosen to get it was to send in Griffin Caine to hold them all hostage while she took off with the device they'd brought for Kahlil.

Cuckoo was a woman scorned. She'd been cast out and humiliated by Raven in front of Swallow and it had been too much for her to handle. All of them had considered it odd that she'd gone so quietly. Knowing now what had gone down after she'd been evicted, her demure reaction made more sense. The crafty woman was concocting a plan, probably from before she left Swallow's apartment.

Caine hadn't told them that. He'd told them that

Cuckoo was taking the device to a buyer, but not who that buyer was. He'd claimed not to know and given how Cuckoo liked to tease and keep him at heel, they'd concluded she probably had kept her puppy in the dark about what she planned to do. If she and Sikorski had connected, their allegiance would've given the Kindred a much larger problem. Disaster averted. Wow, and it was so rare for them to catch any kind of break.

"What happened?" Tuck asked because it made sense to. He knew exactly what had happened.

"She didn't make the rendezvous," Sikorski said, squeezing his fingers around his knees. "Stupid woman left herself open to attack. The whole place was up in smoke by the time we got there."

The explosion that left Zara near death. "She's dead?" The Kindred had no confirmation on that either way.

Sikorski shrugged. "We didn't bother to dock, saw an explosion, maneuvered round and saw the building filled with smoke. When we saw Bandini on the ground, we took off. It was a setup."

"Always a woman," Tuck said, glancing at Kadie who was focused on the floor.

Sikorski paid no attention to the woman he'd summoned to sit at his side. "Bandini doesn't know when to quit. Grant McCormack told me that."

Many people had told Zara that, too. Didn't slow her down. "So Bandini's dead?"

At least if he thought that, Sikorski wouldn't be going after her. The Russian just shrugged again. "I assume not if you have all of this information and access to the device."

"Didn't say any of it came from her."

Sikorski's gaze shrank. "He was working with a partner. Kahlil Samara, he brought in a man he said had been watching Sutcliffe for him. I could tell they weren't close, but there was a history between them. The partner was the one who got my men into Sutcliffe's compound after Grant McCormack's death there. That was the start of my association with Kahlil Samara. We found nothing."

So the fleet of vehicles and men who poured into

Sutcliffe's compound after them were Sikorski's men.

"Must have pissed you off," Tuck said.

His brows went up in slow assent. "That was when Kahlil revealed he had secondary information that could get us the device from those who had stolen it. I don't know if his partner knew the information, but he certainly knew it existed. His partner took off on the same morning I told Kahlil our association was over, when I thought Corvi was going to deliver Game Time."

Sikorski was right. Kahlil should never have come to the Kindred meeting. But he was out of options, believing he could hoodwink them was his last hope. "Interesting."

Taking a breath, Sikorski became impatient. "I have been forthcoming. Will you tell me now how you obtained the device?"

"You haven't told me anything I didn't already know."

"You didn't know about Kahlil's partner," Sikorski said, believing that he'd triumphed.

Tuck released a whispered laugh. "Benedict Leatt? I know all about him."

It wasn't easy for Sikorski to disguise being impressed. "You do know your stuff," Sikorski said, spoiling Tuck with more condescension. "Then I must assume Ms. Bandini is alive or Mr. Leatt is your source."

Tuck would rather that Sikorski believed the second, except tracking down the latter was part of his reason for being here. "Assume what you want... Have you seen Leatt since?"

"Not since the morning he left Kahlil. He got a call, a more important or lucrative job I'd assume. Then he was gone."

Kahlil had told them that Leatt was watching his back from a distance. Quite a distance if Leatt had taken off earlier in the day. Another lie. "Got to look out for number one."

"How is Ms. Bandini, I trust her injuries weren't too great."

If he confessed to knowing Zara, Sikorski might suspect he had nefarious motives for being here. But he did.

"She's alive. She doesn't know I'm here."

Tuck didn't need this guy to think that he was trustworthy. So it didn't matter if he believed Tuck was double-crossing Zara. Sikorski's laugh took him aback. "Anyone who wants to screw over Zara Bandini rates highly with me."

Kadie glimpsed him, but he didn't look at her. "Got to watch your ass though, heard her boyfriend isn't the forgiving type."

Tuck's shoulders rose. "That's not my problem if you're the one bringing the device to me."

Sikorski was happy for him to risk his life to bring Game Time here. If Tuck was the one doing it, Sikorski's name didn't have to come up and he'd be the one facing down Raven if Zara sicced her lover on the threat.

"Okay," Tuck said, ready to round up proceedings now that he had Kadie in his eye line. "I want three things from you, two million dollars and the current location of Benedict Leatt."

Sikorski leaned forward. "Two million? You're seriously lowballing it."

"That's how much I want Leatt," Tuck said, because it was the truth.

"What's the third?" Sikorski asked.

Raising his attention, he fixated on Kadie. "Her."

They'd talked about not making it obvious to Sikorski that he cared about her. But this was the deal. His chance to ensure there wouldn't be a stream of bullets following her when he busted her out of here.

Sikorski looked over his shoulder then back at Tuck. "Why her?"

"I like what she did for me last night."

"You weren't the only one," Sikorski muttered as he sat back. Alarm straightened Tuck. What the fuck did that mean? Tuck knew what it sounded like and that would explain why Kadie was so nervous and shifty this morning. Without jumping to conclusions, or blowing his stack without all the facts, he clenched his hand to a fist and reminded himself to breathe. "Take her, she means nothing to me."

Good. So Sikorski wasn't going to put up a fight. "I'm leaving now and I'm taking her with me." Sikorski was suspicious. Tuck had to get out of here, there was no need for him to stay another minute and there wasn't a chance in hell he was leaving Kadie. For one thing, he wanted to know what was wrong with her and what Sikorski was implying. "Think of it as a gesture of goodwill. I don't want to share… I have uses for her."

Taking a moment, Sikorski narrowed his gaze. "I'll give you Leatt."

Sikorski had resources and his network extended to back streets and alleyways across the globe. That kind of intelligence would take time for the Kindred to collate, Sikorski could get it done faster. "And my money?" Tuck asked.

The Kindred didn't care about money, but it was expected that they would demand a fee, so they did. Most missions entailed a similar requirement when property or information was being exchanged.

"You'll get that too," Sikorski said. "In fact, I'll give you ten."

"Why would you do that?" If he was increasing the price then this negotiation wasn't as over as he'd thought.

Sikorski thought about it a minute, like he was measuring him, either because what he was about to ask was extreme or because it mattered to him so much that he didn't want Tuck to say no.

"Bring Zara Bandini to me. You have access. I want her. Bring her to me."

Swallow. Sikorski really hated the Kindred's only gal. Kadie's chin was down, but her eyes were high in her sockets, monitoring him. Her scrutiny didn't prevent his smile. "Done."

NINETEEN

"I CAN'T BELIEVE that you just agreed to give up your friend," Kadie said. "Just like that, no fight, no nothing. This is the same Zara you spoke to on the way to Gwen's party?"

"Don't worry about it," he said and tried to reach for her hand, but she pulled it away.

Sikorski had offered them a vehicle and Tuck had practically laughed in his face. To her it was odd that Tuck found that offer so ridiculous, but when it came to trading up a woman he was supposed to care about, Zara, he hadn't blinked.

They'd been told there would be a car waiting on the road to take them into town and Tuck accepted that. Walking all the way back down the mountain would be insane, especially when she was wearing kitten heels.

"How can I not worry?" she asked, traipsing down the driveway beside him. The house was getting smaller the farther away from it they went and her dread grew. "Why rescue me just to betray her?"

"It's not a betrayal," Tuck said. "Swallow has been itching to get into the field."

"Into the field? Are you going to try and make me believe that a sane woman agreed to go into that house, to be with that man, out of desire?"

"Not sexual desire, but yeah, Swallow has an appetite for retribution."

Some of the things he said were enough to make her pause. "Retribution?"

"Do I need to get some of my own?" he asked, and she forgot about Swallow for a second.

"Some what?"

Turning around, he stopped walking to match his focus to hers. "What the fuck did Sikorski mean, I wasn't the only one who liked what you did last night?"

Oh God, she didn't want to be having this conversation on a driveway. Glancing back at the distant house, she hoped no one could see or hear them. "Last night, I woke up with you, but I couldn't stay, so I went down to the basement where I was supposed to be."

"And?" He didn't apologize for letting her fall asleep when she'd been explicit about not sleeping with him.

She couldn't soften the truth or lie to him. "Madame sent me to his bed, to Nicky's bed"—Tuck's mouth opened, but she rushed to explain—"Nothing happened, he was already asleep. It was a power play, it had to be. I left at first light, went back to the basement. He and I didn't even speak."

"That motherfucker," Tuck snarled. "I said exclusive and he screwed me over."

Was he pissed that he'd been lied to or that she'd been in another man's bed? "Are you pissed at me or at him?"

"Him," Tuck snapped, and grabbed her to shove her down the driveway in front of him.

Maybe this walk would end up being a good thing, it would give him a chance to cool off because she didn't need him acting on foolish impulse.

They kept on going, all the way to the end, and got out onto the street where there was a jeep and a driver waiting, just as Sikorski had promised. Choosing a diner about five miles from the bar, she and Tuck said nothing to each other on the journey. But she was obsessing about her own problem.

Since Tuck came back into the picture, she'd been

worried that their relationship would be uncovered and they'd be exposed as vulnerabilities for the other. Tuck moved faster than she'd bargained for, she hadn't had the time to explain to him why it was important for her to stay in the house. If she'd put up too much of a fight, she'd have drawn attention to the second fact that she didn't want known. Her association with Howie.

Getting away from the oppressive reign of Nykiel Sikorski was a relief. But she couldn't do it at the expense of a youngster's life. She hadn't seen Howie for a few days. He was still in there. He had to be. And she had to get him out.

Once they were dropped off at the diner, Tuck offered to buy her breakfast, she refused, but he got takeout anyway. It seemed like he was killing time as opposed to feeding his hunger. Keeping note of everything in their surroundings, he was twitchy enough to make her aware too.

Much to her surprise, he took her a few blocks over to where he had a car parked, like he'd planned for this. On their next journey, there wasn't much conversation, they drank the coffee he'd bought and ignored the food, and the only thing she could come up with to do next was be honest with him.

When they pulled in to a motel, she figured he'd just found somewhere convenient to stop. They parked, she grabbed her food and her purse and climbed out after him, expecting him to head for the office. That he'd chosen the farthest corner of the lot to park in meant they'd have a walk, so she just hoped there were rooms.

"Wait here," he said, snagging her hand and pulling her into the covered porch that ran around the lower level of the double-story structure.

Wait here for what, she wondered, but she didn't have to wait long. Going to the penultimate door, he crouched and slid something metallic into the lock, he fiddled with it for a second, then the door popped open.

"What are you doing?" she hissed because it looked damn like he was breaking and entering.

"Wait," he said, opening the door just enough for him to squeeze in and twist around it.

Creeping closer, she didn't want to leave any fingerprints or place herself at the scene of a crime. But loitering out here might be obvious to anyone peeking through their curtains, so she plastered her back to the wall and kept look out, begging that no one would catch Tuck in the act of anything illegal.

About twelve seconds later, the door swung back, and Tuck hung out to gesture her in. "Safe now, come on."

Safe? Why he would break in to somewhere that was unsafe and then invite her inside was beyond her. But this was Tuck, so she suckered in a breath and twisted to follow him inside. The room was large, containing two double beds. Both had been shoved off to the corners and a folding table had been set up in the middle of them. A couch under the window was covered with a sheet, which she thought was odd.

The table had a pile of papers in the middle and three laptops stacked beside them. That neatness wasn't reflected in the rest of the room. Pizza boxes and beer bottles were interspersed with other food containers and paper coffee cups. What looked to be bullets were grouped in one corner, the sight of the ammunition made her eyes flare and she stepped forward.

Tuck closed the door behind her and crouched, but she didn't turn to see what he was doing. The features of the room, the crumpled beds and scattered clothes, intrigued her.

"She's tidier at the manor," Tuck said, rushing past to scoop a bra from the floor. "Though I guess we're not."

He grabbed up a tee shirt too and tossed both items of apparel onto the farthest bed. Keeping his momentum going, he went to the central table, but paused to pick up a slip of paper. He read it and exhaled a smile. Kadie edged closer to see what it said, but all she saw were senseless letters and numbers.

"What does it say?" she asked, assuming it was code. He glanced at her then back at the paper.

"That they've gone for breakfast and if I'm not back to read their note they're launching a full assault extraction. Falc and Wren are on standby. They called Rigor too. They are serious." He shook his head then crumpled their note.

That his colleagues cared for him enough to have such little patience was a testament to the intensity of what they did and how dangerous Sikorski was. But it only made his agreement with Sikorski all the more tasteless.

"What did he do?" she asked.

Rounding the table, he pulled out a chair and she noticed a pillow and blanket on the floor between the table and one of the beds. Someone was sleeping on the floor. "Who?" Tuck asked, sitting down and reaching over to pull a laptop from the stack.

"You said that Zara wanted retribution. What did Nicky do to her?"

"Around here he's called Sikorski or the Russian fucker," he said, his brow snapping down as he turned on the machine he'd just opened. "And you won't hear us using our names either."

"Why not?" she asked, putting her things on the table.

"Habit," he shrugged. "It protects us when we're not in the manor."

"What manor?"

"Kindred Manor," he said, glancing up at her. But the batter of his fingers on the keyboard told her she didn't have his full attention.

There wasn't really anywhere to sit except at this table and the long bullets were a little too close for her to be comfortable sitting with them. "Raven is dangerous," she said, fixated on the ammunition.

"Yep."

"He cares for Swallow," she muttered.

"Loves her," he said, pausing with the tapping to read something, then he carried on. "God knows why, she talks too much."

"What's to stop him from killing you when he finds out you've set her up?"

Flicking his gaze to hers, he stopped typing, and she waited for him to explain the darkness in his glare. It didn't fade. Curling his fingers over the lid of the laptop, he pushed it down. As soon as it clicked into place, he rose in one fluid motion and came to her.

For a breath, he stood near enough that she could inhale him without their bodies coming into contact. When he seized her arms and hauled her up, she gasped.

"Get one thing straight, Toots. The Kindred don't set up their own. We take opportunities. Having a man on the inside with me gives me an advantage. Sikorski can think he's getting her, but she'll be mine, working with me."

"You didn't ask her permission."

Sneering, he shook his head. "You don't get it at all. We do what's asked of us. We force each other into danger when it's necessary. We do what the others ask of us. We don't blink. We don't ask questions. We agree and we act."

"Even when it's insane? He'll kill her… if she's lucky."

Sikorski didn't just kill people quick and painless. He got to the position he was in by building a ruthless reputation. Rumors told of torture, or prolonged rape and imprisonment. Anyone who crossed Sikorski would be delivered to the hands of hell before begging for death.

"If she dies, I die. Raven dies… We can't lose another man. We won't survive it."

Another man. Grief. That was what drove him now. Taking her hands to his face, she searched for the truth behind his steel. "You lost someone… Before you came back to me."

His distraction, the trouble plaguing him that weighted his every move during their last reunion, had concerned her so much that she'd thought of it frequently. Something had changed him because his pain was obvious. But he didn't share it. He kept her out. Locked himself up and pushed her away.

"The chief. We lost the chief. He was the closest thing I had to a father and there wasn't a damn thing we could do to save him."

Tuck's loyalty ran deep and disappointing a man he'd respected so much must have torn him apart. "Oh, baby."

Running her hands up his neck, she pushed her fingers into his hair and pulled him down. Their kiss started slow, but the tenderness didn't last. Shunting her around, he strode forward, forcing her to go backwards and then he was pushing her down onto one of the rumpled beds.

The sheets smelled like him, but she couldn't care less who had slept here when she wrapped her arms around the man who was finally letting her in. Her shoes fell from her feet and he bent her knees to close her legs around his hips.

This was a communal room. They could be discovered by dangerous people who didn't know her and might see her as a threat. But Tuck was here. On her. Above her. Kissing her with a ferocity that pushed her skull deep into the mattress.

"Take this off," he said, sitting astride her to fumble with the buttons on her dress. Opening the fabric, he exposed her breasts, pressing his thumbs to their tips, circling, and squeezing until they were tight points.

Bowing to suck on one peak, he came back to her mouth, letting his hands continue the stimulation of her chest. His hands were large and her breasts modest, his span exceeded her flesh, but that meant he could tease every part of the responsive flesh all at the same time. His typing skills gave him excellent dexterity. Practiced moves of opening and closing fingers, extending and curling, he pampered her with a range of sensations while accompanying his every nuance with the talent of his amorous tongue.

"Tuck," she whispered against him, and he drove his tongue into her mouth again. She wasn't supposed to use his name, but his was the only name she'd used in bed for years. Saying the name of another man, even if it was the same man, felt wrong and dulled some of her arousal.

He rose onto his knees again, lifting her torso to work her dress up over her head. Glancing around as he pulled off his own tee shirt and began to work on his jeans, she became aware that they were in someone else's space.

"Is it okay?" she said, spreading her own hands on his solid chest. "To do this here?"

"I'd say so," he said, pulling her legs open to shift himself between them.

Taking his lack of reluctance as a positive sign, she relaxed because it suddenly hit her that there were no crazy mob bosses compelling her to be here, to be anywhere. She'd left her life to find Tucker Holt and here he was, between her thighs, massaging her intimate flesh with his familiar fingertips.

"I've wanted this," she said, opening her mouth for his when he kissed her again. "For so long, Tuck, I didn't... I thought I lost you and—"

Covering her cheeks with his hands, he kissed her eyes, the end of her nose, her lips, and then her forehead before he looked at her again. "You've got me now. You've got me back."

She'd tracked him down once, if she had to do it again, she would. Tuck had better resources and more experience, meaning if he wanted to leave her and disappear again, he could. Trusting him wasn't straightforward. Like he'd said, if the Kindred lost another man, the band would be devastated. The loss of the chief he'd referred to had driven him to terminate their relationship and that was when he had the support of the Kindred to rely on. If that vanished, she didn't know what kind of man he'd become.

Stroking her hands over his body, she'd always loved his definition, the planes of his pecs and the strength of his arms urged her to touch, to test his resistance. She pinched and caressed, then licked and nipped at him when his mouth descended onto her neck.

Last night had been incredible, but this was better. He'd come for her. Rescued her. And for this moment, in this second, she chose to ignore the fact that she'd have to go back to that horrible place. Dreaming of a reunion with Tuck had dominated most of her adult life. Even when they were together, she craved him because they were so often apart. This was like one of those times.

Forcing her hands to stop their exploration of him, she trailed them down the line of hair beneath his belly button and found his jeans open. Taking control of the moment, she grabbed him with a sure fist and began to pump.

"My dick doesn't need help," he grumbled, moistening her with his breath.

"Sure it does," she said, turning her face against him. "It's not inside me yet. That's slacking."

"Always in a hurry," he said, and one of his fingers glided into her, making her hiss.

It wasn't his dick, but it wasn't bad. Working her juices, getting her slick enough to accept him, wouldn't take long if he kept finger-fucking her at this varying pace. When he had two fingers all the way inside her, he began to roll her clit with the heel of his hand, the flat surface pushing into the sensitive nub and all the tingling flesh around it.

He didn't normally make her beg, and she wasn't capable because the way he kept moving his hand sped up her journey to near completion. "Want me to stop?" he asked, but the amusement in his voice said he already knew the answer.

"Don't you fucking dare."

"I love it when you swear," he said, sinking his mouth onto hers to quiet her protests when his hand fell away from its task. Probably because she so rarely did lose composure enough to curse.

She was there. Right on the cusp. So close. But her frustration was short-lived. The thick length of him didn't linger. One second his head was at her opening and before she could breathe in, he was all the way inside her.

This was safety. His body on top of hers, making love with her. The world locked outside their door. If she concentrated hard enough, she could erase the last nine months.

Intent eyes hovered over hers, he wasn't kissing her, just watching her. Getting faster, his thrusts hit deeper. Fury strengthened a glare on his face, his troubles weren't far from his thoughts. Smoothing a hand over his shoulder, she pushed his hair back from his forehead. Getting to a new, secure place in their relationship would take time, but she couldn't surrender and give up.

"I love you," she said. The words inspired his hips and he propelled in fast, the hard width of him giving no reprieve to her fiery core as it closed around him, tight as a vice that wanted to absorb his being into hers.

Giving her all he could of himself, he pumped through her orgasm until his own crescendo filled her with the seed she needed to sate her. Warmth and contentment didn't fade even after her heart began to slow and with sweat marring her skin, she felt alive for the first time in months.

"I love you too," he panted, and kissed her before settling down on the bed.

"I have to take a shower," she said, patting his chest and wishing that she could stay here all day, but she was focused on the door beyond the end of their bed now and preoccupied with the idea that it could open at any time.

"I have work to do," he said, but didn't slacken his arms from her body. Content to be plastered to him, she didn't push away. Didn't separate them because she didn't want this moment of joining to be over. "The bathroom is through the back. Swallow has all kinds of shit in there, you can help yourself."

Using another woman's toiletries didn't bother her, not after her experience at Sikorski's house. Though until she knew more about Zara and her temperament, Kadie had also learned to be cautious around other women. Some were spiteful. Some were jealous. Some just wanted to fight.

Zara had a close relationship with the Kindred, she was Kindred, Kadie was not. The only female member might like being just that and not want another woman on her turf. In their own way, the Kindred men belonged to Zara, who was a formidable woman in her own right. Kadie might not be able to face-off with such a force.

Tuck trusted her. So Kadie would too. At least until she got the chance to size up the woman herself.

TWENTY

THEY DID EVENTUALLY force themselves to get out of bed and Tuck went back to the laptop he'd been on before while Kadie enjoyed a long shower. Without a time limit or concerns that she may have to share the water with others, Kadie embraced the freedom Tuck had granted her.

He gave her a tee shirt to wear and tucked her into his bed, the one they'd had sex on, telling her to relax and get some rest. Though she still had to tell him about Howie, she could see that he was intent on his Kindred laptop, so she gave him the time to deal with that. After vowing to herself to tell him the truth at some point before the day was out, she must have drifted off to sleep in the sanctuary he provided.

Regaining her consciousness came in time with a yawn and a stretch and when she opened her eyes, she expected to see Tuck working at his laptop, as he had been when she fell asleep. Instead, she saw a woman sitting in the same chair, except she wasn't facing a laptop on the table, the chair was turned and she was staring right at Kadie's sleeping form.

Feeling exposed, she pulled the blanket up to her chin and tried to regain some equilibrium. Tuck wasn't here, no one was. No one except her and the woman in the chair, who was frowning at her.

"Who are you?" Kadie asked.

The woman took a breath and folded her arms above her already crossed legs. "Strolling up to Nykiel Sikorski and throwing yourself at his mercy may be the most insane thing a person has ever done."

The raven-haired woman was calm, but there was a warmth about her that put Kadie at ease. Waking up to being watched was weird, but this woman didn't come across as a maniac. "If you're here to tell me that I have a crazy death wish, someone already beat you to it."

Tuck hadn't hidden his displeasure at where she'd ended up.

"I'm not here for that," the stranger said.

But she didn't offer why she was sitting, watching, in the way that she was, or where Tuck had disappeared to. "If you want to point out that I'm naïve and inexperienced—"

"Actually, I think you just proved you've got balls," the woman said, and smiled as she leaned forward. "Your guy is livid and it could have gone the other way, your body could've washed up somewhere Jane Doe and he'd never have known. It was an insane risk to take."

Curiosity narrowed her eyes. "Then why do you sound so impressed?"

"Because if it was Rave, I'd have done the same thing. If he'd cut me off and walked away, I wouldn't have given up and made escape easy for him. I'd have taken whatever risk I had to, to get back to him."

At least Kadie had won one person's respect in this, even if it wasn't the person she was aiming for. "Thanks."

"If you're going to be a member of the Kindred there are two things you need to know."

"The Kindred?" Kadie asked.

This woman had to be Zara Bandini, Swallow, no other woman would be allowed into what was the Kindred's safe house and she wouldn't guess Tuck would leave her with someone he didn't trust. The only woman he'd ever referred to was Zara. Her impression so far was good, Zara was direct, she wasn't forthcoming about what was going on exactly, but she shared her thoughts without compunction.

"One," the woman carried on, "the men always have to believe they're in charge. Whether they are or not. It takes a little bit of practice if you're trying to manipulate a mission, but I can help you."

"What's number two?" Kadie asked, still not sure if joining the Kindred was what Tuck had in mind for her or if it was something she definitely wanted. "The chances are you're going to get yourself dead or you'll lose someone close to you."

Tuck wouldn't have told anyone where she was, whatever the status of their relationship, he wouldn't put her in danger. This had to be Zara. "You're still here."

"I am," she said with a nod. Amusement wrapped her expression. "But I wasn't so long ago. I lost my life for the Kindred. It's a good thing we have a doctor on the team who pulled me back."

"You… you died?"

"That's not a big deal," the woman said, rising to her feet and waving a dismissive hand. "What is a big deal is that you're here, that you got this far. That's impressive."

"Tuck doesn't think so," Kadie said, thinking of their last conversation. "He's pissed that I got myself mixed up with Sikorski."

"He is and he left me here to talk some sense into you."

Yet, she'd just spoken about Kadie joining the Kindred. "Is that what you're doing?"

"I want you to know what you're getting into. It's not an easy life and sometimes we have to watch our men take risks that endanger their lives. All we can do is watch them go. Eventually, you'll have to walk into danger too and Swift's not going to want you to do it. He's going to do everything in his power to talk you out of it and tie you up at home."

"Swift?"

"It's how you should refer to him when you're off base. Just as I have to refer to Brodie, my man, as Raven. We only use aliases off-base."

Yes, she'd heard Tuck use the names, but it still felt

odd for her to think of him by another name. "Where is he?"

"They're doing a supply run, they'll be back soon."

Sitting up, Kadie saw that the light was fading beyond the partially closed curtains. She'd slept longer than she'd intended to. The stress of clipped sleep and ominous orders hadn't allowed her to get a full night since she'd joined Sikorski. Before that, she'd been so concerned with finding Tuck that sleep hadn't been a priority.

"You're Swallow, right?"

Zara nodded and left her seat to go over to the couch that was still covered up. "That's right."

"You're in love with Raven."

"Sure am," she said, sliding a hand under the cover to pull something out that Kadie didn't see.

Strength and confidence bled from Zara, but she didn't seem superhuman. Raven was trained to kill, and yet the woman he took to bed every night wasn't hard and didn't come across as evil. There was so much that Kadie didn't understand.

In the duration of her sleep, Tuck would have given the others a report on what happened at Sikorski's. Mortified by the idea that she'd been drooling into her pillow while the Kindred Circle had an intimate debrief, Kadie wasn't confident she'd made a great first impression.

Zara might have been left here to look after her and talk her out of doing anything stupid, but Kadie was glad of the opportunity to talk to the woman alone because the chances were, she was the only one who might understand.

"I have to go back," she said.

Only half-listening, Zara was doing something with whatever she'd retrieved from beneath the couch cover. "Swift and I will handle it," Zara said, keeping her back to Kadie.

It wasn't going to be that simple. Tuck knew what Howie looked like, at least they had met once, she didn't know if Tuck was paying attention enough to recognize the boy if he saw him again. But he wouldn't know the layout of the house like she'd been learning since she figured she and Howie might have to make a dash for freedom.

"No, I can't let you do that. I have a friend. A man in there who I can't abandon."

Twisting around in her crouch, Zara laid a level gaze on her. "You have an asset on the inside?" Kadie nodded. "Did you tell Swift?" She shook her head. Zara's chin fell. "Shit," she whispered, and that was when a knock on the door brought her onto her feet.

Zara went to the door and pressed a code into a panel mounted beside the frame that Kadie hadn't noticed before. She unhooked the wire attached to it and touched something on the underside of the doorknob before whirling around to look at her again.

"Before I open the door I should tell you, Raven's in a bad mood," Zara said, pointing at her then turning her hand in a short calming sweep. "But it's nothing to do with you. It's to do with me and a joke I laughed at. It's nothing." Her nervous smile didn't reassure Kadie. "The Kindred guys can all be scary… well, except Wren. But the others, yeah, they have their harsher edge. But you're Swift's girl so, you know, you should be fine."

The knock came again and Zara spun to yank open the door. "Quit your yapping," the first guy who came in said as he shoved Zara aside and stormed into the room.

Kadie held her breath. Large and scowling, she was terrified to make eye contact and yet couldn't tear her gaze away from the fearsome scowl plastered on his face.

"How you doing?" Tuck was next in and she was the only thing in his sights, he came right over and sat beside her. "Swallow look after you?"

For the five minutes she'd been awake, yeah, Swallow was great. Kadie nodded, letting her eyes flick to the first man who'd entered. She was quickly distracted when another came in. This guy had blue eyes so bright they chilled her from across the room. He wasn't frowning as the first man had been, but the bump in his nose and the scar on his neck indicated he'd been messed with in a serious way and had lived to tell the tale.

Zara closed the door and twisted her arm around the latest entrant's arm. "This here is Griffin Caine. He owes me his life."

"Yeah, yeah," he said, shoving her away and stomping to the corner where he propped a foot on the wall and pulled a pack of cigarettes from his pocket.

No alias for that guy and he didn't look happy to be here, but none of them did. Zara was the only one whose expression was relaxed. At least it was until it landed on her. They hadn't finished talking about her revelation that Howie was trapped with Sikorski.

"That's Raven," Tuck said, tipping his chin toward the first man who'd come in.

Raven shed his coat and went on his way to the couch. After hunkering down, he pulled up the sheet, and she squeaked when she registered the weapons laid out. The sheet on the couch had struck her when she'd first seen it, but she could never have guessed what it hid.

The guy didn't even turn around, but something else was on his mind because he reached over to where Zara had been crouched before the knock and picked something up. Only when he held it out to Zara did Kadie see it was a gun.

"What do you need this for?" he asked his girlfriend. "What have I told you about shooting people?"

Did Zara have a penchant for murder too? She seemed so normal. Kadie couldn't envision her being trigger-happy. Zara tiptoed over to him and snatched the gun away. "It's mine."

"Actually it's mine," he said, and Kadie relaxed when she saw his form loosen now that it was in proximity to Zara's. "It's Kindred property just like you, baby."

"You gave it to me as a gift." Zara hugged the weapon to her chest.

"For protection," Raven said, pushing up to full height and towering over the woman he'd just been beneath. "That's obsolete. You don't need to carry a gun. I am your weapon."

"*You* don't need a weapon to kill someone," Zara sneered at her partner.

He opened his arms. "Neither do you. I'm right here."

"You weren't a minute ago."

"Did someone threaten you?" Raven asked, glancing at her for the first time, compelling Kadie to snatch for Tuck's arm.

Instead of reassuring her, Tuck laughed. "He didn't mean you. If someone threatened Zara then they threatened you. You can trust Rave. He's a good guy."

Her wide eyes weren't as sure. Tuck toed off his boots and kissed her, although his mouth wasn't a sufficient distraction for her to blink her eyes away from Raven, who'd just seized the back of Zara's neck to haul her against him. They were a couple with a lot of passion sparking between them and volatile tempers, she could read that those fueled their dispositions.

"We have a variable that we haven't factored in," Zara said, glimpsing all the men. "Swift, your girl has an asset on the inside."

Her mouth fell open. No finesse. No breaking the news gently. There it was thrust out there into the open in front of these lethal strangers. Tuck whipped around to her. "What? Who?"

On the way over here she'd chastised Tuck for making decisions for Zara without consultation. For a while, Kadie thought he was really going to hand his colleague over to Sikorski in order to obtain what he wanted. What she saw now was that this group was open with each other to the point of blunt. Zara had information therefore she was obliged to share it without delay.

"Howie," she said, choosing to look at Tuck because she couldn't deal with everyone all at once. "He followed me. I went to Sikorski looking for you. I got his name from your computer, well, Howie did."

Tuck stood, horror and disappointment tensed his shoulders. "You're with that fucker for me?"

"I wasn't with him for you. I intended to talk to him and walk away. Howie got involved. I didn't ask him to, he just showed up. But when he was stupid enough to tell Sikorski what he could do…"

"What can he do?" Zara asked, coming up behind

Tuck.

"He's a software engineer," Kadie said. "Not up to par with… Swift." She forced herself to use his alias because if she had any plans to hang around, she'd have to get used to it. "But Sikorski's been using him for low-level stuff. Howie's a good kid. He wouldn't do anything wrong if he wasn't scared. I can't just leave him in there."

"No, you can't," Zara said, squeezing Tuck's arm then turning, presumably to seek out Raven.

Waiting for a reaction from Tuck seemed to take an age, yet, when it did come, she was relieved. "If you want to get this Howie kid out, then we get him out." Kadie hadn't expected Tuck to leave the kid there. Considering that Howie knew Tuck's real name, it wouldn't make sense to abandon him.

"Thank you," she said. "I should've told you."

"Yeah, you should've," he said, and from the brief scowl she read that he wasn't over the deception just yet. "You should never have gone near Sikorski. He'd never have led you to me."

But she couldn't agree. Clutching him closer, she pulled herself out from under the covers. "But he did. Whatever we have to do, it will be worth it because we're together again."

"Say that to me again when we're all splitting town alive."

Losing him, losing any of these people, would be a high price. Zara told her to prepare herself for it, but Kadie wasn't sure how to go about that. If Tuck was hurt, she'd be alone with these strangers and it would be her fault.

Howie made a mistake in following her to the meeting with Sikorski, but she couldn't fault his intentions. He'd thought he was doing the right thing by watching her back. Maybe if he'd had some of Tuck's experiences he'd have known to hang back and observe from a distance. One good intentioned mistake shouldn't sentence a man to death.

Although she didn't enjoy disappointing Tuck, she'd rather do that than forget about Howie just to win her boyfriend's good favor. "You don't have to endanger your

people," she said, because she had to give him an out. "I can—
"

"What? What was your plan? Wait until you got him alone then make a run for it?"

Effectively, yes, she had considered distractions and how they might get some time to themselves that would give them a window for slipping out. But she couldn't do either until she got eyes on Howie and the chance to talk to him alone, which she hadn't since the night they'd arrived at Sikorski's mansion.

"I couldn't just leave him there," she muttered.

Maybe she wasn't the world's best strategist, and she knew nothing about weapons or killing, but she'd been brought up in rough neighborhoods around delinquent kids, so she wasn't starry eyed.

Tuck slipped a hand up to her face, his stroking reassured her, lifting her mood a fraction. "I told you not to get attached to him. Pets can cause a lot of mess."

It didn't seem like an appropriate time to tease, but maybe it was gallows humor. Making light of a bad situation no doubt made it easier for these cynical veterans to push through the mission.

For years they'd been doing this. Tuck had known these people from before he'd known her. Eager, almost to the point of desperation, she wanted to get to know them all and to find out if their experiences with Tuck complemented hers. He couldn't be that different around them personality-wise. Yet, the tasks he was required to complete in the disparate extremes of his two lives were so contradictory that he quite possibly had to compartmentalize his qualities.

The man who made love to her, cooked dinner with her, took her to the movies, he had no place in this weary world where he had to be detached and battle-hardened. If what Swallow said about losing people was true, Kadie couldn't imagine what Tuck had gone through, and alone no less. He didn't ever come home to her to say that he'd had a hard day at the office, let alone to confess the loss of a trusted colleague.

Finding out about the loss of the chief had shocked

her. Witnessing these people together, their efficiency, their bonds, Kadie figured what she knew so far was just the tip of the iceberg.

TWENTY-ONE

"SWIFT, I WANT the board meeting minutes," Zara declared, laying her hands on the table on either side of the laptop she'd been using for a couple of hours.

Tuck hooked a leg around his chair and leaned over to snatch the computer so he could slide it down beside the one he was using. "You know that you don't work there anymore, right?" he asked, without hesitating to accommodate her request. "Your obsession is unhealthy."

Kadie had been watching them all interact and it was fascinating. Spending the night with the group was a daunting concept, until she experienced it. For the most part, they worked quietly, their focus was so intent that Kadie craved a task of her own.

When they did talk, they often joked or jibed, especially Zara. Raven wasn't much of a jokester but his wit was dry, and although it took her longer to get the joke when he delivered it, Kadie was beginning to see Raven wasn't as scary as she'd thought.

Tuck tapped away on Zara's laptop as Zara drummed her fingernails on the table. "It's my obsession that keeps the Kindred interesting."

"Which is her way of saying, they get into shit because

she can't keep her beak out," Caine explained.

Kadie had noticed him watching her. He didn't say much. Wasn't as involved as the others. She wasn't sure why he didn't have a codename or why he was here. But he liked to watch. For hours. Sometimes he did nothing but look at everyone else doing something. He watched Tuck work. Watched her as she went through the clothes Zara had offered her. His favorite thing to watch was Zara and Raven together, but Kadie couldn't judge him for that, she was sort of mesmerized by the couple too.

Zara leaned back in her chair to look past Tuck's back to Caine who was slouched on the couch with his legs stretched out in front of him. Raven had moved all the weapons and was cleaning them on the table opposite where Zara and Tuck were working on their computers.

"You do know all I have to do is give Rave the nod and he'll rip out your tongue for me," Zara retorted.

"He'll do more than that," Raven muttered.

Caine didn't react, and it was odd that Zara delivered such a threat with a broad smile on her face. If Kadie was going to get to know these people, she had to start somewhere. "Why does he owe you his life?" she asked.

No one had expected her to say anything, maybe they'd forgotten she was there, because everyone in the room spared her a glance. Tuck smiled and went back to his typing. "I warned him about a concealed weapon an enemy was carrying," Zara said. "Smart guy turned it around on the fucker."

"What a change of tune," Tuck said, pausing. "You liked Kahlil."

"Not as much as she liked me," Caine said, and winked at Zara.

Zara laughed, but Raven's head rose. His back was to her so she couldn't read his expression, but she could gather he wasn't smiling. "You move on her one more time and I won't wait for a nod," Raven snarled.

"I've been telling you to make something of it for three months," Caine said, crossing his ankles and stretching his hands to the back of his head. "You're the only guy in the room who's stolen another guy's girl."

Oh, that was interesting, confounding, but interesting. "You and Zara used to…?"

Tuck shook his head fast. "Not Zara, previous girlfriend."

"She's dead now," Zara said, stretching over the table to pick up a piece of the weapon Raven had just dismantled. She only had it for a second before Raven took the piece from her and in profile, Kadie saw him growl at his girlfriend, who rolled her eyes.

"We think," Caine said.

"Still holding out hope?" Tuck asked, shunting the computer to Zara who pulled it toward her with glee. Tuck twisted to look at Caine. "If she's alive, she's pissed."

"If she's alive and I find her, she won't stay that way for long," Caine snarled.

Venom inspired hatred, yet no one else blinked an eye. Kadie was confused. If Caine had once loved the woman, and Raven had seduced her away, it was a wonder that Caine didn't want to kill Raven when it was clear he held a grudge against the female.

"You would kill the woman for cheating on you but not the man who tempted her?" Kadie asked.

Tuck turned, showing her concern. "I wouldn't push on that particular button, Toots."

Right. Probably best not to incite a riot in the room that was supposed to be a safe house. "Right, sorry," she said. "None of my business."

"If you're Kindred it's all your business," Zara said, peering closer at her computer, still reading as she contributed. "These guys like to drip feed information. I'll clue you in… Do you drink wine?"

"Uh, yeah."

"You're not getting drunk, Swallow," Raven said, stern like a boss rather than a boyfriend. "When you drink too much, you flirt, and I end up shooting people."

"You shoot people anyway, no matter how much alcohol I have in my system," Zara said, glancing at her then at Raven. "One is not related to the other."

"Sutcliffe's kid was."

Zara didn't buy it and folded her hands in front of her keyboard. "Tim was Sutcliffe's nephew, and you didn't shoot him for kissing me, you did it so he couldn't get close and manipulate me into handing over the device because that was going to be your play. Dove should know what she's getting into."

"Dove?" Raven asked, and the others looked at a proud Zara.

"Sure, it fits," Zara said. "Swift said he liked her innocent of this stuff."

"But she's not anymore," Raven said. "She's here."

Zara shrugged. "You don't fuck random women for information anymore, but we still call you Raven."

"That's more to do with the angel of death stuff now," Tuck said, lifting one shoulder. "I'd agree that the name fits, 'cept we don't know if she's hanging around with the Kindred yet. She has a cousin she can go back to, a safe life."

A safe life with Dempsey, was that Tuck's plan? Shipping her back to the business she'd abandoned would return them to their previous state. Except now that she'd been a part of it, she wasn't sure that she wanted to go back.

Curiosity about these strangers was growing. But she hadn't stopped to take much time to think about what they knew of her. If Tuck had told Zara that she was innocent of this stuff, that suggested she'd come up in conversation.

Zara's interactions with the men were certainly the most intriguing. She knew how to work them all and could get each of them to give in to her. Kadie had seen it throughout the night she'd spent with the team. From Caine handing her the remote and Raven giving her the last slice of pizza, Zara knew how to get what she wanted from them. Tuck obviously cared for her too, and there was something deep between the pair that Kadie couldn't decipher yet.

That exact observation was showcased when Zara shuffled her chair over and grabbed Tuck's arm, yanking him so that he leaned toward her. Kadie read his expression as Zara whispered in his ear, her plump lips just half an inch from the ear of the man Kadie loved. Tuck went from loose, to a frown, then a brow moved, and he exhaled when Zara sat back, still clutching his arm, waiting with an expectant expression.

"You actually need me to come with you?" Tuck asked her, and Zara just bobbed her brows. "Okay." He got up, grabbed keys from the middle of the table, and looked at her. "I'll be back soon. Do what Raven tells you. Everything Raven tells you."

Everything. That was unnerving. Getting over her initial intimidation was taking time, but she didn't want to beg Tuck to stay. Staying with Sikorski had taught her the value of exuding confidence, even when anxiety was all that was holding her together.

"He's low maintenance," Zara said, following Tuck to the door. "He won't tell you to do anything unless it involves revealing your most intimate secrets and betraying everything you've held dear in your life."

Tuck unhooked the alarm system before glancing back and giving Zara a shove. "She's kidding, Toots, just sit tight."

They departed and the sound of a motorcycle engine roared outside. Caine was the one who got up to reset the alarm, but Raven got there first. "Sit your ass down," Raven said, and the men faced off for a few tense seconds that made Kadie wonder if Tuck had left her alone with the most dangerous elements of the current scenario.

"He's insecure," Caine said, driving his shoulder into Raven's in a hostile shove as he passed to come in her direction. Raven set the alarm, and she stayed utterly still as Caine came over to sit on the bed beside her extended legs. "He knows I've got the right to even the score, making Swallow fair game."

"In your dreams," Raven said, returning to the table to continue his cleaning.

When the room had been full, Kadie had been okay with Raven not facing her, it gave her the chance to examine his movements without him catching her at it or observing hers. With Caine this close, she'd prefer it if Raven had her in his eye line. Intimidated or not, Tuck trusted Raven, he called him his best friend. Zara loved him. If anyone in this room was going to protect her, it was him.

"Raven's in charge here, isn't he?" she asked out of curiosity, but Caine bristled. "If you hate him so much, why are you here?"

"Because he has nowhere else to go," Raven declared, without bothering to offer more than words. "The fucking loser dedicated himself to a woman and a job that got him this close to dead. He's Zara's puppy. Her pet project."

"I'm no one's project," Caine said.

Raven shook his head and Kadie thought she heard a brief laugh. "Then why the fuck are you here, Caine? Still wanna suck my cock, is that it? 'Cause sorry to tell you, that position's been filled. It ain't ever gonna happen."

This wasn't good. Tension ratcheted higher and Caine surged to his feet. Raven was up and halfway over to them before Kadie saw him move. She didn't know who hit first, all she remembered was the sound of the table splintering when the men crashed together on top of it. For protection, she scrambled backwards off the bed, moving it enough to allow her to fit between it and the wall.

One man hit the other after they pounced back to their feet. One lunged left, the other grabbed fabric that ripped, and they both stumbled. Everything that had been on the table was scattered, being stomped and kicked without consideration as they pummeled each other.

The two of them fell to the floor. Raven landed on top of Caine, he punched again and again. Caine fumbled for a knife and swiped it around, catching Raven across the shoulder, and he seized the opportunity to roll Raven to his back.

The table was flat on the floor, the legs broken, another casualty of this brawl. With every kick and thrust of the men, the equipment was spread further and damaged more. Caine punched and blood spurted across the broken laptop nearest Raven's face.

With a twist of his legs and superior strength, Raven got Caine off him. Before one could gain an advantage, Raven whipped a weapon from somewhere behind him and swung it around to land the barrel between Caine's brows.

Their huffs and pants were as fueled by anger as they were by exertion. Kadie held her breath, clutching the edge of the mattress to just peek over it. "Do it," Caine said, wiping a hand over his bloody mouth. "Years you've been waiting to pull that trigger. Do it."

Raven cocked the gun and she believed he was going to shoot. The men were in profile to her, showcasing the rage on Raven's face. But Caine was loose, like he couldn't care less how this moment ended.

"Worried about what your woman will say?" Caine asked, shifting to his knees and pushing closer. "Fuck her. Pull the fucking trigger, chickenshit. Not even you can miss this shot."

"I could take you out from three blocks away," Brodie growled.

Caine sneered. "Bullshit. My aim drunk is better than your aim sober."

"You're full of shit."

"Prove it. Pull the fucking trigger."

Raven's lips narrowed, he squeezed them tight and a growl of frustration sounded but stayed lodged in his mouth.

"You owe me," Caine said, a perverse smile that made her think of evil twisted his lips. "Your girl saved the day 'cause of me."

Raven bowed, shifting the gun to Caine's throat so he could get in his face. "My girl nearly died because you sent her there."

"I gave her the information, not my call what she did with it," Caine said, slumping back to pull his cigarettes from his pocket. The gun was still trained on him, Raven could end his life in a flash, still, Caine didn't muster any attempt to ask for mercy. "You didn't pick up your fucking phone."

There was more to that statement, something deeper behind it. She could tell from the way Raven tensed that Caine wasn't the sole source of his torture. "You're here because you fit right in with scum like Sikorski," Raven snarled. "You're not Kindred."

"Wouldn't want to be," Caine said, tilting his head

after lighting his smoke. "Long as you trust your lady, we don't have a problem."

Zara wouldn't cheat on Raven, so Caine could make all the plays that he liked. Innuendo wasn't going to be enough to tempt Zara away. Caine enjoyed playing with Raven. Kadie didn't understand it. Holding the tiger by the tail was bound to end bad for him. But if what she'd just seen was any indicator, Caine didn't fear death.

Caine took a long, slow draw on his smoke. "Course she'll be less likely to trust you now that you've made such a good impression on your newest member."

Caine's eyes trailed over to her and Raven's followed not too long afterwards. So they did remember that she was here. The three of them stayed quiet. She couldn't claim that she wouldn't tell the other two what had happened because the place was a mess. They were going to find out.

"Are you finished?" Kadie asked the men.

Unhappy as he was about it, Raven released the hammer of his gun and dug it into his waistband then stood up. Bending over, he grabbed Caine and hauled him onto his feet. "We're getting this place cleaned up."

"She's still going to kick your ass," Caine said, holding the cigarette in his lips as he picked up the chair that had skidded away to the couch.

"No more fighting," Kadie said, standing up and creeping around the end of the bed.

Raven's hand went to the back of his head as he observed the mess they'd made. Crouching to pick up the pieces of the weapon he'd been cleaning, he tossed them to the bed she'd been on. "Get rid of the table," Raven said to Caine who began to pick up the broken pieces. "Take the truck."

"Want me to rustle up a new one?" Caine asked, shifting the heavy slabs of the top surface up to lean them on the wall by the door. The tabletop was heavy, but the fold-away legs weren't sturdy at all.

"No," Raven said. "We're gonna be heading out soon." Picking up one broken laptop, he pushed the other with it. "Swift's gonna take this hard."

Drawn in by the whisper of apology in his voice, she went over to kneel beside him. "If you give me a phone I'll call him, break the news gently."

His computers were like his children. To anyone else, they might all look the same, but to Tuck, they each had their own personalities, their own strengths and weaknesses. Only certain ones were allowed to be touched by others, even in their life together she'd learned how he valued them. At least she knew now that one part of his personality was the same no matter where he was or who he was with.

***

CAINE WAS GONE. She hadn't seen him since he'd taken the pieces of table out of the room. When Kadie had called and told Tuck that his computers were gone, he panicked, not for the electronics, but for her. He started spouting instructions about staying with Raven, keeping her head low, doing as she was told. It took a minute to calm him down and explain that no external threat had caused the damage.

The terrifying performance could've ended worse than it did. She could've found herself dealing directly with a deceased Raven victim, not his first maybe, but it would be the first time she'd been involved in disposing of a body.

With the adrenaline dwindling, she was exhilarated. These powerful men could spin on a dime and it would be worth always remembering that. But now she was a part of the team. Those vigilant men had turned their backs on her to beat on each other and in doing that had revealed so much about themselves and their relationship.

She was sitting on the edge of the bed with a shirtless Raven when the door opened to reveal Zara and Tuck. Raven's hand was on his weapon, which lay by his thigh. They hadn't bothered to reset the alarm after Caine left the room, so he was prepared to respond to threats, which Tuck and Zara were not.

Taking gauze from the open first-aid kit, Kadie paused before cutting a strip when Zara marched over with a face full of ire. "What the fuck did you do?" Zara demanded, sparing a brief glance at the shoulder cut Kadie had just cleaned out.

"Sit your ass down, Swallow," Raven said. The patience he'd had while she treated him was gone.

"I told you not to fight with him," Zara said. Kadie gasped when Zara thrust a fingernail into the slash on his shoulder. Raven hissed when she twisted it. "Is that what you want, beau? You want pain? I can give you pain."

Instinct made Kadie snatch Zara's finger to pull it away. Tuck swooped in to get hold of her and drew her back. "She's hurting him," Kadie said, stumbling as he directed her to the opposite bed.

"Let them worry about them, are you okay? I can't believe they got in a fight when you were—"

"It's okay," she said, shifting down the bed away from him. "Yeah, it was unexpected but, hey, they're physical guys who have beef. I've seen plenty of fights."

When she was a kid, fights were a part of her daily life. "They should've kept it together while you were here."

"No," she said, shaking her head and taking his hand when he tried to touch her face.

Zara shoved Raven and he snatched her hips, hauling her down into his lap where, despite her slapping protests, he kissed Zara hard.

"No?" Tuck asked, but Kadie was still distracted by the other couple in the room.

"I wasn't in any danger," Kadie said, watching Zara loosen and sink her hands into her lover's hair to relish their kiss. "They had to get it out." At least it wasn't as awkward in the room after the guys had vented some of their pent-up friction.

"What's wrong with you?" he asked when he tried to sidle closer and she slid away again. "You won't sit still. You won't look at me. Are you pissed I left you? I won't do it again if—"

"I don't want to go back to Dempsey," she said, forcing herself to look at him.

Since helping Raven put the room back together and carrying table legs out with Caine, she had decided. This was where she wanted to be: dealing with the mess and the missions of the Kindred. Their bond was undeniable, they were closer to Tuck than she was and she couldn't love him all the way, not until he proved he trusted her enough to take her into battle with him.

Grasping his wrist when he tried to soothe her cheek, she straightened, taking his hands to her lap. "We can talk about that—"

"I don't want to talk about it. I'm telling you. I've made my decision. I'm not going anywhere. You want to send me back to him because you think that it will be safer. I don't want to be apart from you anymore. I don't want you keeping me separate, or innocent of this."

He squirmed. "Zara should never have said—"

"I like that you talked about me. It would've been better if you'd talked to me about them. But you didn't. Telling them who I was, it made me real in this part of your life, even if I didn't know anything about it."

"I didn't say anything bad," he said and when he smiled, she let him have his hands back so he could grasp her face.

When he leaned in, she tried to lean back, but found herself pressed into the headboard, thus unable to avoid his kiss. Tuck didn't restrain himself. Pulling her body to his, he opened her lips with his tongue and the weight of it tested and coerced hers. She couldn't stay rigid while his mouth tormented her hormones, so she melted against him. The immediate impulse of her body to yield to his was unstoppable.

One of his arms insinuated itself under her thighs and he brought them up onto his lap. The bulge at his groin made her pull back. Raven and Zara were in the room, so it seemed sort of wrong that Tuck should be having this reaction to her when there was an audience.

"They don't care," he said, reading her mind and threading his fingers through her hair to join their mouths again.

She couldn't deny that when she twisted to observe that couple enjoying a tug of war kiss that included Raven's hands under Zara's skirt. The door opened again and Caine came in, coming to a stop, he folded his arms. Both couples parted to look at his scowl but no one said a word. He spun around and walked straight back out, closing the door behind him.

Kadie made eye contact with Zara. "Do you think he's coming back?" Kadie asked.

Zara shrugged. "Maybe. Maybe not."

"No one cares," Raven grumbled, earning himself another shove from Zara. Seizing her in his arms, he squeezed her tight. "You gonna tell me you care about him? The guy held you at gunpoint. He threatened you. Cornered you in an alley. Why are you so hell-bent on me giving him a break?"

"Because he was used," Zara said, not shrinking despite her lover's annoyance. "Because that woman tormented him, made him believe in something that wasn't true. She humiliated him for her own ends." Opening her hands on his shoulders, she curled her nails into him. "Besides, I can understand how someone can be obsessed with you. I'm addicted. I'd follow your every move across the world, watch every breath you took. Only difference is, I keep you to myself, Caine shared you." She scrunched her face and then licked his lip. "I don't do that."

Raven's hands splayed flat on her back. "You can suck my cock any day of the week."

Kadie got what he meant. He'd told Caine that he couldn't have that privilege, Zara could. Zara was perplexed but went with it. "Thank you, beau," she said. "It's an honor."

Tuck let his linked hands rest on her hip. "You need to tell us everything about Howie, Toots. Everything you know about where he is and what he's doing for Sikorski. Pinpointing his location before we go in is the only way we can guarantee to get him out. But he has to be there."

And in Sikorski's place, there was always the chance of last minute jobs or trips. She'd be honest about that and about everything else she'd learned while she was living there. Being one of the girls, she could move more freely about the place than these strangers could. Kadie would insist on going back with him and with Zara. After they liberated Howie, she'd do whatever she could to help the Kindred complete their plan, if they'd trust her with it.

TWENTY-TWO

"SOMEBODY'S SCREWING AROUND."

Phoning Sikorski was better than going back to that house, and it was nice to hear the guy shocked. "Who…? Who is this?" Sikorski stuttered over the line of his own personal cellphone.

The choice had been made for him to leave the motel to make the call. In the unlikely event that Sikorski could trace the origin, they didn't want to lead him back to the place Kindred had set up base. They could move, but this was easier.

So he was in the parking lot of the bar he'd met Sikorski in, Hell's Waiting Room, without any intention of going inside. Far as he was concerned, this was as close as he'd ever like to get again to the room where he'd seen Kadie come so close to being violated.

"Swift," he answered, because this would screw with the guy's head enough and playing games wasn't the point of making this connection. "And you've been playing dirty."

Quickly getting himself composed, Sikorski's tone went deep. "I don't know what you mean."

"Someone's been trying to hack my system, and since you're the only one I'm doing business with at the minute…"

"What? You think it was me?"

Tuck didn't have a static system as such, not anymore. Sikorski didn't know that. He also didn't know that despite Tuck's various redundancies, none of his digital proximity shields had fired. No one had been trying to enter his system. Plenty of fools had tried in the past, but no one had ever succeeded.

After learning how Kadie and Howie had found him though, he'd have to be more careful about cleaning up after himself. What was left on the machine in the basements back home couldn't have been more than an echo, shades of light and dark, fragments caught in the filter on their way to the trash like algae imprinting on glass.

"What is it you want to know, Sikorski, do us both a favor and stop dicking me around."

Kadie wouldn't leave his mind. Witnessing the fight between Raven and Caine should have scared her, instead it reinforced her certainty that she wanted to be a part of his Kindred life. Tuck couldn't figure out how he felt about that. Would it be nice to have her around all the time? To have her there to lie with every night? Sure, it would. But was it worth the risk?

Leaving her was supposed to insulate her. Keeping her safe away from harm felt like the right thing. As much as he loved Zara, seeing her in danger didn't do the same thing to him as seeing Kadie in it. But he had wondered in the past, how Raven did it, how he watched the woman he loved putting herself in perilous situations without wanting to step in and barricade her from harm.

"Whatever you think you know, you don't," Sikorski said over the line, and he had every right to sound confident because Tuck was making a false accusation. What Sikorski couldn't know was that the claim was meant to achieve something other than conflict in their association.

"Then one of your people is working alone," Swift said. "I bet a bunch of guys know I was there. They know your guy Warta didn't come home, your driver too, did they have friends in your place? 'Cause if one of your men is coming for me—"

"My people don't work on initiative," Sikorski said,

blustering into offense. "No one would act without my permission."

Turning up the heat, Tuck gave Sikorski a second to stew then added some menace to his voice. "I don't trust you, mafia, this deal is starting to stink… There must be someone on your payroll smart enough to think they might be capable of this."

Tuck knew for a fact that there was. It wasn't easy and had taken him most of the rest of the day, but he'd found a digital signature they were sure was Howie's. Kadie was worried for the kid's health. He was supposed to meet her in the bar on the night Tuck had first run into her and hadn't made the meet. If he'd been discovered sneaking out, it was possible he'd been executed for his insubordination.

Zara had been amazing with Kadie. She'd talked about other possibilities with her, helping to lessen Kadie's concern. Saying that he might just have missed his chance, been too scared to take the risk, or been cut off before he had the chance to walk out, were all plausible alternatives to the boy getting a bullet to the brain.

Sikorski didn't have many lines into the house, he had his private cellphone, and there was a hard line into the mansion, which was rarely used, making Tuck believe few people knew about it or had access to it. But Howie did, he had to if Sikorski wanted him to commit criminal acts for him.

Busting Howie out was what Kadie wanted to do, and Tuck would follow through as he promised. But they would have to quiz the boy on what he'd done for Sikorski. As scared as he might have been by the threat aimed at him, it would tell the Kindred a lot about Howie's integrity to learn what he had been willing to do to stay alive.

Tuck was capable of just about anything when he had access to a computer and an internet connection. But there were some things he just wouldn't do and would elect to eat a bullet before betraying kin and country.

"No one as smart as you in this regard," Sikorski sneered, it was amazing just how quickly the bullshit fell away. Now that Sikorski knew Tuck had no interest in joining his ranks, all the simpering and pandering was gone.

"But there is someone," Tuck said, because he knew there was and took the chance to act like he'd heard a concession in Sikorski's words. "Some punk who thinks he can get into my shit? I want to meet him." Sikorski said nothing. "Whoever your whizz is, I want to see him at our meeting."

"Why would you be—"

"Professional curiosity," Tuck said, and it worked perfectly because he'd said it before so Sikorski already thought of him as the curious type. "I want to look him in the face and laugh at how pathetic he is."

"If I do that, I expect you to bring the girl to the meet," Sikorski said. "The one you took from me, I want her there."

Fighting with Kadie about her presence at the meet was a battle he expected, Sikorski's request was not. "Why?" Tuck asked. "Why do you want her there?"

"I want her to see what men like us do to those who betray them," Sikorski said. "I want her to see the horror you are complicit in."

Because he wanted to put a wedge between the couple or just because he enjoyed seeing women shocked? Sikorski couldn't know that Kadie and Tuck were connected beyond meeting in the bar. This was another of Sikorski's games, his famed power plays, he wanted Kadie there because it would piss Tuck off and give Sikorski an audience for whatever he planned to do with Zara.

"I don't—"

"It's not too much to ask. More witnesses means more protection for me."

Ah, so the Russian thought Tuck would spare his life if the woman he was sleeping with was there to watch them interact. Sikorski shouldn't be so sure of that. Though Tuck would likely not be the one holding the gun.

"Okay, you bring the money and your weekend gamer, and I'll bring Saffy."

This would be a test. If he could handle Kadie standing there during this confrontation then maybe he could see her integrating into his Kindred life. If not, their relationship would slide back into jeopardy because he'd never be able to make her see that leaving her with Dempsey was his way of protecting her not segregating her, and it didn't mean he loved her less, it proved he loved her more.

"When?"

"Two days," Tuck said. "I'll forward you the coordinates. You come with your buddy and only him."

That would never happen. Sikorski didn't go anywhere without at least a couple of human shields. Tuck couldn't argue. He would show up with the women, they would be the only visible people at the meeting, but they wouldn't be alone.

"You bring Saffy and Bandini, and I want her alive."

"No problem."

Tuck hung up the phone and pulled out the battery. They'd yet to decide if he'd stroll up with Zara at his side or if they were going to make a show of restraining her like she was there against her will. Two days would give them time to make plans and set up. Kadie wasn't wild about the delay. She was worried about her friend. But they'd only get one shot at this and they had to do it right.

***

THE OTHERS COMMENTED on how quickly two days went by. For Kadie, the minutes dragged, but she didn't complain, at least not in public. On the rare occasions Tuck took her out for food or they got a minute alone, she expressed her concern for Howie because she didn't want him to think she'd abandoned him and they had no idea what he was going through.

Tuck kept his cool, they all did, so Kadie did her best to make out that she was handling everything without concern. Sometimes she got close to freaking out. Having Tuck nearby always helped to soothe her.

There were times when she looked at him that she wanted to smack him in the head. They'd come so close to being apart forever. He'd given up on them, chosen the Kindred and left her in the dust. It didn't matter how many times he told her that he did it to protect her, she still got irritated by his arrogance. But it was nothing knew, so it was on her. When they'd met, he'd had all the confidence in the world and that hadn't changed in the duration of their relationship.

Getting through the next few hours was going to hinge on them being able to trust each other. Kadie hadn't been initiated into the Kindred, though they treated her like an honorary member. Since telling Tuck that she wasn't going anywhere, they hadn't talked about their long-term plans. Knowing that he had to keep his head in the mission, she elected not to push the issue. Maybe when all of this was done and they had a better idea of how working together would play out, they could decide about their future.

As it stood for her, she couldn't see her future without him in it. But if today went wrong, if one of them was hurt, or they lost Howie, she wasn't sure what impact that would have on her or on the Kindred. More was at stake today than their lives.

Tuck was driving and she sat in the back with Zara. Every detail had been accounted for from what would be said, or not in her case, where they would stand, even their positions sitting in the truck had been thought about and orchestrated. The group thought not only of safety, but of perception and psychology as well.

"They've been doing this a long time," Zara said, making Kadie wonder if her worry showed on her face. "You have nothing to worry about."

Involving others in her dilemma did alleviate some of the burden on her. But it was amazing how it altered her feelings about the situation. When she'd left home to seek out Tuck she'd been willing to do anything to find him and felt little concern for her safety because she only had to worry about risking herself. When Howie got involved that changed and the guilt compelled her to be more careful because she wasn't only risking her own life anymore, she was risking his as well.

Not long before Tuck showed up in her life again, she'd concluded that she couldn't choreograph a situation where she and Howie would be guaranteed a clean escape. It was impossible to ensure he'd be a hundred percent safe if they made an attempt to flee and that made her hesitant to try it.

Somehow—maybe because like Zara said, they'd been doing this a long time—Brodie and Tuck managed to forget that the players were real live people who had families and loved ones. Switching off their feelings for the women involved probably helped them to make sound decisions. Kadie would need more practice.

Watching Tuck drive today reminded her of the limo trip. Not because this was stressful or they were in any danger, but because she remembered the feeling of dread that night. During the course of the accident, she hadn't known that it wasn't an accident at all. For those terrifying seconds before the car stopped, she had to come to terms with the fact that Tuck might lose his life saving hers.

She felt the same way today. Dusk was the chosen time for the meet, just when they were starting to lose the light of the day. Choosing this time made her uneasy, but Tuck explained that every choice they made was considered before being finalized. Apparently, dusk was the time to meet when exchanging goods for people. Zara might be in on the plan, but Kadie was concerned for the woman seated beside her. If Sikorski got his hands on her, got her back to his mansion, he wouldn't show mercy. It didn't matter that Brodie and Tuck would rip the place apart to get her back, Zara may have to endure horrors before they got there.

Rounding the ridge that shielded the open ground they were meeting on, the first thing she saw was a long, black limo. Sikorski went everywhere in those luxury cars. Learning that they weren't suited for off-roading, and were easy targets, hadn't put him off using them. It was probably bullheadedness that made him continue to drive in such impractical vehicles.

"They're already here," Kadie said, though she hadn't meant to say it aloud.

"So are we," Zara muttered. A new determination settled over her expression; her gaze fixed on the view out the windshield between the two front headrests. "Are you with me, beau?"

"I'm with you, baby." Raven's low voice came through the earpiece Kadie had been given to wear.

Raven had left the motel before the rest of them. Kadie hadn't been expressly told where he was going, but she didn't need it spelled out. Raven was the assassin, the sniper of the group. With their limited numbers, they had to utilize everyone's skills. Raven wasn't expected at the meet, but that didn't mean he wouldn't be there.

His position would be lofty, she was sure of that, and it was probable that he'd have his weapon trained on the scene. Kadie wasn't sure how she felt about that, about being at the end of a scope, in someone's crosshairs. Swift trusted Raven. Swallow loved him. Dove was still learning the ropes and standing in target range would take some time to get accustomed to. As would listening to a disembodied voice in her ear, especially one that wasn't talking to her.

It was unsettling how his husky tone sounded so intimate, as it should because he was responding to Zara. Yet the words slid through the canal of Kadie's ear in a series of sensual vibrations direct to her mind, which couldn't match the voice to any source of arousal. Tuck's voice could turn her on, Raven's just made her shiver.

Sikorski didn't get out of the car. In fact, they saw no one and when Tuck pulled up near the front of the limo, blocking it in, they all stayed in the truck.

"We wait?" Zara seemed to be asking either Tuck or Brodie.

"Let him sweat a minute," Tuck said.

"Something doesn't feel right about this," Zara said. "I don't think I like it."

Swift twisted around to scrutinize his colleague. Raven's voice came to her ear. "Want me to pull out?" he asked.

Zara smiled. "There's something you've never said to me before," she said, and Tuck almost laughed. "No, I just don't think we should give him time for his monologue. He thinks he's smarter. He thinks he's better. He wants to rule the world. We get it, we've heard it before. Can we just get the boy, the information, and split?"

"Whatever you want, Swallow," Raven said, and Tuck nodded.

"Want to get this over with?" Tuck asked.

Zara thought for a second, catching her tongue between her teeth. They weren't too far from Sikorski's place, he could have reinforcements on the boundary somewhere, ready to storm in. Except if everything went as Sikorski thought it was supposed to, he should be taking Zara back to his place, and shouldn't need an army.

Discovering that Zara was uneasy made Kadie edgy. Raven and Swift had been doing this a long time, sure, but Zara wasn't far off being a veteran herself. If she'd been part of the group before Kadie and Tuck split up, that meant she'd been doing this for around a year. Swallow's instincts were more honed than she probably realized.

"Yeah," Zara said, and bent to retrieve a glass soda bottle from the backpack at her feet.

"What's that for?" Kadie asked when Zara twisted off the cap and gulped down some of the liquid.

"Want some?" Zara asked, offering the bottle, but Kadie shook her head.

"No thanks."

There had been plenty of time to eat and drink before they left and while they were in the car. The bottle could be used as a weapon, but it would be a pathetic one and wouldn't last long. The most she'd get out of it was a single hit, maybe Zara assumed that was better than nothing. But for a group who didn't leave any detail to chance, this was one Kadie couldn't figure out.

"It's game time," Zara said, and Tuck shook his head as he turned to get out of the car first.

Again, this had been planned. Zara wasn't going to be trussed up in the trunk, for one thing, they'd loaded a large box into the back before leaving, so there wouldn't be much room, and it might be dangerous to put Zara in there if the item in the box was heavy. Kadie didn't know what it was, only that it was important that they took it with them.

The deal she'd heard Tuck and Sikorski make

included the Game Time device that Tuck had told her was dangerous. Thinking about carrying such a thing to a man as dangerous as Sikorski made her mad and scared at the same time. Under any other circumstances, she'd never let Tuck risk bringing something like that here. But Howie's life was at stake. If that meant giving Sikorski what he wanted in order to get the kid back, then they'd have to deal with the fall out after Howie was safe.

Tuck came to the back of the car and opened it to reach in and haul Zara out. Keeping her locked in his grip, his scowl reminded her of the man she'd seen in the bar, that dangerous man only out for himself.

"Get out," he said to her, not loud enough for anyone except Zara to hear, but he was abrupt just in case.

Kadie shuffled along the backseat and climbed out, staying beside Zara as Tuck pulled her out into the open space. Beyond the limo was a drop, they were on one of the mountain ledges, if they kept on going up then they'd come to Sikorski's place, but that would mean going back out onto the road they'd used to come here. There was only one road in, one road out. Tuck's parking was no mistake. There wasn't much room behind the limo, so backing up without going over the edge would be difficult. Tuck was blocking the front of the car. If they needed to make a quick getaway, he could back up a few feet, swing a wide turn, and get back onto the road faster than the limo could and they'd be first, because the limo couldn't move until they did.

The ridge that rose beside the road was at least thirty feet high and was covered with trees and grass. Part of her wanted to turn around to see if she could decipher where Raven was, but she guessed he knew how to camouflage, and if she looked then Sikorski might too. So she kept her back to the ridge, and watched the limo, waiting for Sikorski to emerge.

Time ticked. Kadie felt every second. The limo didn't move and her pulse began to panic. Could this be a decoy? Were Sikorski and his people waiting somewhere else? But no, there was nowhere to hide on this large, curved ledge, there were some trees on the other side of the road, but they thinned to nothing by the time the road opened onto the plane.

"He's trying to make us sweat," Tuck murmured, and Kadie stole a look at his impatient glare. "We wait thirty more seconds then we get in the car and go."

TWENTY-THREE

OUT OF NOTHING more than her instinct for survival, Kadie wanted to flee. But as soon as she remembered Howie, she wanted to argue with Tuck. Did he want to go because he, too, thought this might be a setup? She doubted that because if he did, they'd be leaving now, not after a set period of time. Meaning the only conclusion left was ego. Tuck wanted Sikorski to know who was in charge. They were still vying for power.

Kadie didn't know why it mattered whose balls were bigger. But Raven made a sound of agreement, so she guessed he was affected by the power play too. Men, sometimes no amount of sense could alter their primitive instincts.

Before the thirty second countdown was up, the front door of the limo opened. The man who got out was one of Sikorski's more skilled security men, not a driver, and another two got out from the front to move in around the back door as the driver opened it.

She expected Sikorski to come out, maybe with companionship in a show of nonchalance like this was no big deal for him to be here and he didn't see Tuck or the women as a threat. These men had made a deal with each other. She'd have assumed that they would be civil because each wanted something from the other. Instead, they acted like enemies, proving how thin the trust was that existed between them.

Sikorski didn't get out first, one security man did, then another. Three men came out of the back of the car when Kadie had never known him to travel with more than one male in the back at a time. If this was a show of strength or intimidation, she doubted it would work. As a female without training, she was concerned about her safety. But knowing what she did about the Kindred, they'd be more likely to take this as a sign of insecurity.

Sikorski was surrounding himself with force, and these men were formidable, but all he was proving was that he had no skills of his own and no way to defend himself. The Kindred were a threat to him and he'd never be able to convince them that he thought otherwise while he was cowering behind a squad of security agents.

Only after the men were in a V formation, did Sikorski get out of the car. He wore a droll expression like he found all of this absurd, yet he was the one who'd just put on a performance. In a face-off, Sikorski said nothing and Kadie wondered how long they would spend standing here, staring at each other.

"Maybe you've got all day, we don't," Tuck called out. "Show us what we want to see. Let's get this over with."

Sikorski was obviously in no hurry because he smiled a slow smile and didn't move in the direction of the car, as he would have to if he planned to show Tuck what he wanted to see. "Why such a hurry?" Sikorski said. "We have plenty to keep us entertained right here. You'll get what's owed to you, Swift."

He said the name with a layer of sarcasm that Kadie didn't like, and it helped her to understand Zara's unease. As much as they weren't supposed to be acquainted, and as such couldn't openly acknowledge each other, Kadie did feel herself move slightly closer to Zara. Though she couldn't identify in that second whether it was because she wanted to protect the woman Sikorski wished to hurt, or because she knew Zara could defend herself and Kadie was worried about her own safety and sought protection.

Tuck was on Zara's other side and before Sikorski had got here, Kadie had reassured herself about where Raven was and what he was doing. But, somehow, he seemed so far away, so she didn't feel particularly protected by the sniper. Maybe that was just her lack of experience because she'd never seen his skills in action. She'd been a party to them by proxy when he'd killed the driver and Warta. If that was truly him who took those shots, then he knew what he was doing. He was capable, he could protect them.

Knowing those things intellectually didn't mean much to her as she stood in this windswept place, staring into the ice-cold eyes of the man she'd feared she'd have to share her bed with. In this position, with Raven on the peak behind them and Sikorski in front, she hoped they weren't blocking Raven's shot, should he need to take one.

"Ms. Bandini," Sikorski drawled.

His satisfaction made her sick. The girls at the mansion had told her what he was capable of and it had disgusted her when she was thinking of him doing them to strangers. But knowing he wanted to hurt the woman standing with her, a woman who Tuck trusted and cared about, who had been a part of his life for a long time, it made her feel protective. She almost wanted to get in front of Zara to shield her, and she was surprised by her own courage.

Kadie could defend herself, she knew how to hold her own, though she did tend to try and avoid trouble because she'd seen how easily it could spiral out of control. In her most recent years, she'd lived quietly, and Tuck was the only drama she knew.

For so long, she'd worried about disappointing Dempsey. Kadie worried about toeing the line and proving she was a good girl for fear that one day, she might be found out as a fraud, that she didn't belong in the slick office, in the beautiful building in the upscale neighborhood that had been provided for her. She didn't belong there. She belonged here, in the dirt, with Tuck. She just hoped that he would see that when this was finished.

"You summoned me," Zara said. "This asshole came, told me you had information for me. So… spill." That was the plan, to feed Sikorski the story that Tuck had tempted Zara here on the promise of valuable information from an old foe.

"Did he?" Sikorski asked, and almost seemed impressed when he flashed a look in Swift's direction. "Information. Yes, I have information for you."

Breaking away from the security men, although he didn't venture far toward Kadie and her group, Sikorski moved forward a step. Maybe he was feeling cocky, felt a bit more confident that he'd managed to get out of the car and stand tall without being taken out. Maybe he was just ignorant and didn't realize who Zara was connected to.

Kadie was a bit fuzzy on who knew what and who didn't, so her instruction for today had been to keep her mouth shut and for now, she was more than happy to go along with that. Sikorski looked at Zara, examined her face, her hair, her clothes, her shoes, and gratification bled to his gaze. Kadie didn't understand it. Apparently, Zara did.

"You're pleased to see me," Zara said. "It's been a long time, Nykiel."

Like they were old friends, Sikorski responded with joviality. "The Grand Hotel. You were so refined, so meek that day. I really believed that you were an innocent little desk flunky. I believed you were what McCormack told me you were. Believed that you were on his side, that you understood what was happening, understood business, understood deals, negotiations, and honor."

"I understand honor," Zara said. "I understand exactly what went on in that room that day. I know everything there is to know about you and about your intentions."

"I don't believe you do," Sikorski said, tipping his chin up and losing some of his good humor. He took another step toward Zara. "I don't think you know what I intend to do at all."

"I know you got yourself mixed up with him," Zara said, turning a sneer on Tuck and stepping away, which had the inadvertent consequence of nudging Kadie closer toward the truck that they'd arrived in.

Kadie stumbled out of the way, but nobody seemed to notice, she was incidental. She didn't need to be here.

Sikorski wanted her here because he wanted to exert power, pressure, on Tuck. That was how it had been explained to her.

Sikorski wanted her present to prove he could make a demand and force Tuck to comply, making him uncomfortable in the process, which was probably the same reason Sikorski had asked her to come into the office on that morning in the mansion before Tuck took her out of there. Not that she had a problem with being here, Kadie had intended to insist that she was included for Howie's sake, if not for Tuck's.

Sikorski and Zara were sizing each other up and while they did, Kadie did the math. If all those security men had been in the front and in the back of the vehicle, Howie wasn't here at all. He couldn't be. There was simply no room for him. Then her gaze settled on the rear of the limo. Would Sikorski be so cold? So cruel? As to return the boy to them traumatized or even worse: deceased.

Horrified terror made her tense and she desperately wanted to call out to share her thoughts with Tuck. But Sikorski was coming closer to Zara, closer and closer.

"You shouldn't have come here," Sikorski said. "But I knew you would. I knew he had your ear, somehow you were connected to this. Knew he could get you to this place and I knew you would come because you're just that stupid."

Zara wasn't affected and slowly folded her arms. "Am I?" Kadie couldn't believe that Zara was smiling, she almost seemed to be enjoying herself. "I am that stupid?" Zara said. "I came here to face you because I believe I'm stronger."

"Is that right?"

"Because I believe I'm better than you. Somehow, I'm more superior," Zara said. Kadie could see the humor in Zara's statement because that was what Sikorski thought of himself. He thought he was superior, so he would probably have done the same thing in coming to a meet after being challenged by an enemy. "It's ironic."

Kadie noticed how Tuck began to move in the opposite direction, one small side-step at a time, then forward, closer to the security men, closer to the limo.

"Where exactly is the information I asked for?" Tuck

asked, taking Sikorski's attention away from Zara for a moment when he stopped. "We had a deal. I have shown you Zara. You show me the information. You show me the guy who thought he could get into my business. I want to see his face. Bring him to me."

"Mm," Sikorski hummed. "I don't think I will. My employees rely on a certain amount of anonymity, which I'm sure, Mr. Swift, you can understand as you operate in the same way. I can't simply trot them out and hand them over because it suits your needs."

"Actually," Tuck said, looking surprisingly relaxed given the situation they were standing in. "It serves your needs right now because unless I see the guy standing here in front of me, you get nothing."

"I get nothing?" Sikorski asked, switching back to look Zara up and down. "You've brought me what I want. You've brought me the problem. You've brought me the woman who caused all of this and who is responsible for the death of a good friend."

The death of a good friend, who could he be talking about? Kadie didn't know. "Grant McCormack," Zara said. "It's the only man you can be talking about, you're certainly not talking about Albert Sutcliffe. You couldn't stand him. Despite both of your desires to rule the world and be worshiped by all, you couldn't be more different. Of all the men that stood with me in the Grand Hotel, the most interesting and probably the most honest, was Kahlil Samara, and he died a sad, pathetic death because he was greedy and scorned, not because he wanted to rule the world. He wanted to do what he'd been told he couldn't, which I assume is the reason I'm standing here."

"Is that why you think you're here?" Sikorski asked.

"You were told you couldn't have me and now that I'm here, you feel like you've got me. You can't have been that close to Grant if he snubbed your bid," Zara said. "And you know nothing of loyalty, you left Kahlil hanging out to dry because Corvi offered you a better deal. You're not a man of honor."

Sikorski's lip curled in disgust. "You don't know

anything about me."

"You can't see what's right in front of your face. You like to play games."

She and Tuck were forgotten again as Sikorski fixated his hatred on Zara. "I've heard stories about you," Sikorski said. "Kahlil told me you were sarcastic, above your station, confident beyond what was reasonable. You overestimate your ability and underestimate everyone around you, and that is what brought you here and what will get you killed."

Sikorski spoke like some knowledgeable giant who had experience in the world beyond anything the rest of them could ever imagine.

"I don't mean to interrupt your pathetic trash talk," Tuck said, unimpressed and unamused.

He remained as distant as he had before, acting like he couldn't care less what happened to Zara, that she was standing on her own, or that these security men were eyeing him as if he were some sort of human bomb who could explode at any moment.

They had no intentions of sacrificing themselves. Kadie knew the plan, she'd heard Zara say she didn't want Sikorski to have his time in the limelight, singing his song about how fantastic he was and how he would triumph. But they had to get Howie before they could cut him off and Sikorski had just admitted that he wasn't here.

"Where's my information?" Tuck asked. "Leatt, you're supposed to tell me where he is? Did you even try to find out?"

"Perhaps," Sikorski said, taking a sauntering step backwards from Zara. "It's curious…"

With his focus averted, Zara got closer to Kadie. This was like a dance, everybody moved in subtle motions when the others weren't looking. One side step, one forward, one back, go left, go right, be ready at all times. Tense, relax, smile, frown, all of these different discreet movements, as slight as they often were, conveyed a message to everybody else who was present.

Men on security stayed tense and alert, prepared to pounce at any moment. Yet, they had too many targets who were spread too far apart. Kadie wondered if that was why Tuck put so much distance between himself and Zara. Surely, he'd know he could protect the women if he was standing beside them. Except by distancing himself, he created a different target, away from the women who would probably be viewed as no threat.

By putting that space between them, he gave them a clear shot to the vehicle and escape. Zara was probably under orders to scamper if things went south. Kadie hoped that wasn't the plan because she wouldn't be able to leave Tuck on his own, not with all of these men, even with Raven up on that hill.

"You tell me you're a man of your word, we made a deal," Tuck said. "You tell me you don't have the guy I want and now you're gonna tell me you don't have the information."

"Most people in this situation," Sikorski said, carrying on with his previous, unfinished thought. "Most people are interested in the money. There should be ten million dollars, sitting in that car, waiting for you right now and you haven't asked about it once."

"Some things are more important than money," Tuck said. "I have a feeling that that's the most likely thing you'll have brought. Money is something that you have plenty of, something you can hand over as you see fit. You don't even need to think about it. Ten million's nothing to you, it's a drop in the ocean, you won't even miss it. But your guy, the one I want to see, you'd miss him."

"Is that your intention?" Sikorski asked. "Your intention is to kill him?"

"I didn't tell you what my intention was, just as you didn't tell me what yours was with Bandini. I didn't ask, and I don't care."

"That's what you want me to believe. I don't know how you know each other or how you got your hands on Game Time. But to me, right now, that's the most important thing. I have Zara right here and you're going to give me that device. If you don't, I'll make sure you pay."

"And how will you do that?" Tuck asked.

"I'm going to bet that device is in your vehicle. You brought the device and I'm looking at Bandini, everything I want is here."

"So it was your intention to screw me over all along?" Tuck asked. "You were never going to give me Leatt, never going to let me speak to your minion, never going to pay me? I think we know who we're dealing with now, what kind of man you are."

"There's nothing you can do about it," Sikorski said. "You're outmanned and you're outgunned."

"I wouldn't be so sure about that." Zara glanced toward Kadie. "Come and stand here," Zara muttered, coiling a tight arm around Kadie's shoulders.

She only moved them a foot and a half to the left, so Kadie didn't understand why the movement was important.

"He still hasn't figured out that the limo shooting was a setup," Tuck said, sharing a smile with Zara.

Panic made Sikorski's gaze dart between them. "What?" he demanded. "That was your people? But… you could've been killed?"

Tuck shrugged. "Those are the risks we take. Erasing scum like you makes it worth it. Swallow?"

Zara extended the arm that she didn't have around Kadie to the right and with a wide smile, she opened her fingers to release the glass bottle she'd been clutching since they left the truck. Before the glass hit the floor, a piercing whoosh hit the air and Zara's hair was displaced.

Sikorski's body fell, and although Kadie gasped and tried to drop, Zara held her tight. "He's not through," Zara murmured from the corner of her mouth. "Don't move a muscle."

The security men began to drop one at a time and Kadie squeezed her eyes closed. This was trust unlike any she'd known before. Bullets were flying one at a time, very precise, in every direction. No one knew which way to run because nowhere seemed to be safe. Nowhere except right here, beside this woman standing in the middle of it all.

TWENTY-FOUR

WHEN THE SHOOTING stopped and the dust began to settle, Kadie relaxed enough to open her squeezed-tight eyes. She almost couldn't breathe having never seen so much blood or so many lifeless people lying in the dirt.

But Tuck and Zara didn't blink. Tuck was already at the limo, searching the trunk and then the interior. Zara made a beeline to help him after giving Kadie a shove toward their truck. "Get in there, Dove," Zara called back. "Get the engine going."

Kadie wanted to help, but she didn't know quite what had happened. Shock still slowed her down. Zara slammed the front door of the limo and the sound shook Kadie from her daze enough that she could stumble toward the truck. Clambering inside, she somehow got the truck running, though it took her quite a few attempts to turn the key because her fingers were shaking so much.

The back door shut and she glanced in the mirror to see that Zara had got in. The driver's door opened at her side and Kadie gasped, but it was Tuck who shoved her across to the passenger side and took her place at the wheel.

"Buckle up," he said. The truck was already spinning backwards in a fast, efficient arc. He slammed on the brakes, jolting her forward, and then suddenly they were racing ahead. "None of it's here. But we have bought some time. We're going to the house."

"Meet you there," Raven said in their ears, sounding as aloof and withdrawn as ever.

The house, they were going to Sikorski's mansion. Tuck was focused on the road, hunched over the wheel. Despite their galloping speed up the mountain, he wasn't wearing his seatbelt and she didn't feel the need to fumble for hers because they were almost there and she was still frozen in time. Tuck was driving, she was safe.

"What the hell just happened?" she gasped.

Sikorski was dead. His men were dead. And they were racing toward the house to find Howie? To get the information on this Leatt guy that the Kindred wanted? Kadie wasn't sure what their objective was, maybe both, maybe neither. Whatever it was, they were on a clock. Sikorski had been stupid enough to bring the majority of his security force to the meet. Chances were, they wouldn't come across any at the gates.

As they sped through them, she saw that she was right. They got there, raced up the driveway, then Tuck spun the car in an almost handbrake turn to face it down the path they'd just come, probably to facilitate and easy escape.

"Wait here," he said, but she was already out of the car, racing around it toward him.

"Not a chance. I have to find him and he might not come if it's only you."

Tuck wasn't putting up much of a fight because he was running up the stairs instead of trying to force her back into the vehicle. Kadie followed, not keeping pace with his fit physique, but she did her best. "Oh he'll fucking come with me, even if I have to knock him unconscious," Tuck said.

Going in the front door, he darted through the hallways, he was searching rooms, opening doors. Clattering around the place, knocking things over in his haste, without a care for the noise he was making. Kadie knew the layout of the house. Grabbing his arm to stall him, she needed to give him focus.

"Stop it," she said. "They'll hear you and they'll come for us." Sikorski had brought his best men to the meet, but there were still staff here who would note their odd behavior and call up those who might be left. "Take a breath. I know where he'll be."

The first thing she had to do was avoid the basement because if she didn't do that, Madame would see her and she would ask questions. Madame was the only one on the premises who'd probably been told Kadie wouldn't be coming back, that she'd been bargained away.

There were offices in the rear part of the building that linked to the basement. She knew this because Howie had been kept in the basement for a while near to, but not with, the girls who she trained with. It was these offices she was heading for.

The trouble was, she also knew that there were sometimes other people in those rooms. Sometimes they were overcrowded, sometimes they were empty; it just depended on what work was being done and where Sikorski had allocated his resources. But there was nothing she could do to change what they'd find, they had to take the risk, this could be their last chance to extract Howie.

Zara wasn't with them and Kadie wasn't sure where she was. But Howie consumed her concentration now. They had to get Howie and get out. As far as Kadie was concerned, he was the most important thing.

Keeping hold of Tuck's hand, she led him through the house, through corridors, down stairs, and into passages that were almost invisible to those who didn't know they were there. Because she'd lived in this house for a month, she knew her way around. But she'd never had the free reign to run where she wanted to go.

While Sikorski wasn't on the premises, the security men usually congregated in their own part of the house, which was in the other wing. They were supposed to do rounds, and probably would eventually, but there was complacency around here because Sikorski projected an air of being untouchable—despite incidents like the supposed attempt on his life in the limo.

Usually being chaperoned by security, Madame, or Sikorski, she'd always been under someone's watchful eye. Now she had the run of the house. On getting to the office door, she stopped and turned, forcing Tuck to crash into her under his momentum. She grabbed on to him so as not to fall flat on her ass.

"Listen," she said in a discreet whisper. "Sometimes there are people in here, sometimes there are not. Howie will be here or in his bedroom. I haven't spent much time in here, but one of the times we managed to talk for a minute at a party when I was being shown how things work, Howie told me this is where they make him work."

"It's okay," he said, twisting his arm around his back, he pulled a gun from his waistband that she hadn't noticed until this moment.

"Oh, God," she whispered, not because she didn't trust him with the weapon or because he might have to kill to protect her and Howie, but because his weapon meant others might go for theirs and put his life in jeopardy. "I love you." Consumed by the desperate need to make sure he knew how she felt before they walked into what could be their end, the words tumbled from her.

"I love you too," he said. Grabbing her head, he gave her a quick, hard kiss and then he turned her around to push her against the wall next to the door. "Wait here."

He pressed himself against her, out of the line of sight of whoever might be on the other side of that door and she hoped this wasn't the last time their bodies were so close. After turning the handle, he moved fast to burst into the room with his gun outstretched, ready to aim and fire at anyone who might be in their way.

She couldn't breathe, she gnawed on her lip and clasped her hands together at her chest praying that there was no one else in that room. One beat then two, there couldn't be anyone in there, there was no fighting or shouting. Suddenly, as if all of her prayers had been answered, Howie burst out of the room like he'd been shot from a cannon.

Taking one hard step before bouncing forward to clatter against the opposite wall of the hallway. Kadie went over, right on his tail. "Oh, my God," she said, grabbing him and giving him a shake. "Oh my God, you're alive."

Pulling him into a tight hug, she wanted to apologize for everything that had happened, wanted to ask what he'd been through. They'd had so little time to talk during their forced stay, there was so much to share, but this was no time for stories.

Tuck grabbed both of them by the back of their necks and began to throw them down the corridor. "Wait!" she called. "Wait! Wait!"

"No," Tuck said, gruff and impatient. "You're going with Zara."

"But the girls," she said. "We have to let them go. We have to get their passports and—"

"No!" Tuck was insistent.

Zara appeared at the end of the hall, but didn't come toward them, just gestured for them to follow. Somehow, she'd found them, maybe they had GPS, maybe there was something in the earpiece that helped them track each other, Kadie didn't know.

Zara was a lifeline, the reprieve of support that she needed. "Go with her," Kadie said, pushing Howie toward Zara who was positioned at the end of the corridor, gesturing for them to hurry. Kadie stayed with Tuck to beseech him. "We have to get the girls. They weren't part of the mission, but we're here and—"

"No," he said. "I know that you made friends down there. We can't mess with this. They'll be freed after Sikorski doesn't come back. They'll know something is wrong and they'll have their chance to run."

"But we have to get their passports," she said, knowing that Sikorski confiscated them to keep the women compliant.

Tuck exhaled his irritation. "You'll have to go through the Madame and security too," Tuck said. "Are you willing for me to hurt those people to get you what you want? I'll do it, but I'm telling you, it could get bloody."

Madame didn't deserve to die. But then, Kadie didn't know much about the security agents, perhaps most of them didn't deserve to either. Although, they may have been mass murderers and psychopaths, she had no way to know specifics.

Nodding, she came to terms with what being Kindred meant and it meant making hard choices. "Okay," he said, just as Raven appeared beside Zara. "Okay, Zara will get you and Howie out. Rave and I will take care of it."

Kadie stepped back. "You expect me to leave you here, in this place? Alone?"

"He's not alone," Raven said, coming up behind her to move past and grab hold of Tuck. "We have limited time and you have to find Leatt."

Tuck shook his head. "Anything Sikorski had on the system I have already. We can trawl through the data back at the manor. No point in tapping the network now."

"I'll get the girls out," Raven said. "If there's a private network…"

"If there was, I'd have found it. But I can check if anything on Leatt was picked up in the last couple of days."

So Raven was going to free the girls and Tuck was supposed to hack the computer to find out what the Kindred needed to know. Sikorski hadn't delivered and tracking down this Leatt guy was important to them.

"Good," Raven said. "Copy everything, you guys can analyze it at base."

"Agreed," Tuck said and whirled to her. "Where are the passports?"

Paling, fear of failure chilled her. "I don't know, in the office, in a safe. I don't know."

From the background, a usually timid voice became strong. "I know," Howie said. "They're under the carpet, beneath the window. There's a safe in the floor. It's just a four digit combination: two, four, zero, one. You'll find them in there, but it won't be easy to hand them out."

"Easy is relative," Zara said, with unwavering confidence in Raven and Tuck.

Going to Tuck, Kadie rested her arms on his chest. "You have to try. Please, Hotshot."

It was a risk, but if she walked away, those women

could end up on street corners across the globe being used by depraved men to satisfy their perverted desires. A fate that could have been hers if Tuck hadn't returned to her life. "Please. Just give them their passports, get them outside, and then it's up to them. Sikorski's not coming back here. Trust me, most of them are desperate enough to run and those who aren't, let them stay."

"She's right," Zara called. "You have to do your best. Think about Falcon and Wren."

Kadie didn't have a clue what that meant, but she appreciated Zara's support.

"You've got to get out of here, Swallow," Raven said with encroaching urgency. "Get Dove and the squirt and go."

Raven gave Kadie a shove that was stronger than she'd anticipated, so she staggered the first few steps toward Zara. The marksman was already pulling Tuck into the office, Kadie just managed to make brief eye contact with her love before he disappeared. The moment the connection was broken, she turned and fled to Zara.

"I'll get you out," Kadie said, because she knew the routes better than them.

"We regroup at the safe house," Zara said, following Kadie as she retraced the trip she'd taken with Tuck.

This warren of a house was meant to disorientate those who didn't know it. Her impetus grew now that they had Howie and were so close to success. They were going to get out of here. She was sure of it. They had to.

Just then, from a narrow facing stairway, two security men descended into the corridor they'd just reached. Clearly, they hadn't expected to see Kadie, Zara, and Howie. All five of them paused, frozen as they processed and tried to decide what to do next.

Zara had a weapon in her hand, but there were two men opposing them, both of whom had weapons on their hips. Zara might get a shot off and be able to kill one, but the other would most likely get to his gun and off one of them before Zara could take the second shot.

Kadie couldn't breathe. Her heart raced. Howie began to sweat. Grabbing for his hand to reassure him, she was glad when he squeezed to reciprocate. Zara had to be assessing the situation, but she wasn't as experienced as Tuck and Raven, so it took her time to come to a conclusion. Before Swallow could get there, there was a bang and one man fell, then another shot exploded and the second was gone from their vision.

Whipping around, Kadie didn't know what they would see because they'd left Tuck and Raven in the corridor behind and those shots came from the left. To her surprise, she could see a figure standing in the shadows at the end of the hallway that could only be Griffin Caine.

He stepped forward into the light, looking only at Zara while ignoring the other two that were there, and said in a rumbling monotone, "We're even."

Without saying anything else, or waiting for a response, he let his gun fall to his side, turned around, and walked away the way he'd come. They hadn't seen him since the day of the fight and she didn't know how he knew where they were or what was happening.

Zara grabbed Kadie's free hand and began to pull her along the hall toward the exit. By the time they got to the end and turned the corner, Caine was already gone.

"What?" Kadie asked. "What happened? How did he—"

"He watches," Zara said, her words as hurried as her steps. "I don't know how he knows. But he does. Watching Raven is. What he did. For a long time. And then. He started watching me." The quick words and abrupt cutoffs matched the twists and turns their trailing snake took. Zara was still holding Kadie's hand, and she was holding onto Howie at the rear. "I guess he needed closure. And he just got it."

Zara was through thinking about it, or through talking about it, because that was the last she said about Caine. They got to the main doors, then outside, and ran down the exterior stairs and across the drive to dive into the truck they'd arrived in.

Kadie gasped when Zara began to drive away. "What are you doing?" she shrieked, desperate to know why they were leaving Raven and Tuck behind.

"Raven has transport," Zara explained. "We regroup at the motel. Those are the rules. We stick with the plan. I don't like it any more than you do." They bumped down the road at a great speed. "I hate it when he goes off on his own. I hate it when he kicks me off the job. I hate it when he gives me instructions that are contrary to what I want to do."

"So how do you put up with it," Kadie asked, holding her seat and the dash to steady herself on this uneven road.

"I have to because there's times I do things that he doesn't want me to do," Zara said. "He doesn't want me on missions and doesn't want me going out on my own. And the only way that I get to do those things is by trusting him to do his job right. If they need us, we'll get back to them, don't worry about that. But when those two are together…" Zara paused to take a breath and another smile formed on her face before she made brief eye contact with Kadie. "They'd never leave each other behind, they're capable of anything, and capable of getting out of every jam."

Driving away from Tuck while he could still be in danger felt alien. But she had to get used to this, just as Zara had explained. Kadie had to get used to letting Tuck work as he had for all the years that they were together. Just like when he left her to go off on jobs while she was sitting at home running their legitimate business, this is what he'd been doing all that time, every day, and she'd been oblivious to the risks he took.

He would be okay; Raven would watch out for him. But Zara had told her that she may lose the man she loved, and Tuck had told her there were risks. This could all go wrong, but she couldn't ask him to trust her if she wasn't willing to trust him, just as Zara had stated.

So with a single breath, she sat back and turned to glimpse at Howie. Kadie had completed her mission of getting him out safely. God only knew what he'd been through or how long it would take him to recover. But he was out and so was she. Now all they could do was go back to the motel and wait for Raven, for Swift. Only when they were all back together could they start to figure out what came next.

TWENTY-FIVE

WAITING WASN'T HER forte. She probably had other strengths, waiting wasn't one of them.

Howie had been grateful at the motel and Zara had settled them in and then gone out for food. Kadie didn't know how she could think of such a thing because the adrenaline made it difficult for Kadie to even sit down let alone think about putting something heavy or greasy in her stomach. But Zara said it was tradition.

Kadie read a brief glimmer of worry in Zara's countenance and she speculated that doing something, even if it was just retrieving food, gave Zara a distraction. Keeping busy stopped her from thinking about Raven and the danger he might be facing.

Howie was buzzing too and was full of stories that he tried to share all at once, barely managing to finish one thought before he bounced to the next. It didn't matter because she wasn't really listening. Once they were away from here and back in their lives, there would be time to look back and commiserate. As far as she was concerned, the two men who were still in the field were central to her thoughts and they'd stay there until they came back.

Trying not to think about how she would cope if they

didn't reappear, or even what kind of rescue mission she and Zara could mount on their own, Kadie tidied up the room and sent Howie into the shower.

It was while the youngster was in there that Zara came back. Kadie was full of questions and she took over Howie's role of bombarding the listener.

"What will we do?" Kadie asked, wringing her hands and watching Zara set out food on the blanket she'd laid on the floor.

"It's fine," Zara said, sitting down with a cooler and a handful of glasses, a finger in each one held them together in the middle. "We usually have a table and the guys will moan, but if we remind Rave that he's the reason there's no table, he'll shut up fast."

"What?" Kadie asked. She hadn't registered that Zara was setting a picnic in the middle of the floor or that it might be awkward or unusual for the battle-hardened Kindred to eat this way. "No, I meant, what will we do if they don't come back?"

"Kick their asses," Zara said, opening the cooler to take out a bottle of wine. "Withhold sex? I don't know, we'll coordinate punishment." Another smile joined Zara rising onto her knees as she twisted a corkscrew into the bottle. "It's going to be fun having another woman around."

Hunkering down, Kadie set the two wine glasses side by side. "What could we do? You're more capable than I am, and I'll do whatever it takes, but could we be effective in getting them out? Alone?"

Zara put the bottle on the floor but didn't push down the arms of the corkscrew because she was fixated on her new colleague. "We're not alone. They'll get out of there, just give them time."

"And if they don't?" Kadie asked.

Zara put a hand on her cheek to stroke and soothe. "We're not alone," Zara said. Kadie took her loose hand. "The Kindred is more than just who you've met. If we have to mount a mission to save their asses, we'll have plenty of help."

"We leave you guys alone for two seconds and you're getting it on."

Kadie hadn't heard the door open, these men had to still be in stealth mode. When she whipped around, Tuck was inside with Raven behind him who was closing the door. "What have I told you about the alarm, woman?" Raven said, scowling at Zara.

Leaping from the blanket, Kadie flew into Tuck's arms, jumping up to loop her limbs around him and kiss him deep. "Phew," he said, taking his lips away. "This is like one of our hellos, how long do you think I've been away this time?"

Every time he was away from her and she'd greeted him like this for returning, it was because she missed him and needed the connection. Now she knew that he deserved it for saving the world in silence so many times. Pride and gratitude made her kiss him again, he was an incredible human being, capable and skilled, and all hers.

***

THEY ATE DINNER, discussed what had gone on, and expressed great frustration at not getting the information they needed from Sikorski about Leatt. Apparently, that was important, the Kindred were wary of him, confused by him. Kadie could tell that they didn't like to be in the dark because that set them behind.

A few times she made eye contact with Tuck and wished she could ask for them to be alone. As much as she appreciated what Zara and Raven had done and how pleased she was to have Howie safe, she still wanted time alone with the man she loved.

Somehow, she felt his need to be alone too, though given their circumstances, there was nothing either of them could do to achieve their want. She'd expected them to spend the night where they were in the motel and make plans for the future tomorrow. But the Kindred didn't hang around.

At least, Tuck didn't. He disappeared, leaving her alone with Raven, Zara, and Howie. As soon as he was gone, Zara started to pack up, she said they were going back to the manor. Kadie wasn't sure what that meant, but she helped to tidy and pack, helped to wipe fingerprints from the room while reassuring Howie that everything would be okay.

As it turned out, the reason Tuck left, was to get a wad of cash and a vehicle, which he handed over to Howie the minute he got back. Making the boy swear to never discuss what had happened here, what he'd seen, or who he had interacted with, Tuck told him to get himself home. Kadie had more to say to the youngster who'd wanted to be her shining knight. She wanted to talk to Howie alone and she could tell he wanted to talk to her as well.

But just because they said goodbye now, didn't mean they were saying goodbye forever and that was how she reassured him during her short talk with him outside next to the car Tuck had procured. She said some of the things that she wanted to and once Howie was resigned to the fact that he wasn't going with the Kindred, Howie was eager to get in the car and get on the road.

She could understand his want to put as much distance between this area and himself as possible. Neither of them had had a time they wanted to remember. After watching Howie leave the parking lot, she turned around to see Tuck, Raven, and Zara coming out of the motel room with the last of their things.

"That's it," Zara said.

The truck was packed and beside it was a motorcycle that Raven tossed a leg over before kicking away the stand. "Are you coming with us?" Tuck asked Zara. "It's a long way on the back of a bike."

Zara nodded. "If you guys don't mind a gooseberry."

Tuck laughed. "For all the times I've played that role with you and Rave, I think you're owed a shot."

Zara kissed Raven and then got in the back of the truck. The journey was long and she understood why they'd started it when she was told that they wouldn't get where they were going until the next night. They drove through the night and into the daylight, and still they kept on going.

Zara took a turn at driving, Kadie offered, but Tuck said no, which made sense because she didn't really know where she was going. They stopped for food and it seemed that Raven was always close by, on their tail or scouting ahead on his bike.

They stopped at diners where they could view their vehicles at all times. Whatever was in that truck, they were packing precious cargo that they wanted to monitor. The Kindred didn't like complications, just as she'd always known from Tuck.

As she'd been told, by the time they reached their destination, it was dark. Not that she recognized where they were. But they slowed on a street right by the shore, that she would've put money on being abandoned. It didn't look much to her like there was a property here and she wondered if the Kindred resided in a secret cave.

The land rose in a sharp cliff that jutted out onto a peninsula that she couldn't see. A wall ran almost parallel to it then carried on beyond the landscape in a long straight line that faded into the darkness. The motorcycle roared away and for half a second, Kadie thought Raven had crashed because he vanished in a blink. When the other two didn't bat an eye at the magically disappearing, suddenly-invisible motorcycle, she assumed that that was part of the plan. They carried on at a trundling pace and it was odd because what had been a jovial journey became somber.

Tuck slowed the truck and she almost missed the large black gate to their left that was opening ever so gradually. Yet, when it was just open enough for them to turn, they did. The gate wasn't even fully open, it was still retracting. But in the mirror, she noticed it stalled and began to close before they were all the way through.

"You always think of him, don't you?" Tuck said, his eyes turned up to the rearview to examine Zara who was in the middle of the backseat.

Zara's mood had dropped and she was distracted by the side window. "I don't know why, but I always think of the first time I came here. I was defeated, so sure that I would never see Brodie again and then, there was Art opening that gate to let me in, standing in the beam of his headlights like some kind of sinister savior. At first, I was terrified, I didn't know what he was going to do, I still thought he hated me then. But he welcomed me here. If it wasn't for him, I wouldn't be here now."

"And neither would the rest of us," Tuck said. "You've saved our asses so many times. He would be proud of you."

"Of all of us," Zara said.

The chief. Kadie almost said it aloud. It was something about the way that they shared the memories that made her feel like she should keep her mouth shut. She didn't want to ask questions, she would learn what she needed to know in time.

"Five people," Zara said and leaned forward to rest her forearms on the back of the front seats. "Art told me five people had set foot in this house in the last twenty years. He asked if I wanted to be the sixth. So…" Zara straightened one arm so she could put her hand on Kadie's shoulder. "I guess you'll be the seventh."

Seven people in twenty years, that was a daunting prospect. Whether or not she was going to be accepted into the Kindred, she had their trust. The house that emerged at the end of the tree-flanked road was large, gothic, and completely unexpected. They drove downwards into an underground garage that looked surprisingly modern given the exterior.

Going up spiral stairs, they paused at a doorway that Kadie expected to go through, but Tuck caught her hand so that she didn't. "This is my stop," Zara said and gave Kadie a quick hug. "You guys settle in." She made eye contact with Tuck. "You know where we'll be."

"One of three places," Tuck said. "One of which I'll avoid at all costs."

They shared a hug and then Zara disappeared through the door. "Where will you avoid?" Kadie asked.

"Their bedroom," he said and winked before bobbing his head sideways. "Come on."

Taking her hand, he led her farther up the stairs, through another door into a hallway. They went one way, then the other, and kept on going. The house had been large from the outside, but she hadn't comprehended just how confusing it would be inside.

"Don't worry," he said, letting go of her hand to put an arm around her shoulders. "You'll get used to it."

"Will I?" she asked. They stopped and he pressed his thumb pad to the center of a doorknob to open the door attached to it. Gesturing her inside, he stepped back to give her a good view of the room she was about to enter. "Will I get used to it? Will you give me the chance to do that?"

Her breath was stolen when she scanned the room they'd gone into. The room was huge, the ceiling had to be twenty feet high. It was filled with beautiful, antique furniture that was made of real, heavy wood that had to be extortionate. There was a huge dresser and the bed was bigger than any she'd ever seen, suggesting it was custom made.

Doors stood in opposite corners and she speculated on where they might lead. Just behind her, on the same wall as the door, was a massive TV mounted on the wall with an entertainment center below it.

"This is…" she stuttered. "This is like a hotel. Like some luxury, twelve-star resort."

He exhaled a laugh. "Don't worry about it. We won't get slapped with a bill, this is our room."

It was a wonder that he ever came back to her if this was his alternative. But he was unfazed by the opulence and went over to sit on the bed to take off his boots. Pulling his tee shirt over his head, he gave her a glimpse of the body she'd been thinking about all night, then flopped onto his back.

He exhaled. "It feels good to be home."

A spike of irrational hurt made her self-conscious. "So this is home?" she asked. She'd always believed that the apartment they shared together was the place he called home and felt safe. Kadie couldn't understand how that would measure up against this opulent manor with its upmarket décor and exquisite furniture.

Here he had tech and tools and friends. As she moved toward the bed, she caught a glimpse of the vast ocean beyond the towering pointed arch windows. "It's incredible here, the house is amazing, and Zara, Brodie," she said, using Raven's real name felt odd. "You have quite a life here."

"Yeah," he said, lifting his hand. Kadie took his offer and allowed herself to be yanked forward on top of him. Tuck absorbed the impact of her fall, but she quickly recovered and sat up to straddle his hips. "It just got better, having you here makes it better."

"You had all this and I never knew," she said. "I'm not surprised you walked away from me."

"Hey now," he said, crunching up to cup her face with his palms. "This was nothing. Toots, you were home. It feels good to be here. But it feels better to be with you, no matter where the hell that is."

"How will we explain this to Dempsey?" she asked.

While he was sitting up, she straightened her legs to then crook her calves around his back, crossing her legs to keep him inside the circle of her lower limbs.

"Well you'll have to call him and tell him that you're safe," Tuck said.

"He always believed I was," she said, running her hands over his chest and into his hair. "But we have to decide what comes next. Are we going to do this here? Are you coming home with me? Or is this it for us?"

"Is that place home for you?" he asked. "Is that how you think of it? Could you be happy elsewhere? If that's the place you want to be then you have to go there. You can have the business, have the apartment."

"And you?" she asked. "Would you come with me or is your life going to be here?"

His certain gaze became less assured and dropped to her cleavage, not in a show of desire, but one of contemplation. "I love you," he said. "But I can't walk away from them. When we lost Art, the chief, Brodie had a meltdown, we nearly lost him. And then his brother died and so much shit has gone wrong. The only reason we've got through and we've managed to keep fighting is because we know we can rely on each other."

Stroking him, she sensed his internal conflict. "I'm not asking you to choose. I understand that they're important to you." And it was important to her that he looked her in the eye, so she made him by scrunching his hair in her hands and urging his head back. "I want to be with you. But I can't pretend I match up to what you have here and I don't have the same skills as your friends. I'll give you my all. I'll do everything I can—"

"You always have," he said. "And you do give me everything I need, just by being here, being patient."

Patience was something she'd always had to have with him. Patience that he would come back. Patience with his lack of explanations. Patience that, while he gave her everything in the world she could possibly ever dream of, he wouldn't trust her enough to tell the truth.

"So I guess what we're saying," she said. "Is that our life is here. We just have to figure out how we'll make it work. How we'll work."

"You'll learn," he said. "Zara knew nothing when Raven appeared in her bedroom and told her that the end of the world was coming. But she stuck by him, she persevered, she took crazy risks that I don't even want you to think about taking. But she learned and they're stronger for it."

"Then we will be too," Kadie said, tightening her legs and resting her elbows on his shoulders. "I already feel closer to you. In all the years we were together and how crazy in love with you I was, I didn't believe I could love you more and now I know that that was just the beginning and there's still so much to come for us."

"Yes," he agreed. "So much to come."

Tuck's hands went under her top and he managed to pull it off over her head. Kadie hadn't meant more sex, but she wasn't going to say no. It felt like they hadn't been alone in weeks, even though it had only been a few days.

He rolled her to her back and began to tease her body with his mouth. Kissing her lips, her face, her eyes, he brushed his hands across her neck, down her arms, over her breasts. As he slowly stripped her clothes from her body and discarded his own, Kadie felt content in this warm veil of security shimmering over them.

She didn't have to worry about Sikorski. Howie was safe. Dempsey was running the business, and probably in his element without her there to constantly get on his ass or tell him what he was doing wrong. And here she was, with Tuck, her mission was complete. She had set out to find him and somehow, they'd found each other. In horrible, despicable circumstances, but still they'd found each other.

As he moved inside her, she felt that this was new. He was the same man she'd always known, the same man she'd always loved, and yet there was so much more to him. There was a strength to his character, and a resolve in his eyes that she'd either never seen or failed to identify. Tuck had purpose and he was sharing that purpose with her.

The shaft of his dick was thick and insistent in its objective. He wanted her to yield to him and her body was powerless not to.

"Tuck," she said. "Tucker Holt."

Calling his name aloud liberated her, she was tired of using the alias. She would get used to it, she'd have to, as the Kindred had their rules. But here in this house, on this land, Zara had switched from Raven to Brodie as soon as they'd crossed the threshold of the gate. So it was safe here, they were safe here, and that meant she could be with her man in any way she chose to be.

Slowing his pace to take his time in fondling each of her breasts, he lowered his mouth to them. Sucking, licking, teasing the pampered flesh, his attention made it hard for her to concentrate on breathing. One short breath followed a deep one, and she couldn't find her rhythm, but his stimulating behavior carried on, sending her into an endless loop of torment. Hormones fizzed, buzzed, and ached inside of her.

They'd been doing this for so many years and yet he could still enliven every cell in her body, every part of her being wanted to reach that peak he strove to drive her over. "I've missed this body, my pet," he breathed. "I love you and I'll never leave you again. I'll never let you out of my sight."

That seemed almost impossible, but she appreciated what he was saying. "No," she panted, tightening her thighs around his hips. "Because I won't let you go. I want you here. I need you here."

"Inside you?" he asked, while wearing an almost half-smile.

"Inside me," she whispered and pulled him down to kiss her again.

It didn't take long to lose control. Just like in their frantic joinings after he'd been gone for periods of time, that insistence, that need, burned and built until the pressure was too much for either of them to contain. Moving faster, he hit the wall, and in one long satisfied groan he compelled her into climax, making her body cease into static, matching the white noise buzzing in her ears.

Her breath stopped, her heart stopped, the only thing that bloomed was her love for him and the fountain of pleasure gushing through her, warming her blood, searing her insides, branding the heart that belonged to him.

He didn't let their bodies part when he rolled away to save her from taking his weight now that he was spent. Satisfied, and probably exhausted, he'd been strong throughout this and held it together for her. Now he could relax.

In the Kindred motel, they'd shared a room with Raven and Zara, now they were alone for the first time since they'd been in Sikorski's mansion where she'd awoken in such a panic about breaking the rules.

But there was nothing to panic about now. So when he stroked her hair and kissed her head, she closed her eyes because she was allowed to sleep. This was her new haven and she was with her man. There was no safer place.

TWENTY-SIX

AT BREAKFAST TIME, Tuck took her from their bedroom. Every minute that she spent in this house intrigued her more and she was eager to explore. If Kadie had to pick a guide, she'd select Zara because being the newest arrival, she'd have looked on it with fresh eyes most recently, and from a woman's perspective too.

He took her into a large kitchen that she was still scrutinizing when Zara put a mug of coffee in her hand. Raven was at the island eating bacon and eggs, so Tuck rounded to sit by his friend while Zara went to dish out food for him and put a plate down for her too.

"Sleep well?" Zara asked, inviting Kadie to sit with an open hand.

"Yes," Kadie said, going where she was put. "This house is incredible."

"I know," Zara said, drinking her own coffee. "I think these guys take it for granted."

Tuck did move through the house without paying much heed to how wonderful it was, so she guessed Brodie was the same. "How was your night?" Kadie asked, because it was polite and she had noticed the charged glance Brodie and Zara shared.

"Great," Zara said and Brodie nodded, putting his cutlery down to sit straighter. "We made a decision."

"Oh yeah?" Tuck asked, digging into his food. "You set a date?"

"No, we're taking a break," Zara said.

Tuck stopped eating. "From each other?" he asked.

Zara made a face like that was a ridiculous and unfunny joke. "No, a break from the missions... Not a forever break, but, yeah, a break."

"Finally taking that vacation?" Tuck asked, examining them both.

Zara grinned. "Yes. We just figure that, well, Kindred work is never-ending. There will always be someone trying to catch up with us, or someone that we're after. Leatt will wait, Caine is off our tail, so yeah, it seems like the right time."

The right time, Kadie had just got here and now the other Kindred couple was leaving. "It's about time," Tuck said. "I think it's a great idea. Gives me time to settle Kade in too."

Settle her in, did that mean some kind of training? Either they'd have a lot of sex or fight constantly, maybe both. "You guys have to stay here," Zara said. "Look after the place for us. It's your home too. You don't have a girl to go anywhere for, now she's here with us." Zara bowed to squeeze Kadie's hand.

"I hope I haven't scared you away," Kadie said. "If it's inappropriate for me to be here—"

"No!" Zara exclaimed and got off her stool to come over and put an arm around Kadie. "The mission's not over. It's just on pause."

So the Kindred that she knew were taking a break, giving her time to get up to speed and learn her man again. Tuck left his stool and came over to cup her face and direct their mouths together. "Buckle up, baby, your adventure's just beginning."

Fitting in would take work, it would take time, but being in the embrace of the man she loved bolstered her. Joining the Kindred was right, wherever Tuck was based was her home. This was a new beginning, a stronger foundation, and nothing would tear them apart again.

TO BE CONTINUED...

Thank you for reading this tale!
If you can, please take the time to review.

~

Ask your local library for more Scarlett Finn novels!

~

For all things Scarlett Finn
check out:

www.scarlettfinn.com

BOOK FIVE

He's in hiding... until her.

FALCON

Kindred Book Five

SCARLETT FINN

OUT NOW!